paparazzi princess

SECRETS OF MY HOLLYWOOD LIFE

a novel by

Jen Calonita

LITTLE, BROWN AND COMPANY
New York   Boston

Little, Brown and Company

Hachette Book Group
237 Park Avenue, New York, NY 10017
Visit our website at www.lb-teens.com

Little, Brown and Company is a division of Hachette Book Group, Inc.
The Little, Brown name and logo are trademarks of Hachette Book Group, Inc.

First Edition: March 2009

Library of Congress Cataloging-in-Publication Data
Calonita, Jen.
    Paparazzi princess / by Jen Calonita. — 1st ed.
        p. cm. — (Secrets of my Hollywood life)
    Summary: Wanting only to mourn the end of her television series, seventeen-year-old Kaitlin, under pressure to choose her next acting project and study for her SATs, is drawn into the Hollywood nightlife by publicity-loving "It Girls," while her friendship with Liz flounders.
    ISBN 978-0-316-03064-9
    [1. Actors and actresses—Fiction. 2. Interpersonal relations—Fiction.
3. Celebrities—Fiction. 4. Self-confidence—Fiction. 5. Paparazzi—Fiction.
6. Hollywood (Los Angeles, Calif.)—Fiction.] I. Title.
    PZ7.C1346Pap 2009
    [Fic]—dc22

                                                        2008016440

10 9 8 7 6 5 4 3 2 1

RRD-C

Printed in the United States of America

Book design by Tracy Shaw

Secrets of My Hollywood Life novels by Jen Calonita:

SECRETS OF MY HOLLYWOOD LIFE

ON LOCATION

FAMILY AFFAIRS

In honor of my grandmothers, Kathleen Calonita and Evelyn Horn, who always inspired me to dream big.

Week of December 30

Family Affair's favorite daughter talks about life after a hit TV show.

By Steven Diamond

TV TOME: Pretty soon *Family Affair* will be no more. How are you coping?
KB: It's hard, you know? I've been on this show practically my whole life. Let's talk about something happy, like where I'm going for my winter break.

TV: Sure thing. So where are you going on vacation?
KB: *(laughs)* I'm glad you asked, Steven. My family hasn't been on a major vacation in years so I'm re-ally excited to turn off my cell phone and veg — *(Kaitlin's flack, Laney Peters, interrupts and is heard insisting Kaitlin not reveal the location.)* I'm sorry. Where was I? Oh, I was saying I can't wait to get away.

TV: Guess you can't say where, huh?
KB: Um, I don't even think I'm allowed to reveal what hemisphere I'll be in!

TV: If the paparazzi knew, they'd probably turn up in droves.
KB: I'm no Angelina and Brad, but a few faithful always seem to know where I'm going before I do. The paparazzi have cut me a lot of slack over the years, so I don't mind too much when they want a picture — as long as I'm not in mid-bite!

TV: It has to be hard to deal with. The press courts you like you're their personal princess, but they seem to like when you fall from grace too.

KB: *(Muffled voices again.)* Um, well, yeah, I have had some scuffles, haven't I? But that's what happens when you're seventeen and you live your life in public. You're going to mess up and everyone's going to know about it. I'm just thankful that I've learned from my mistakes. I never want to get completely out of control, which is why I keep a life outside of work, and stick close to my family and friends. They keep me grounded.

TV: And don't forget the boyfriend, Austin Meyers. How are things between you and the hottie high school lacrosse player?

KB: Good! He's amazing. Austin makes it easy for me to think about more than just work. He's fun to be around and he makes me laugh. I couldn't ask for better.

TV: You're going to hate me, but we have to talk about *Family Affair* now.

KB: *(sighs)* Okay. It's just that you're the first reporter to ask me about the show ending since it was announced publicly. I'm still in denial.

TV: What are you going to miss most about *Family Affair*?

KB: Definitely the people I work with. FA is my second family. It's going to be really hard not seeing them practically every day anymore.

TV: Can you tell us anything about how the series will end?

KB: Your guess is as good as mine! Our executive producer, Tom Pullman, is keeping the final scripts under wrap. None of us have seen it yet.

TV: What about you? What do you think your life will be like post-*Affair*?
KB: I know I want to do projects that will help me grow as a person and as an actress. Beyond that, I'm not sure. Hopefully a restful vacation will help me figure out the rest.

Family Affair *airs Sunday nights at 9 PM EST. Kaitlin's next film,* Pretty Young Assassins (PYA), *costarring her ex, Drew Thomas, hits theaters this May.*

one: *The Great Escape*

"Okay, Kaitlin, just relax."

"I am relaxed," I insist.

Okay, that's a lie. I'm petrified.

"There's no need to be nervous," Pierre says soothingly.

I'm starting to think my Greek God of a parasailing instructor, Pierre, is a mind reader. He's sitting in the driver's seat of a Winch boat that is seconds away from pulling my parasail chair off the back of his boat and hundreds of feet into the air above the waters of Turks and Caicos Islands, where I'm vacationing. Pierre may be used to doing this, but I'm completely freaked out.

Pierre starts the motor. "Ready, Kaitlin?" he yells over the humming. My bodyguard, Rodney, and my brother, Matty, are sitting behind Pierre, their heads bobbing as the boat rocks back and forth in the relatively calm ocean. "If anything goes wrong, just pull your cord and we'll bring you down," Pierre adds. "Got it?"

I attempt to say yes, but when I open my mouth, it feels like I ate a fistful of cotton. I fidget in my chair, which is thankfully still grounded on the back of the Winch boat. When the boat takes off, a suspiciously thin tow cable will be my only lifeline as the air catches my parachute and sends me flying.

How did I get myself into this?

I try to calm myself by focusing on my outfit. I adjust the straps on my cute white lace Dolce & Gabbana bikini, which feels itchy under my life jacket.

Oh God. What if this all goes terribly wrong and this is the last piece of clothing I ever get to wear? I can see the tabloid headline now: **Teen star Kaitlin Burke plummets to her death parasailing in the Caribbean wearing this season's sold-out lace bikini by Dolce & Gabbana.** I grab my straps and prepare to unhook myself.

"Hey, Kates!" my younger brother, Matty, yells over the loud engine. "You look like a ghost!" I glare at him. "Listen, if you wimp out, I won't tell anyone — except *Celebrity Insider*," he adds with a devilish grin. "Rod, hand me my cell. I'm sure Brian Bennett would like to hear that Kates chickened out of parasailing."

WHAT? Over my dead body. Maybe literally. Ha, ha. Ahem. I will *not* be tomorrow night's lead story on *Insider*! I take a deep breath and close my eyes. "GO!"

I hear Pierre rev the boat to full-throttle and I scream as

my chair begins to lift off the back of the boat. Within seconds I feel the wind pick up and my parachute rises into the air. After what seems like an eternity of screaming, I open my eyes and look down.

WHOA.

I am sailing high over the Caribbean! The bright blue water is so clear, I can actually make out rocks and coral below the surface. I can see the beach near our hotel, people jet skiing and swimming, and look! There's my Winch boat with Matty, Rod, and Pierre. It looks like a Matchbox car from up here. I quickly shut my eyes again.

This. Is. Terrifying.

Yet . . . kind of exciting too. No one can see me up here, not even the paparazzi with a long camera lens. That's a parasailing plus, for sure. I'm used to living my life under a microscope, so this ride is pretty freeing — even if only for a second.

Don't get me wrong — I love being a Hollywood "It" girl. I've been playing cotton-candy-sweet Samantha on the hit TV show *Family Affair* since before I started kindergarten. I get invited to the best parties, I'm on a first-name basis with Zac (as in Efron), and I have Stella McCartney on speed dial for fashion emergencies.

Being a teen star is like winning the lottery, but it does come at a price. When my non-celebrity best friend Liz breaks curfew or fights with her dad, she loses Sidekick, cell phone, and TV privileges for a week. When I screw up, Perez Hilton knows before my parents do, and then when they do find out what I've done, they can download my embarrassing moment on YouTube.

The light blond hair on my arms stands on end. It's sort of chilly up here. The wind picks up, smacking me in the face, and my chair suddenly lurches right. I'm flying high above the exclusive Parrot Cay resort again now, which is where we're staying. The villas look like dollhouses and I can see the pathways to the pools and tiny people lounging on the beach. I wonder where Mom and Dad are right now. Hopefully they're not anywhere they can see me. Before I know it, my chair sways to the left and then I'm descending.

Of course! Just as I start to enjoy myself. Within minutes there's a loud thud and my chair lands on the back of the boat as if I'd never even left.

Ahhh . . . land, sweet land (well, sort of). I've missed you.

"That was awesome," my brother Matty says as we disembark a few minutes later and walk onto the beach boardwalk. His Ralph Lauren bathing suit is completely soaked from the quick jump in the water he just took to cool off. He shakes out his hair and water pelts me in the face.

"Watch it!" I laugh.

"What?" Matt protests. "I want to look good in case we run into anyone." He slicks back his hair. Honey-blond locks, fair skin, green eyes — looking at Matty is like looking at a mirror, except, well, he's a thirteen-year-old boy and I'm a seventeen-year-old girl. But still.

"You mean like Maya?" I tease. Matty met this cute redhead at our resort and has been drooling over her all week. The two of us are so busy taunting each other that I don't realize someone else is talking to me until they're blocking my sun.

"You're Kaitlin Burke, right?" a girl asks. She's wearing oversized Dior sunglasses and a teeny brown Versace bikini. Her long blond hair is pulled into pigtails. She's holding a tiny, yappy Pomeranian — which is growling at me. I didn't even know they allowed dogs at the resort.

I suddenly realize I know this girl. She's Ava Hayden. There's not a party in Los Angeles that she's not on the invite list for. Ava had her own reality show on VH1 for two seasons, but her real claim to fame is having an endless stream of money, thanks to her parents' popular, upscale steak restaurant chain, and her uncanny ability to live her entire life in the presence of the paparazzi.

"Ava, right?" I say. "This is my brother, Matty, and my personal security, Rodney." Rodney (who hates the word bodyguard, which is why I avoid it) just grunts. Matty is speechless so I keep talking. "How are you?" I ask.

"Hot," she whines. "This island is way too humid. I'm hoping parasailing will cool me off. I'm not sure Calou is going to like the boat though," Ava adds, gesturing with her small, wound-up pup.

A girl walks up next to her. "Maybe we should throw him

overboard." Seeing the look of horror on my face, she laughs. "I'm just kidding," she says. "I love this annoying little guy." She rubs his head and he tries to bite her. "Calou goes with Ava everywhere. Even if we have to sneak him on and off the resort every day."

The girl is Ava's sidekick, Lauren Cobbs. She's an heiress too — her parents own a major electronics company — and she's had her own show on E! She's also been in a few slasher films, usually playing the part of the girl who dies an awesome death two minutes into the movie.

Ava rolls her eyes. "Of course I take Calou on vacay. He deserves one just as much as I do, don't you, sweet pea?" The dog yaps in agreement.

"Well, if something happens to you during parasailing, you better not leave your fortune to some dog," Lauren says as she twirls her long, brown curly hair around a red manicured finger. "I want your four-carat diamond hoops." Lauren's wearing an itty-bitty bikini in navy blue with a sheer, long-sleeved cover-up covering, well, nothing.

I laugh. "I wouldn't count on getting those earrings," I tell Lauren. "I just finished parasailing and I survived. I was petrified, but once I got over it, it was exhilarating." The two of them just stare at me and nod.

"I'm sorry," Lauren says finally. "It's just, we love you. Seriously, we're big fans. *Family Affair* is like the best show ever!"

"I can't believe it's going off the air. Fifteen years!" Ava complains. "My mom cried for an hour when we heard about it on *Celebrity Insider*."

"Yeah, I was pretty broken up too," I admit. I haven't thought about *FA* much while I've been on break, but hearing Lauren and Ava talk about the show's soon-to-be demise brings the emotions flooding back. "I've grown up on that show. I'm really going to miss it."

"I'm sure you'll get a new show in a second," Lauren says. "You're huge! And not just for *Family Affair*. I mean, everyone is still talking about you going all *Hannah Montana* and enrolling at that high school last year. Pretty fresh."

"And about how you dated two gorgeous guys at once," Ava adds. "How did you manage both Drew Thomas and that high school hottie?" Matty snorts.

"Oh, I wasn't dating Drew," I say quickly. "That was this silly publicity stunt the people on my next movie, *Pretty Young Assassins*, came up with. I'm dating the, uh, high school hottie." They nod. "How do you guys know all this stuff?"

"I live for Page Six," Ava says solemnly. "And I never miss an issue of *Sure*."

"Or an episode of *Access Hollywood*," Lauren adds.

"You guys watch and read that stuff?" Matty is stunned.

"Of course," Ava says. "Don't you?"

Matty and I look at each other. I mean sometimes, yeah, when it has to do with our family, but I don't live and breathe the rags. "Not every day," I say awkwardly.

"It's always good to stay on top of your publicity so you can get more of it," Lauren says knowingly. Suddenly she notices my bathing suit and squeals. "Where did you get that bikini? Ava, that's the one I was looking for, wasn't I? Just last week at Bendel?"

"It looks so good on you," Ava says admiringly to me. "You can pull off white. I look pasty."

I blush. "Thanks." I've met both Lauren and Ava before, but I don't think I've ever said more than two words to either of them. Their party girl reputations precede them, but they actually seem pretty nice. "I got it at that cute store on Melrose."

"The one with all the great bangle bracelets?" Ava asks.

"That's the one," I tell her.

"I love that store!" Ava gushes. "One time I spent an hour just trying on bracelets."

"My sister's done that," Matty interjects.

"Hey, have you ever been to —" Ava stops short at the sound of a camera flash.

Everyone turns around and we see a tall, bony photographer in a sand-colored tee and camo shorts hiding behind a nearby bush. Where did he come from? I haven't seen a single paparazzi all week. Rodney makes a swift move to rustle him up. Even in ninety-five-degree heat, Rodney is wearing a black tee and black jeans and looks completely terrifying in those Terminator glasses.

Before Rodney reaches the photog, Ava screams, "Gary,

get over here! Where have you been hiding out? I told you I was parasailing at two sharp."

"You know him?" Rodney points menacingly.

"Know him? I invited him," Ava replies. "He's sending my parasailing pictures to X17, aren't you, Gary, my love?"

"Anything for you, Ava," Gary says, as he continues to snap pictures. "Hey, how about one with your friend here?"

Matty jumps in front of me and puts his arm around Lauren.

"I meant the ladies," Gary says.

"Typical," Matty mumbles.

"What do you say, Kaitlin?" Ava asks. "One picture?"

"Make it two," I tell her, looking at my brother. "As long as one includes Matty."

We're in the middle of posing for the second shot — which is more like the twenty-second since Gary shoots so fast — when I hear a familiar voice.

"Kaitlin? Matty? Where are you?" It's Mom and she doesn't sound happy. Calou must hear her too because he starts to growl again. I look around. My parents aren't on the beach boardwalk, but they must be close by.

"We should go." I grab Matty's arm roughly. "It was good seeing you guys."

"What are you doing later? We're having a little party at my cabana," Ava says, oblivious to the yelling coming from the bushes. Any minute Mom and Dad are going to push through those palms and come face-to-face with us.

"Thanks," I say hurriedly, "but I have some studying to do. My SATs are in another month and I'm so behind." My personal assistant, Nadine, who is very pro-education, bought me these practice books and I've been lugging them to the beach every day. Even so, how are you supposed to memorize thousands of words for one test?

"Nerd," Matty mutters under his breath.

But Lauren and Ava don't look offended. Lauren looks sympathetic. "That's smart. I have my GEDs next month and I haven't even opened a textbook yet."

"We'll take a rain check." Ava smiles. "Maybe we can meet up in L.A.?"

"That sounds good," I say distractedly as my parents' voices — and Calou's barking — grow louder.

Ava, Lauren, and Gary make their exit just in time. Two seconds later, Mom and Dad emerge between two palm trees and step onto the boardwalk. Mom's honey-highlighted hair is hidden under a wide-brimmed straw hat, and her beach cover-up conceals her beautiful, size-four Prada bathing suit. She's wearing oversized black Gucci shades, but if I could see her eyebrows, I know they'd be raised in annoyance. Dad towers over her in a Tommy Bahama shirt, navy Calvin Klein swim trunks and a frown so sullen I'm afraid it's been tattooed to his face.

"Your father and I have been looking everywhere for you two!" Mom points a pink manicured finger in our direction. "Are you trying to kill me before I turn forty?"

"Aren't you forty-two?" Matty asks. I elbow him in the ribs. "OUCH!"

"We were just taking a tour around the island with Pierre," I tell her in my best sweet-as-pie Sam voice. "We should have told you where we were going."

"Don't actor us, Kaitlin," Mom says coolly. "We saw your limited-edition Dolce & Gabbana bikini flying over the island when your father and I were coming back from our scuba lesson."

Oops.

"How did you and Matt get past the waiver?" Dad wants to know.

Matty and I look at each other guiltily. Then Rodney coughs, which makes Mom give him the evil eye as he's gathering up our swim bags. We silently begin the short walk back to our golf cart, which will take us back to The Residence, the private villa where we're staying. The Residence is a five-bedroom mansion with two three-bedroom villas that is about a seven-minute buggy ride from the main Parrot Cay resort. The place has a full kitchen with butler service, an indoor and outdoor dining area, a media room with a plasma TV and DVD player, and a deck with a heated swimming pool and beachfront access. Anyone can stay at the world-renowned resort, but it's usually Hollywood folk and computer geeks with cash to burn that ante up the $16,500 a night price tag. Which leads me to the first of many new secrets I want to spill.

HOLLYWOOD SECRET NUMBER ONE: Where do stars vacation? To be honest, the same places you do. We head to Hawaii or the Caribbean for a good tan, the mountains for the fresh powder and ski action, and Europe when we want a change of scenery. But the reason you probably don't bump into us is because of how discreetly we travel. While some stars go commercial first-class (Brad Pitt and myself included), many prefer private jets. And as for where we stay, when we want a little R&R and very few autograph requests, we pick high-end resorts known for their zipped-lips staff and guarded quarters to keep the prying eyes of the paparazzi away.

"Parasailing is like driving a Ferrari." Dad's tone is strict as he begins to reprimand us, slipping into an analogy from his car salesman days. "Sure, it's exciting, but if you get in a fender bender, the car will never be the same. Need I remind both of you that you're under contract with *Family Affair* whether you're on vacation or not? I don't think you're allowed to do something this dangerous! If one of you got hurt there would be huge repercussions."

"Sorry," Matty and I mumble at the same time.

"You should be," Mom says, sounding exasperated. "At least if I knew, I could have had Laney set up some sort of exclusive with *Access Hollywood!*"

Matty and I look at each other. Then we look at Rodney and the three of us burst out laughing. Mom and Dad look at each other and start laughing too.

"Mom, I love you, but you're insane!" Matty hiccups, holding his stomach. "Work is all you think about!"

My mother has been my manager since I started my career. When Matty got into the business a few years ago, she became his as well. Mom says that no one would be able to look out for our interests as well as she does, but Nadine thinks my mom is obsessed with my career and that her managing style suffocates me. I don't think she's *that* bad, but sometimes I do worry my mom is more concerned with whether I win a Kids Choice Award than how I do on a chemistry test.

Mom is still laughing pretty hard. "I can't help it. My brain is hardwired to be your manager and when I see an opportunity, I have to take it!"

"We're on vacation," I remind her. "This is why we confiscated your cell phone."

"Sweetie, that's not enough to keep your mother away from Hollywood," Dad hoots. "She's had a backup phone on her the entire time." Mom blushes furiously.

"Speaking of calls, you've had a few while you've been flying over the island." Mom holds up my cell phone. I was so nervous about parasailing I guess I left it back in the villa. "Liz called from Hawaii and Austin called and said he'd see you after work on Monday." She raises her eyebrow again.

"I missed Austin and Lizzie," I groan. I've spoken to Austin every day, but with the major time difference I've only spoken to Liz three times. She sounds like she's having fun, though. She met this girl from Los Angeles the other day and they were going hiking together.

"More importantly, Seth called from Vail. He needs to talk to you."

Seth is my agent and for him to be calling me from his first vacation in three years, it must be major. Everyone I know is away this week. Hollywood sort of shuts down in late December and Los Angeles becomes a ghost town. Nadine is visiting her family in Chicago; my publicist, Laney, jetted to Cabo with "Drew and Cameron"; and Liz and her dad, my entertainment lawyer, are island-hopping in Hawaii. With no one left to bug, Mom and Dad even let us leave town (especially after they found out the Beckhams cancelled their New Year's Eve party).

"Did he say what he wanted?" I ask.

"Now that vacation is over, he wants to set up a meeting to discuss your post-*FA* plans," Mom explains. "He says we have to move if you want a chance at a new show."

"Already?" I squeak. I promised to make decisions about my future after this break, but I didn't realize we'd be diving in so soon. "I can't believe we have to worry about a new job. I'll still be taping the show for another few months."

"Your decade-plus of regular paychecks is running out soon," Dad jokes. "Where do you think we're going to get the money for our next luxurious, private villa-style vacation if you don't find a new project for me to produce, Matty to star in, or Mom to manage you on?"

Mom and Matty laugh, but the joke feels like a punch in the stomach. I never thought about my *FA* career in that way before, but I guess Dad has an unsettling point. I've been this family's breadwinner for a long time and soon I'll be unemployed. What happens if I don't find the next *Ugly Betty* or a *Harry Potter* franchise to carry my family for a few years? Will I have to let Rodney go? Give up Nadine? Yikes. Now I'm getting depressed.

"We should probably set something up for next week," Mom is saying. "I want to find your next project and announce it as soon as possible." I nod.

"Okay then," Dad says as we reach the golf cart we've been using to get to and from the main resort. "Let's get back to the villa, wash up, and rendezvous back at the cart at seven PM for our last dinner in paradise." He smiles at me. "You better enjoy it, kiddo. I have a feeling the next few months are going to be a blur."

I smile weakly. I thought I'd have time to get used to all these changes, but I feel like I just stepped onto an express bus speeding toward the end of *FA*. I just hope when I make the final stop, I'm ready to get off.

Friday, January 2
NOTE TO SELF:

Call Seth back.
Look up definition of aerostat. Pack SAT books 4 the plane ride!
Saturday flight home: 4 PM
Monday: FA calltime 6 AM
Movies w/A: after work, time TBA

12. INT. BUCHANAN MANOR KITCHEN—DAY
The kitchen island is covered with a large breakfast spread.
It's a bright, sunny, Sunday morning and PAIGE, SAMANTHA, and
SARA are in high spirits after a round of tennis.

                    SARA
    What's with the lavish breakfast? No offense, but I
    usually just eat a banana.

                    PAIGE
    I thought it would be nice if the four of us had
    breakfast together. We're all running in different
    directions lately. I feel like I never see you girls.

                    SAMANTHA
    Same goes for you, you know. What's with all these
    secret rendezvous with Dad? I still can't believe you
    two flew off last weekend and didn't say where you were
    going.

                    SARA
    They're always whispering on the terrace too. What's up
    with that?

DENNIS walks in wearing a dark suit and carrying a briefcase.

DENNIS

Good morning, my beautiful ladies. (He kisses each of
them.) I guess it's time we 'fess up. There's a reason
your mom and I have been so covert lately. (He looks
at Paige.) I've been asked to become the CEO of the
Bluestone Group. They're building an advanced
computer technology system for NASA.

SAMANTHA

(Sam hugs him.) Dad, that's incredible! This is what
you've always dreamed of doing!

PAIGE

This is an amazing opportunity for your father,
girls, but before you get too excited, there's
something else you should know. The company is
based in Miami.

SARA

Cool! Can I come with you sometimes? I hear they
have great shopping in South Beach.

DENNIS

Well, it wouldn't be to visit, Sara. If I take this,
we'd have to move there full-time. I can't run a
company this size via satellite and BlackBerry.

SAMANTHA

(shocked) You're joking, right?

PAIGE

We need a change, girls. Your father and I have felt
this way for a long time. After everything that's
happened this past year, and the Buchanan Manor
fire a few years ago, we want to make a fresh start
and we feel this opportunity is the way to do it.

SARA

You can only have a fresh start if you move to
Miami?

DENNIS

You girls are going to be off to college in two years
and then it will just be your mom and me. We have to
think about our future too.

SARA

What about the future of Buchanan Enterprises?
Or Granddaddy? He needs your help running the
company, Dad. And Mom, what about Aunt Krystal and
Aunt Penelope?

PAIGE

We've thought about all of these things, girls, but
the truth is, sometimes you have to take control of
your own life and to do that you have to put your
own needs first.

SAMANTHA

(choked up) That's it then, isn't it? This isn't some
big family meeting where we all get to take a vote.
You two have already decided!

PAIGE

If this is about Ryan, he can visit whenever he
wants. You'll work it out.

SAMANTHA

This isn't just about Ryan! It's everything! How
could make us move during junior year?

SARA

It's not like schools in Miami don't have a yearbook
committee, Sam.

SAMANTHA

(to Sara) How could you be okay with this? I thought
you loved living here!

SARA

I do, but South Beach is electric. I could work on my
tan, meet some cute boys ...

SAMANTHA

(snaps) You can do those things here.

                    PAIGE

I'm surprised at you, Sam. If anything, I thought
Sara would give us a tougher time with this decision.
You're always up for trying new things.

                    SAMANTHA

This is different! I'm not going. Aunt Krystal or
Granddaddy will let me stay with them.

                    DENNIS

Samantha, if we go, we're going as a family.

                    SAMANTHA

Well, then maybe I don't want to be part of this
family any longer!

(Samantha runs from the kitchen in tears. Sara moves to
follow her.)

                    PAIGE

(to Sara) Let her go. She needs time. She can't hide
from the future forever.

TWO: *Back to Reality*

"There you are!" Paul yells exuberantly as I enter the *FA* makeup room. "How's our little star? Did you have a good break?" I give him a huge hug. Paul is my hair designer (he's banned the word "hair dresser" from my vocabulary).

"Your skin is glowing," marvels Shelly, my makeup artist, as she wraps her large frame around me. "How was Turks and Caicos?"

"Great," I tell them. My vacation was incredible, but it feels good to be back in my comfort zone. "The weather was perfect every day," I gush. "Matty and I even went parasailing. Don't tell Tom," I add quickly.

"You made it back in one piece, so who cares?" quips Paul. He helps me up into the makeup chair and begins spritzing my wavy hair with water. My phone rings and Paul sighs. "You can answer it, but don't blame me if the curling iron singes your Motorola."

"HI!" Lizzie squeals when I pick up. "I told Mr. Harris that I needed to use the bathroom so I could sneak out and call you. Our flight from Hawaii was delayed last night and I didn't get in till late."

"That's okay. I missed you!" I tell her. "When are we getting together?"

"How about tonight?" Liz asks. "Slice of Heaven at eight?"

"I can't," I say guiltily. "I have a date with Austin." I grab my Sidekick and scroll through the week's schedule. "Tomorrow I'm working late. Thursday I have a meeting. How about Wednesday?"

"Wednesday I have a kickboxing tournament." Liz sounds bummed. "Thursday I have this thing with Josh and Friday night I'm hanging out with Mikayla."

"Who's Mikayla?" I ask as Paul comes dangerously close to burning my ear.

"She's that girl I met in Hawaii," Liz explains. "She's awesome, Kates. She's a freshman at NYU. Her family just moved to Los Angeles so she's out here for winter break. You have to meet her before she goes back."

Liz has been obsessed with getting in to New York University ever since she assisted me on the set of *Pretty Young Assassins* and began working with the film's producer. Now Liz's goal is to be a major Hollywood producer. Someday we want to team up and create our own production shingle. It could happen. Having a production company is the hot star trend these days.

"Well at least I'll get to see you this weekend at the Cinch luncheon," I say. Cinch is this high-end handbag company that stars drool over. Their annual invite-only luncheon is one of Liz's and my favorite events. The money from every Cinch handbag we buy goes to charity, which means I can spend and not feel guilty about borrowing from next month's allowance. "Maybe we can meet up with your friend afterward."

"Perfect," Liz says. "I'll call you later. I better get back to class before Principal P. catches me."

When I hang up and look in the mirror, my hair is full of big, bouncy curls that have been finished with a high gloss. The look works with the outfit Renee gave me in wardrobe. I'm wearing a Zac Posen denim skirt and a pale pink halter top. But together, neither my hair or my clothes seem right for a scene where Sam is supposed to come from just playing tennis. "Paul, this looks great, but isn't it a little dressy?" I ask tentatively as Shelly applies my foundation.

"I'll redo your hair before the first scene," Paul explains as he runs a comb through my curls one more time. "First you have the promos to shoot."

"Promos? What promos?" I ask.

"There you are," Nadine says as she strides into the room. I jump out of my chair and give her a tight hug. Nadine is more than just my longtime personal assistant. She's my Yoda. While Mom and Laney, my publicist, are consumed with me doing the best thing for my career, Nadine is the one concerned about me doing the right thing for *me*. She worries

when I get caught up in work stuff, always has my best interests at heart, and keeps my life organized better than any assistant I know. I don't know what I'd do without her.

"Did you hear about the promos yet?" Nadine asks me.
"That's why I'm late. I had to go pick up your script from
Tom." Nadine's balancing a huge stack of papers on top of
her bible (aka the binder that holds my schedule) and her
personal cell phone and work BlackBerry are ringing and
vibrating simultaneously, but at least she looks relaxed. She's
wearing makeup, her collarbone-length red hair is pulled
back in a ponytail, and she's sporting a black ribbed shirt
and green cargo pants with her Adidas sneakers.

My face must look confused because Nadine adds: "Don't
worry. Your lines are easy. The network wants you to shoot
some clips about *FA* going off the air so that everyone and
their mother tunes in. You're meeting Melli and Sky on the
set in fifteen minutes." Nadine hands me a paper and I look
at the brief script.

SARA: Will I finally get my act together?
PAIGE: Will I convince my family I know what's best for them?
SAMANTHA: The only way to find out is to tune in. Don't miss the
final eight episodes of *Family Affair*.
SARA: You know you'll kick yourself if you do. (Paige looks at
her) What? You know they will. (Faces the screen again) Don't
miss what everyone is going to be talking about.
PAIGE: She's got a point.

SAMANTHA: Eight episodes left. Don't say we didn't warn you.

PAIGE, SAMANTHA, and SARA: *Family Affair.* Sundays at nine.

Gulp. EIGHT episodes left? Is that really all there is? I thought there were more, but I guess this makes sense. It takes us more than a week to shoot each episode and we only shoot through March even if the episodes air through May.

"These are your interview questions for *Seventeen.*" Nadine is still talking. "I asked them to send them over before your phoner. A lot of the questions are going to be about the end of *Family Affair,* but you can't give away plot info. After that you have a meet-and-greet with the winner of a studio contest and another phone interview. Then I thought we could do an SAT practice test. I assume you've been studying every night." She hands me a script. "And this is from Seth. He wants you to look over this TV pilot."

My head is spinning. Interview, meet-and-greet, SATs, meeting. Oops. I still have to call Seth back! "Nadine, you're really on your game for the first day back," I kid.

Nadine doesn't laugh. "I know," she says seriously. "You're looking at a new and improved Nadine. I made a New Year's resolution for myself while I was in Chicago: I'm going to be more than just your personal secretary from here on out. You need someone to guide you into a future without *FA,* and I can help you do that. I want you to reach your full potential both professionally and personally. No more slacking off! That's why I've developed a Kaitlin Burke game plan."

She pats her binder and smiles. "We're going to get you a great SAT score so you have a college backup plan, and we're going to look at as many projects as possible to find the right one for the more grown-up you." She puts her arm around me. "Think of me as your own personal life coach."

Huh? I know I said I trust Nadine completely, but that doesn't sound anything like the Nadine I know. Nadine wants me to do well, but she's never been consumed with molding my life the way the rest of the team has. She's my friend first. I'm sure Nadine means well, but it's not like my life is hanging in the balance. Shouldn't I be able to achieve my potential on my own? Sure, I lose it sometimes — okay, a lot — but I don't need Nadine to babysit my life. I'm just going to ignore that last statement. Maybe she lost oxygen on her plane ride back to L.A. Or she could just be feeling the strain of the show ending, like I'm starting to. Suddenly I feel sad. I'm going to really miss everyone at *FA*.

"Are you done?" Sky appears in the doorway, snapping her gum. Her raven hair is curly and she's wearing a khaki Prada dress I recognize from their spring line.

Well, I'll miss *almost* everyone.

Okay, that's not nice. Sky and I have never been friends (She may play my fraternal twin, Sara, but she's more the Wicked Witch to my Glinda), but after twelve-plus years of working together, what happened at *FA* last fall helped us see eye to eye. This guest star named Alexis Holden wanted a permanent role on our show and when she was told the cast roster was full, she planted vicious lies about us in the press. I guess she thought Sky and I would blame each other for the bad karma and get ourselves fired. But for once, we worked together, and saved our jobs. Well, till the end of the season.

Shelly gives me a quick coat of Bobbi Brown lip gloss and I hurry after Sky. We walk the long corridor in silence for the first few minutes, which is really awkward.

"How was your break?" I ask, trying to be friendly. "We went to Turks and Caicos. It was beautiful. What did you do?"

"Stuff," Sky says stiffly.

I stop. "Sky, this is silly," I say. "After Alexis, we were getting along better, weren't we? We don't have to be BFs, but we can still be friendly on set."

Sky sighs. "I guess. I only have to see you for a few more months anyway."

Okay, a slight improvement — for Sky. "Let's start over: How was your break?" I ask again.

"Super busy," Sky says, her eyes bright. "My agent set up a ton of meetings and I've got a few offers, but I'm not making any sudden moves."

Whoa. She's done all that already? It's January fifth!

"I heard you're going after that show based on the book, *I'd Hate You If I Didn't Love You*, about girls who live in a Chicago hotel. I'm meeting with them too."

I haven't even heard about that pilot and here Sky's already heard I'm interested? "I still have to meet with my agent. I'm stuck in *FA* land and don't want to leave," I joke. "Can you believe we're shooting our last eight episodes? I thought there were more."

Sky shakes her head. "Nope. The show is almost finito," she says without emotion. "You better get going if you want another show or a movie this spring."

"How are you so calm?" I'm shocked. "Aren't you upset about *FA* ending?"

Sky shrugs. "I'm over it already. I'm focusing on getting a new show that I can headline. You should do the same. I'm sure we'll be going after the same projects. Maybe that will be fun. I've always liked a good competition."

"You don't say?" I deadpan. We've reached the sound-stage.

Melli, who plays Paige, our TV mom, is waiting for us on the other side. "Girls! How are you?" she asks and pelts us with kisses. "How were your vacations?"

"Great," we say in unison. It feels so good to see her. Melli is like my second mom. The one I can share my fears with. But that's going to change, isn't it? Soon I'm not going to talk to her every day. A lump begins to form in my throat.

Sky's phone rings and she looks at me triumphantly. "That must be my agent with another offer! I'll be right back." She runs off to answer it in private.

"What's wrong, Kaitlin?" Melli gives me a knowing look.

"I don't know." My voice is shaky. "I guess seeing you, being back here, filming this promo. The end of *FA* is really hitting me."

Melli hugs me. "It's okay to be upset. You've grown up here." She looks around. "*FA* is what you know and love, but that will change." She smiles.

"I know," I say, even though I'm not sure I believe that.

Tom Pullman, our creator/executive producer, walks over carrying a clipboard. His bald head is beaded with sweat and his black glasses are slightly fogged. Tom's wearing jeans and a T-shirt that says *The Affair is Almost Over.* "Why the long faces?"

"We're talking about the show ending," Melli tells him.

"Ah," Tom mumbles. "We can't deny it anymore, can we? Especially when we have these promos to shoot." He waves the dialogue at us and accidentally smacks Sky in the face as she walks back over. "Are you guys ready? These are twenty-second promos the network wants to air right away. They'll announce special episodes, show retrospectives, and count down to the final episode. Everyone is taping different ones so the network will be blanketed with *FA* reminders." Tom looks pleased. "Let's do a quick run-through and then we'll shoot. This shouldn't take more than half an hour."

Eight episodes. *Eight* episodes. I can't believe that's all that's left. I try not to think about it as I walk over to my mark.

Tom sits at his director's chair, which is behind two flat-screen monitors showing different angles of our setup. The grips are already in place with the microphone, and two cameramen are focused on us. We rehearse the scene twice before we shoot.

"Promo number one, take one," Tom announces as we start taping.

"Will I finally get my act together?" Sky says with a sneaky grin.

"Will I convince my family I know what's best for them?" Melli smiles.

It's my turn. I stare into the camera. "The only way to find out is to tune in. Don't miss . . ." I can't remember my line! How did that happen? I did fine in rehearsal. "Don't miss . . ."

"Don't miss the final eight episodes of *Family Affair*," Tom reminds me. "Keep going. We're still rolling."

But I can't. I can't say it. I can't say "the final eight episodes." These promos, the thought of losing my on-set family; it all feels too real for the first day back to work. Sky already has a list of projects lined up and I haven't even looked at one. How is she so blasé about this? How is everyone so calm about *FA* going off the air? Doesn't anyone but me feel like this is all happening too fast? Don't they care that our lives are changing?

Tears drip down my cheeks. I start thinking about Dad's bad joke again. I'm not just losing my on-set family. I'm losing my steady paycheck, which shouldn't matter too much to a seventeen-year-old, but I'm one that has a roster of people on her payroll (including my parents). "Don't miss the final . . ." I begin to sob. "I'm sorry."

Melli starts to cry now too and Sky shakes her head. "Will these two ever stop crying? Tune in and find out," she says. "Don't miss the final eight episodes of *Family Affair*."

The crew laughs, but I can see Tom and his eyes are watery too.

"It's okay, Kaitlin." He gives me a hug.

"I'm sorry," I sob. "I can do it. Just . . . just . . . give me a second."

"I can see now it's going to be a hard few months," Tom says softly.

He just figured that out?

*　*　*

Ten hours later, I'm standing in front of the ArcLight theater with Austin.

"Where do you guys want me to pick you up when the movie gets out?" Rodney looks concerned. Paparazzi were waiting for me outside work today. I'm sure it has something to do with the pictures of me with Ava Hayden and Lauren Cobb that were splashed all over the tabloids this morning. They're calling me the girls' new BFF, which is funny considering I don't even know their phone numbers.

36

"Rod, we'll meet you at the car," I say. "I think Larry the Liar got enough shots of me at the airport. I see one guy behind that trash can, but I'm sure he'll leave when we go inside."

"Don't worry, Rodney, I'll take care of her." Austin puts his arm around me protectively.

How did I get so lucky? I met Austin last fall at Clark High, where I masqueraded as a new student for a few months last year, and if you had asked me then if we would have wound up together, I probably would have said no. Austin found out my secret and was really hurt. Even after he forgave me, neither of us was sure how to balance his schoolwork and lacrosse practice with my crazy work hours and appearances on *Jimmy Kimmel*, but somehow we've managed to make our relationship a priority.

Tonight is the first time I've laid eyes on Austin in over a week and I have to wonder: Is it possible he got even *more* good-looking while I was away? His blond, windswept bangs are skimming his gorgeous blue eyes, and he looks Abercrombie catalog–ready in a navy T-shirt over a long-sleeve white thermal and distressed jeans that make his butt look unreal. (I hope he hasn't caught me staring at it.) I was so excited and nervous about seeing him that I agonized over my outfit tonight. My skin is bronzed from a week of sand and sun, so I changed into a crocheted white halter top and hip-hugging PRVCY jeans.

When Rodney is finally convinced I'm not going to be harassed by photographers, he drives away. We're completely alone. Well, alone with that one paparazzi guy and a sea of moviegoers, but they don't seem to notice me or if they do, they don't care. The ArcLight is very celeb-friendly, which is why I tend to go here even if the tickets are fourteen bucks. Plus, this is the only theater I know that lets you reserve actual seats in the theater ahead of time.

"It's just you and me. Finally." Austin grins at me, revealing his perfectly straight white teeth, and kisses me.

For a minute, I forget about work, my SAT practice test (Nadine gave me one today and I did horribly) and the shutterbug taking pictures of us.

When we come up for air, Austin says, "I could stay out here all night, but we should go inside if you want to catch the movie." We're seeing the new Mac Murdoch flick. He played my dad in *Off-Key*, a movie I made last year, and I never miss one of his films. Austin takes my sweaty hand in his and leads me toward the main entrance.

The ArcLight lobby reminds me of Grand Central Station. There is a large "departure board" that lists fourteen or more movies playing in the auditoriums and in the Cinerama Dome (which is this geodesic-shaped theater they built in the 1960s). I'm immediately overtaken by the smell of caramel popcorn, which is a theater signature. The theater also has a snack area and a café/bar that serves meals like tamales with grilled shrimp in lobster cream sauce or Angus beef burgers. We head right to the concession stand

and Austin gets us two sodas, Raisinets (for me), Milk Duds (for him), and a large popcorn.

"How was your first day back to work?" Austin asks when we finally take our assigned seats in the theater.

The smile that's been on my face since I first saw Austin slides right off as I tell him about taping the promo and how blindsided I felt. "I thought I was okay with the show going off the air, but when I saw everyone today, I lost it," I admit. "I can't believe we only have eight episodes left. I've been on that set every week since I was four. Do you have any idea what it feels like knowing your whole life is going to change in a matter of months and you can't do anything about it?"

"I don't," Austin admits. He retracts the armrest (another cool ArcLight feature) so that I can lean on his shoulder. "I guess vacation is really over, huh?"

"You can say that again." I sigh. "On vacation, the only pressing thing I had on my agenda was memorizing vocab words for the SATs, but the minute we touched down in L.A. everything changed. Everyone is hounding me to meet with Seth and find a new job. They've got me worried about making money and keeping a roof over everyone's head. And I am freaked out about that, I really am. But part of me just wants to spend some time mourning *FA* too."

Austin tries to suppress a smile. "Burke, even if you can't find another job for a year, or three, I think your family will still have a roof over their heads."

39

"I know that, and you know that, but Mom and Dad act like finding the next big thing is essential to our livelihood. Every time they bring it up, I get a lump in my throat. I guess I never thought about what my job at *FA* meant to the people around me."

"You can't be so hard on yourself," Austin tells me. "Today was your first day back at work and you're overwhelmed. You'll figure this out. *FA* isn't going away tomorrow."

I stare at the movie screen. They're playing one of those trivia games with questions about celebrities and one about me just flashed on the screen ('What is the name of Kaitlin Burke's character on *Family Affair*?' Answer: Samantha Buchanan). "Austin, that show is my rock," I practically whisper. "I'm not ready to let it go."

He kisses me. His lips taste salty from the popcorn. "I can be your rock," Austin says softly.

I must have the best boyfriend in the world. What guy says things like that outside of a romantic comedy?

"Thanks." I smile and dig into my bag. "I forgot. I got you a souvenir." I break out a royal blue T-shirt and ball cap that says Parrot Cay, which is the name of the resort where I stayed. It's not much, but my funds are low after Christmas. I got Austin this cool, framed, vintage New York City subway sign. He's always wanted one. It was listed on eBay for a hundred dollars, but I got into a bidding war with ICrack-Bax82 and wound up paying $450. Austin doesn't need to know. And, um, neither do Mom and Dad.

But Austin, he got me something ten times better. It's this beautiful, thin white gold bangle bracelet that I'm wearing right now. Inside, he had engraved: *Love, A.*

LOVE, A.

L-O-V-E, A. Sigh.

I still can't believe he's said those three little words to me and I've said them back.

Austin admires the shirt I gave him. "Very cool. I can wear this to practice on Monday."

"Lacrosse season is starting already?" I'm confused.

"We don't officially start till February," Austin explains, "but most of us aren't in a winter sport so we're starting early. I want to be at the top of my game this season."

"You're one of the best on the team," I say proudly.

Austin smirks. "You have to say that. But seriously, I need to work harder. Rob and I are thinking of doing a lacrosse training camp in Texas this summer. We've heard college scouts check out this camp for prospects."

"Wow, it sounds like you should go there then." I try to sound ultra-supportive even though the idea of Austin being halfway across the country for the summer bums me out. Before I can say anything else, the lights dim and the movie trailers start. This is my favorite part of the movies. I love deciding what flicks look good and which ones look like stinkers.

HOLLYWOOD SECRET NUMBER TWO: Movie trailers are an important piece of real estate for a film. A good film trailer can create industry, fan, and Internet buzz months or even a year before a movie's release. A lousy trailer can drive potential moviegoers away in less than two minutes. Movie trailers have become so important that studios actually vie for placement before certain films and even request what order their trailer be placed in the rotation (the last trailer before the feature is typically better than the first one, which most people miss because they're buying Milk Duds). The inside word is that some studios pay big money to make sure their trailer gets shown exactly where they want it. But you didn't hear that from me.

"Do you know why movie trailers are called trailers?" I whisper during a lame-looking romantic comedy trailer with an aging B-lister and a way-too-young-for-him blonde.

"No, why?" Austin whispers back.

"Back in the 1950s movie trailers ran after the movie, not before," I tell him as I steal a handful of his Milk Duds. He swipes a few of my Raisinets.

Suddenly I hear my own voice, and it's not coming from my mouth. What the . . . ? I glance at the screen. It is me! They're showing the trailer for *Pretty Young Assassins*.

"Hey, that's you!" Austin says excitedly.

"SHHHH!" Someone behind us hushes.

In under two minutes, we watch me battle debris, fight with Sky (who plays my backstabbing best friend), and see my character run from Mrs. Murphy, the evil clone doctor, and her army. The last shot is of Drew Thomas, who plays my boyfriend, and me on the run from a speeding car. A loud, upbeat soundtrack plays as the scenes cut fast and furious and our names — director Hutch Adams, Kaitlin Burke, Drew Thomas, Sky Mackenzie (in that order) — flash across the screen. At the end, the screen goes black and the title appears in bloodred letters — *Pretty Young Assassins*, coming to you this May.

A few people clap and I feel myself blush. I know what I said about trailers, but still. The movie shoot might have been a nightmare, but the movie itself looked *good*.

"You looked amazing." Austin kisses my cheek. "Very Princess Leia-like. I especially liked your tight black leather pants."

I giggle. "Keep May open," I tell him. "I want you to be my date for the premiere."

Austin squeezes my hand. "I wouldn't miss it."

FA may be ending, but I guess I do have something fun to look forward to.

Monday, January 5
NOTE TO SELF:

REALLY call back Seth. He's left 4 messages!
Tues., Wed., Thurs., Fri., call times: 6:30 AM
Cinch 4 a Cause luncheon w/Lizzie: Sat.

THREE: *Cinch for a Cause*

Rodney's just dropped me off at the Cinch for a Cause luncheon and I'm standing outside the restaurant trying not to fall asleep standing up. We shot on location last night till eleven so I'm exhausted. Under-eye circles or not, there was no way I was missing this. Cinch's lunch combines two great perks: I can buy a limited-edition handbag and raise money for cancer research at the same time!

This year's event is being held at Mac Murdoch's Cuban-American eatery, Fusion. I doubt Mac will be on hand for the event. Mac once told me that he only drops in a few times a year. That would explain HOLLYWOOD SECRET NUMBER THREE: Most stars don't have time to oversee their own BlackBerry messages, let alone run a restaurant. Many stars in the restaurant biz are usually silent partners who contribute with their wallets and recipes. (What star doesn't want to share their mother's beloved meatloaf with the world?) If a star's eatery is good, the place can be a way to bring in cash in between projects. But if business is bad, get ready for a nasty bashing in the press.

Thankfully, Mac's restaurant is the former. I give myself a once-over before heading inside, checking my eye concealer coverage. The lunch is semi-casual so I'm wearing a strapless navy blue Samantha Tracy dress and three-inch Jimmy Choos. My hair is down and I'm carrying a brown leather Cinch bag. (It's always good to wear or carry something from the designer whose event you're attending.) I'm about to open the door when I hear a familiar ringtone. I pick up on the first ring.

"HOW WAS TURKS AND CAICOS?" My publicist Laney bellows. Laney may be in her thirties (I *think* — she still won't tell me her exact age), but she scares even the most seasoned people in the business. She's known for being loud, brash, and a big celeb name-dropper. ("Jess Alba and I had lunch yesterday at this darling place!") But she'll also defend her clients within an inch of her life, which is what I love about her.

"GOOD," I yell, forgetting for a moment that I don't have to yell back. Laney always seems to find the nosiest locations to call me from so she's always screaming into the phone. "I water-skied and Matty and I . . ."

"WHEN ARE YOU MEETING WITH SETH?" she asks, shouting over a symphony of jackhammers, drills, and falling lumber. Laney's house in Malibu is being renovated.

"I'm calling him today," I say guiltily. I got so busy between

FA stuff and SAT studying this week that I put Seth's repeated messages aside. Not that I'm going to tell Laney that. "How was Cabo with Drew and Cameron?" I change the subject.

"Fab," Laney coos and takes her voice down an octave. "I told the girls they have to do another Angels flick and put you in it. Now about your meeting. I think . . . NOOO! I SAID PUT IT ON THE TERRACE. NOT ON THE DECK."

I pull the phone away from my ear. "You sound busy," I tell her.

"I'm not." Laney sounds offended. "I was calling to set up a lunch for *after* you see Seth. Nadine said she thinks you're putting the meeting off. Are you?"

What? Why would Nadine say that to Laney? She's supposed to be on my side! "I'm not," I insist quickly. "It's just going back was harder than I thought and —"

"I WANT THE JACUZZI THERE!" Laney interrupts. The hammering and the drilling grow louder again. "OVER THERE! Kaitlin, call Seth. No buts. I'll call you later after I deal with *this*." Click.

Sigh. It's just as well I didn't tell her about my crying fit during the promos taping. She'd tell me I was just being dramatic.

I can still hear the jackhammer in my ears as I make my way through the air-conditioned restaurant to the outdoor patio. Fusion's outside area is really peaceful. Ivy is draped over the concrete patio walls, planted trees provide extra shade, and white twinkling lights dot the bushes even during the daytime. A large stone fountain with two cherubs sits in the center of several wrought-iron tables topped with hydrangeas and small votives. For today's event, I see the restaurant's outdoor bar has been converted into a mini Cinch store being run by girls wearing the brand's signature CI logo. I look around. The place is packed with women I know, or have at least seen, on the big and small screens.

Cinch's marketing chief, Enid Euber, greets me warmly. "Hi, Kaitlin! So glad you could make it. You're at table eight." She points to the far side of the room, where Liz is already seated. She sees me and waves madly. "We have photographers documenting the event so keep your smile handy!" Enid adds as I head over to Liz.

Photographers are an understatement. Cinch's lunches get a lot of coverage, so there are four photographers and at least two video crews working the room. Already, Miley and Vanessa are holding Cinch T-shirts for a camera in one corner while Rihanna, Jessica, and Ashley strike a pose with their purchases in another.

A flash goes off as I hug Liz. We both start talking at the same time and laugh.

"Sit," Liz instructs. She looks good in a curve-hugging rust-colored dress that looks amazing against her olive skin. Liz's shoulder-length brown hair is down and curly. "Let's catch up quick so we can shop," she says. "I have my eye on a limited edition snakeskin pochette that one of the Cheetah Girls keeps looking at. Vacation details. Go."

I giggle. "Totally relaxing and beautiful. I thought about ditching it all and opening my own dive shop just so I could avoid coming home and taking the SATs."

"Stop stressing!" Liz scolds. "You've been studying so you're going to be fine."

"If you call doing half a practice test during lighting changes on set studying, then yeah, I've been studying," I say dryly. "I was getting at least an hour of practice a day while we were on break, but now, between memorizing my lines and doing interviews about *FA*, I'm lucky if I can squeeze in twenty minutes."

"Picture, girls?" a photographer interrupts and even before we can answer, begins snapping. "Hold up your purchases."

"We haven't made any yet," I tell him and he looks disappointed.

"I'll come back, then," he says. "And Kaitlin, maybe I can get one later of you with Ava and Lauren too."

"Sure." I smile sweetly.

"I heard about your new BFFs in *Hollywood Nation*." Liz nudges me when the photographer is out of earshot. "You didn't tell me you guys went on vacay together."

"Very funny," I say and explain what happened. "What about you? Tell me about your trip."

"The Grand Wailea Resort Hotel and Spa is perfection," Liz gushes. "You have to go. It's pretty quiet so you need company. I don't think I could have handled two weeks if I hadn't met Mikayla." I nod. "She's been so helpful about NYU and —"

"Excuse me, Liz," Enid interrupts, smiling sweetly. "Your father's business associate is here and I was hoping to get a picture of you two together." Liz's dad is a famed entertainment lawyer whose clients include most A-listers, and a lot of TV stars, like me. Liz and I met when I became her dad's client years ago.

"I'll be right back," Liz tells me apologetically.

While I'm waiting, I survey our table. There are six chairs, but Liz and I are the only two seated yet. Two Disney Channel stars walk over seconds later and quietly say hello. I've met them both at other events, but I don't know them too well. They drop their own Cinch purses on the chairs, pushing aside the pretty pink Cinch gift bags, and head off to shop. I start looking over the luncheon menu and hear a loud crash. A waiter carrying a tray full of beverages has collided with Lauren Cobb and Ava Hayden. Lauren's clear drink sloshes all over her dress. "Watch it!" she barks.

"Sorry about that." Liz slides into her chair next to mine. "What's going on?"

I shrug. "I don't know," I say as I watch Enid rush over to Lauren and Ava and begin apologizing.

"So where were we?" Liz asks.

"Um . . ." There have been so many distractions, I can't remember. "I don't know." We both laugh.

"What about you?" Liz takes a sip of her seltzer. "How is *FA*?"

I'm glad she asked because I've been dying to talk to Liz

about this. Just a month ago, I was feeling so confident about leaving *FA* behind, but now that the end is right in front of me, I'm not so sure. I'm about to tell Liz exactly that when I hear someone behind us clear their throat. I turn around.

Sky is standing behind me with her friend Elle Porter, a C-lister known more for her botched boob job than her body of work. She gives us a half smile. "I need you," Sky tells me as she leans in close and smiles for a nearby photographer. "Enid wants us to do a quick interview together. It's for *Celebrity Nation.*"

"Take your time," Liz insists. "I'm going to buy that bag I wanted before anyone else gets it."

Ten minutes turns into twenty and I rush back to our table, where Liz is making small talk with the girls sitting next to us. "That took longer than I thought it would," I apologize. "Where were we?" I know where we were. I was about to tell Liz about my mini-meltdown on set, but I don't want to be rude and just start talking about myself.

Liz makes a face. "Actually I have to go."

"What?" I protest. "We haven't even had salad yet."

"I know." Liz looks guilty. "I was going to tell you earlier, but we kept getting interrupted. Mikayla's dad's best friend is on the board of directors at NYU and he's in town visiting. Mikayla said I could come over and schmooze. I only found out last night. I'm sorry."

"It's okay," I say, disappointed. "I was just really looking forward to hanging out."

"I know." Liz sounds apologetic. "I've been too. I just can't pass this up, Kates. Meeting with NYU board members is a huge deal. It could give me an edge, you know?"

"You don't need an edge," I tell her. "Your SAT scores were great, you've got good grades and nine million after-school activities. NYU would kill to have you."

"Thanks, but it's so competitive." Liz sighs. "Mikayla says it's important to distinguish yourself. This meeting could really help me. Can you hang out tomorrow instead?"

I bite my lip. "Tomorrow I have my SAT tutor in the morning and a Fever photo shoot in the afternoon." Fever is this cosmetics line I'm a spokesmodel for. "But I really want to talk to you. So much is going on."

"I want to talk to you too," Liz insists. She grabs her new Cinch purchase and the pink gift bag. "I'll call you later and we'll figure out a day to get together."

We hug again and I watch Liz go. A small part of me is upset that Liz left. I know meeting board members from NYU is a great opportunity, but couldn't she have gone afterward? We've had these plans forever. I try to make the best of the situation and talk to the other girls at my table over the salad course, but the conversation is awkward. I get the feeling they just want to be left alone. Maybe I should go mingle. I haven't said hi to Miley yet.

"Kaitlin! Over here!"

I look up. Ava is standing two tables away with Lauren and they're calling me over. Without the spilled drinks and hubub surrounding them, I get a good look at what they're wearing. Ava looks great in a short, canary yellow dress that folds in ripples across her tiny waist and wraps around her knees. Her long, straight blond hair is piled in a low bun and she's wearing what must be at least ten-carat diamond earrings. Why do I have a feeling she didn't borrow them? Lauren is dazzling in a thigh-length silver dress.

I excuse myself and walk over. "I didn't know you were going to be here," Ava squeals as she hugs me tightly, like we're best friends. "We've been meaning to call you."

"Who are you sitting with?" Lauren asks. "Forget them. You're sitting with us."

Ava holds out the chair next to her. I look back at my own table. I'm sure the girls won't mind if I leave. Ava and Lauren smile at me expectantly.

"Okay," I agree shyly.

"Can you believe Oprah is here?" Ava leans over and whispers. "I'm dying to say hi. I worship that woman."

"She is brilliant," Lauren seconds. "I TiVo every episode."

"Me too," I say, perking up. "Her and Rachael Ray. Not that I can cook."

"Shut up!" Ava slaps my arm. "We love her too!"

We get into a lengthy conversation about television hosts, our favorite TV shows and the best reality programs on TV (neither of them mention their own, but we're all in agreement that *The Hills* rules). It turns out that Ava and Lauren watch *Gossip Girl* just like I do, and swear by the two-hour block of *Ugly Betty* and *Grey's Anatomy*. Lauren even likes *Star Wars*. Our chat is only interrupted once briefly when Ava tells off this Nickelodeon actress for having said something negative about her to Page Six. It all happens so quickly that I don't even have time to react. Lauren is too busy grilling me about my favorite *Star Wars* scenes. It turns out the three of us shop at the same stores, all agree that Coffee Bean kicks Starbucks's butt and can't get enough of Pinkberry yogurt. Ava is funny and Lauren, despite her rep for being an airhead, actually seems to have a lot to say. I almost feel guilty for believing everything I read about them. I know I'd hate it if they did about me.

"Okay, enough talking," Ava declares. "It's time to shop." She grabs my hand and I notice several camera flashes go off around us. "Come on! Let's go."

The three of us rush up to the Cinch shop and Lauren and Ava begin plucking bags off their pedestals like they're candy. "Oooh, look at this one! I only have it in blue. I don't own red. Do you make an orange? This one is killer! It's so cute and tiny. I'll take three. What kind of wallets do you have? Do you have a matching keychain?"

I make my way along the display and stop in front of a large leopard print bag with black leather trim and tons of zippers. I pick it up and twirl it around. I've never seen a Cinch bag like it before.

Ava gasps. "That bag is divine," she says, taking it out of my hands. "The leather is so soft, and I love the pattern. You have to get it. It's *so* you."

I laugh. "It's kind of loud for my taste. And big. I don't carry this much stuff."

"Trying something out of character is so now," Lauren says. "That bag rocks."

I put it on my shoulder and look in the floor length mirror standing next to the display counter. The bag is cool. And I don't have anything quite like it. I look at the price tag. Ouch! It's over three thousand dollars.

Ava sees my face. "Don't think about the price. The money goes to charity."

"Even so, it's a lot. My mom will kill me." I have bags that cost much more than this, but they've all been gifted to me. I can't buy this. I can hear Mom yelling already.

Lauren shrugs. "Wait till the bill comes in to tell her. That's what I do."

"I can't do that," I say, surprised. I put the bag back on the pedestal and stare at it longingly.

"Don't think. Just buy," Ava tells me and takes the bag off the pedestal again and pushes it into my arms. "You work hard. You make money."

"But my mom," I start to say again.

"Forget your mom," Ava insists. She looks at me intently. "This is a great bag and you deserve it, especially with your show going off the air. Buy the bag to cheer yourself up."

Maybe I do deserve a pick-me-up. I look at the bag again. No. I can't do it. Mom will freak. She can make a purchase like this, but if I did it, she'd wig out. "Maybe I'll talk to my mom and if she says it's okay I'll get it then," I say a tad sadly.

Lauren pouts. Ava sighs and shakes her head. "Don't you ever just do what *you* want to do? I mean, *without* asking anyone for permission?"

Um. No?

I stare at the bag again and play with one of the zippers. Hmm . . . maybe Ava's right. Everyone is always making my decisions for me. I should be able to buy a bag without having to call a meeting. And Mom did say to get whatever I want. The money goes to charity. Besides which, I *love* this bag. "Okay," I say defiantly. I hand my credit card to the Cinch girl and feel a surge of adrenaline shoot through my body.

The girls squeal in approval. Their loot winds up costing three times more than mine, but neither flinches. When we get back to the table, my Sidekick begins buzzing and I see the message is from Nadine.

FUTUREPREZ: Great news! We got U in2 the *Vanity Fair* Oscars party! U + 1. Guess we need 2 find U a dress. Congrats! (P.S. Don't forget 2 study 4 my SAT quiz on Monday.)

Oh my God. I got in to the *Vanity Fair* party! I've never gotten in before and I've always wanted to go. I may have been annoyed with Nadine before, but all is forgiven now. I want to scream, but I don't think it would be appropriate. "I got into the *Vanity Fair* Oscars party," I tell Lauren and Ava excitedly.

Lauren squeals so loudly that I hear dogs bark next door. "Us too! We have to go dress shopping together."

"Girls, let's celebrate!" Ava lifts her champagne glass to toast. Lauren grabs hers too. I quickly reach for my seltzer and cranberry.

"Hey, girls, smile," a photographer says.

I turn and grin broadly. Today that's not a problem.

Saturday, January 10
NOTE TO SELF:

Date w/A — tonight @ 8 PM. Tell A great news!
Sunday — SAT tutor @ 9AM, photo shoot 4 Fever @ 12 PM
Monday, Tuesday — call time @ 6 AM
*Tues. night. Gina's movie premiere! Red carpet @ 7 PM
Wed. on location — Santa Monica Pier 7 AM
Study 4 Nadine's SAT prep exam. Have Nadine look in2 driving lessons. Again.

BLOGS SIGHTINGS BIOS ARCHIVE

SIGHTINGS   January 11

LEAVING TREMONT PLASTIC SURGERY CLINIC:
Don't think that Hermès scarf and Chanel shades can hide your
face from us, **Alexis Holden.** We saw you leaving Tremont Plastic
Surgery Clinic yesterday with a big, white bandage over your nose.
Has your honker been downsized? Your new publicist says "she
was there researching a role," but we think otherwise. The nose
knows, as they say, Alexis, and once you come out from behind
that Hermès scarf, we'll know for sure too.

CAUSING A SCENE AT YOGA CENTRAL:
Loopy *Pretty Young Assassins* director **Hutch Adams** threw a hissy
fit at his nightly yoga class when a substitute instructor asked him
to move his mat so there was room for another student to join the
class. After repeated attempts to calm Mr. Adams didn't work, he
was removed. Don't think you'll be doing the downward dog there
again anytime soon, Hutchy. Boo hoo.

DOUBLE DATING:
Drew Thomas, you dog, you! Your sweet little dates may not have
realized they had competition for your affections, but we caught
you red-handed. At five PM on Saturday you took a mystery blonde
for dinner at Koi (Too early, dude! What were you doing? Hoping for an early bird special?) and then at nine thirty you had a
brunette on your arm as you entered Shelter. Tsk, tsk. Let's hope
neither of them read this column!

BLOGS **SIGHTINGS** BIOS **ARCHIVE**

NEW BFFS SPOTTED AT THE CINCH FOR A CAUSE LUNCHEON:

Family Affair star **Kaitlin Burke** was shopping and laughing with new best buds **Ava Hayden** and **Lauren Cobb** at the annual Cinch for a Cause luncheon benefiting breast cancer research (see our pictures under the STARS OUT section). Sources tell us the three are inseparable, having vacationed together over the holidays, and Kaitlin may be in talks to do a reality show with the girls, which would follow their adventures in a Malibu rental next summer after Kaitlin's stint on *Family Affair* ends. Unlike Lauren and Ava, the party lifestyle is new for Kaitlin, but she seems to be settling in just fine. She was seen sipping and toasting with an unknown beverage at the luncheon. "I'm not saying it was definitely alcohol," says one witness on hand. "But with those two girls at Kaitlin's side, I wouldn't be surprised."

FOUR: *Kaitlin Burke Kidnapped!*

Bright light! Bright light! I feel like a vampire when I step out of the protected *FA* location trailer after a day of shooting on Santa Monica Pier and face the waiting paparazzi. I cover my eyes to avoid the blinding camera flashes as Rodney pulls Nadine and me through the crowd.

"Excuse us, coming through," Rodney says gruffly. Ever since it was announced that *FA* was ending, the paparazzi have been worse than flies. They hang around outside our studio, loiter near our location shoots and basically get in everyone's faces.

"Kaitlin, doll, smile for the camera!" My own personal pest, Larry the Liar, points his Nikon camera in my face.

If I wasn't afraid the conversation would be printed in tomorrow's *Hollywood Nation,* I'd tell Larry exactly where he can put his request. Dealing with guys like Larry is part of being a celebrity, but this past weekend, he crossed the line. He's the one that took a picture of me toasting with Lauren and Ava at the Cinch for a Cause event and sold the photo to some Web sites. All the sites questioned whether I was drinking. Hello! It was seltzer! There was so much controversy about my thirst quencher, Laney had to make a statement: "Kaitlin Burke is too young to drink. She was sipping seltzer with cranberry juice at the Cinch luncheon."

Can you believe this is the stuff that makes the five o'clock news? Not human injustices or starving children. Me and my beverage choice. It's unreal.

"Beat it, Larry," Rodney growls, revealing his chipped tooth. He's getting a cap tomorrow, but he's not in any rush. The crack is a badge of stuntman honor in Rodney's book. He cracked it rehearsing a chase scene for a Trident gum commercial he's doing.

Larry keeps shooting. "You can't stop me. I have every right to be here."

"Ignore him, Rod," I tell him. I'm not going to let Larry ruin my mood. Today was a pretty good day. Sky, Trevor, and I got to ride all the rides on the Santa Monica Pier in the unseasonably warm (near eighty degrees!) weather. The best part is that no one mentioned *FA* going off the air even once. For a moment, it felt like any other day of shooting. That is, until I remembered we have less than two months left.

"Let's get to the car." Nadine gives Larry a look. "He can't get you there."

We start walking — cars aren't allowed on the Pier — and my phone rings. I reach in my new leopard print Cinch bag (I've gotten tons of compliments on it already) and pray the call is from Liz. We've been playing phone tag for two days, which is so unlike us. I look at the caller ID and don't recognize the number. "Hello?"

"Hey, chickie! It's Ava," she drawls in a deep voice. "Want to hang with me and Lau?"

I smile to myself. I had so much fun with them at the luncheon. I thought Lauren and Ava were going to be pretty self-involved, but they weren't. They wanted to know a lot about me and my relationship with Austin. We must have talked about boyfriends for an hour. (Lauren's single. Ava is on and off with this popular band's lead singer who is known more for being a serial dater than for his group's singles.)

"We're going to Chateau Marmont and then dancing," Ava says. "You can come with as long as you don't drink too much, you lush."

I'm laughing so hard I don't notice the black Escalade pull up next to the street corner we've just reached. Larry jumps out of the way as the car screeches to a halt. The tinted passenger window opens and Rodney grabs my arm. We're prepared to flee when I hear a familiar voice say: "Kaitlin Burke, get in this car right now."

"Mom?" I peek my head in and see Mom and Dad in the backseat. Mom's face is grave, the way it is after a bad Nielsen number, but she looks great, as usual. She's wearing her favorite Dolce & Gabbana cream-colored pant suit and her long hair is curly. Dad looks like he's ready for a day at the office — even if he doesn't work at one — in his light blue Izod button-down shirt and navy trousers. "Is everything okay?" I ask nervously.

"Everything's fine. Rodney will take Nadine home," Mom presses. "Get in."

"Ava, I have to call you back," I tell her quickly and hang up as Larry continues to shoot the bizarre scene. I open the backseat door and barely have time to say goodbye to Nadine and Rodney before we pull away.

"Hi, Kaitlin. How was your day?" Laney is in the front passenger seat. What is she doing here? Laney looks fabulous. Her long blond hair is ironed to flat perfection and she still has a tan from her vacation. She's wearing a black tailored shirt with sleeves she's rolled up to reveal toned arms, her diamond-encrusted Movado, and a tennis bracelet she bought herself. (Laney says the only relationship she has time for is the one with her clients.)

"It was fine up until now," I tell her and peer curiously at the unknown driver veering us to points unknown. "You guys are freaking me out. Why did you just kidnap me? Did you see Larry the Liar standing there? He must have shot a zillion pictures and they're all going to be online later."

Dad frowns. "Hmm . . . we didn't think about the paparazzi."

"I'll handle that," Laney insists. "This is more important. Your parents and I decided the only way to get a real answer out of you is to talk to you in person."

"For the zillionth time — I was drinking seltzer!"

"We know that." Mom sounds agitated.

"I do want to address these new acquaintances you've made at a later time," Laney says ominously.

"This get-together is about your meeting with Seth," Mom explains. "We want to know why it hasn't happened yet. Is there something you're not telling us?"

"I've been busy." I squirm uncomfortably. They don't look convinced and I'm not sure I would be either. I could have met with Seth by now. I make time for everything else. I guess I haven't wanted to face the future yet. I have enough of a reality check every time I step on the *FA* soundstage. "I've had all these interviews and we've been filming long hours and doing promos," I remind them. "I haven't had the time."

"You need to make time!" Mom tells me, sounding annoyed. "Meeting with Seth is more important than anything else, Kaitlin. Finding your next project is crucial if you want to remain at the top of the Hollywood most-wanted list."

I feel my stomach begin to churn, like I'm on the verge of a major ache, and I feel slightly nauseous. Is getting another job that pressing? Does Mom think if I don't get something right away the public will forget about me before the next TV season starts?

Dad takes my hand. "I know you'll miss *FA*. I remember the day I gave up my 1977 Mustang," he says. "I thought I could never love another car as much as that one. Then I saw the 1982 Pontiac Firebird. It had leather seats and fifteen-inch aluminum wheels and I just knew it was the car for me. Sometimes you can open your heart to more than one automobile."

I squeeze his hand. I understand what Dad's saying.

"This is your moment to shine," Laney tells me, sounding like she's a king readying me for battle. "You need to show the world that you can play a part that's different from Samantha. Seth can help you do that."

"I know," I admit.

"If you're going to do a pilot, we need one now," Laney says. "Otherwise all that will be left is bland teenager parts on a bad sitcom with some C-level comedian."

"Or *Dancing with the Stars*," Mom threatens.

I gasp. *Dancing with the Stars* is one of my biggest fears. I don't want my star to fall so far that I have to resort to learning the quick step and the mambo. I have to meet with Seth! I'll tell him what I'm looking for and if he doesn't have something I like, I won't take something for the sake of taking it. Who knows? Maybe Dad's right and I'll find something I like even more than I like playing Sam. "I'll set up a meeting right away," I promise, feeling suddenly confident. "Is that all you wanted? Because I was going to meet some friends for dinner. Maybe you could drop me off at Chateau Marmont."

Mom smiles serenely. "I'm afraid you'll have to cancel. We're on our way to Seth's office now."

"What?" I feel my self-esteem come crashing back to

earth. Now? They want me to meet with Seth now? I'm not ready! My merlot-colored Abercrombie tunic feels like it is suffocating me and my Divine Rights of Denim jeans are glued to the leather seats. Does the driver have the air on? The nausea is coming back, and my stomach aches. I want to argue, but it's pointless. Nothing is getting me out of this meeting. Except maybe jumping from the car. That would hurt. Sigh. "How could you guys do this without asking me?"

Mom shrugs. "We knew you'd understand. This had to be taken care of, Kaitlin."

"Fine. Drop me off then," I say defiantly. "I can meet with Seth myself."

Mom and Dad chuckle. "Sweetie, we need to be there," Mom says. "We can't have you making the wrong decision, can we? We want to make sure your next project is a block-buster, and good for your image, and we don't think you can do that on your own. You need our guidance, Kate-Kate."

"Thanks," I mumble. Mom can be so embarrassing some-times. I know she's looking out for my career, but I hate when she treats me like a child. I sink into the seat feeling defeated and Ava's words echo in my head. When do I get to do what *I* want to do without having to ask for permission? My family doesn't know what kind of role I want. *I do.* Well, I might if everyone stopped hounding me long enough to let me figure it out. Suddenly I feel like I'm six again and I'm asking permission to ride my bike alone around the studio backlot. I wasn't allowed, of course. Mom was afraid I'd talk to a passing studio exec and say something silly.

"Don't be mad," Mom says in a gentler voice. "We're trying to help." She looks at Laney. "Speaking of which, there's also another matter I wanted to discuss with you."

"What is it?" I ask wearily.

"*Fashionistas* wants to profile me in their next issue." Mom sounds excited now. "I'd have a photo shoot and they'd follow me around for a few days and do an in-depth interview. I wouldn't talk too much about you, of course, just my management duties, but Laney thought I should clear it with you before accepting." She stares at me hopefully.

Finally something Mom needs *my* permission for. I'm so aggravated I want to say no on the spot, but I look at Mom's elated face. *Fashionistas* is a big, thick fashion bible. It's incredibly hip and read by most of Hollywood. Mom is obsessed with it. "You should do it," I tell her. "It sounds like fun."

"Really?" Mom looks like she's about to burst. She starts punching numbers on her cell using her long fingernails. "Thank you, honey! I've got to call my trainer and add more workouts, get my hair redone, and set up an airbrush tanning appointment. The photo shoot is next week."

At least one of us is ready for our close-up.

Some celebrities like to be the star of every moment in their lives. They want their charity work chronicled in *OK!* They want their child's first baby pictures to spur a bidding war. When they have a movie, TV show, CD, or documentary to promote, they book themselves on every talk show couch that will let them warm the seat.

As you might have noticed by now, I'm not one of those people.

I like a rave review or an exuberant fan encounter as much as the next person, but the thought of talking about all things Kaitlin Burke at length is embarrassing.

Needless to say, I don't spend anywhere near as much time with my agent, Seth Meyers, as Vince spends with Ari on *Entourage*. I like Seth well enough and I know he has my best career interests at heart (He should. I pay him practically a mortgage payment each month to guide my career.), but I guess I've always felt I didn't *need* Seth. I'm on a hit TV show so I don't have time to let him book me as many projects as an A-list film star or musician.

That's all about to change, isn't it?

When we arrive at the office building and reach Creative Connection's floor, Seth and the rest of the company are waiting for us at the elevator. I feel like a dark cloud is hanging over my head and I wonder if it shows on my face. I hope Seth doesn't know I was forced here against my will. When the agency reps see me they start to applaud. I smile sweetly and try to push my ill will aside. Seth is standing in the middle of the crowd with a huge, laser-white smile.

If you met Seth six years ago, you wouldn't recognize him today. Seth wore Dockers and Old Navy polos and had big, brown glasses that always slid down his nose when he talked in a soft, low voice. He didn't make eye contact much, probably because his brown hair was constantly falling in front of his brown eyes. He was so pale that sometimes when he wore beige, I used to joke that he looked like the invisible man. He was fresh out of college and it was his first year at CC so he was eager to work triple hard, which Mom loved. (My old agent kept pushing for me to leave *FA* and stretch my wings on a "real soap" like *The Young and the Restless*. I'm glad we ignored him.)

Seth envelopes me in a tight hug, giving me a whiff of his cologne. (Armani, perhaps?) "I was worried you were avoiding me," he whispers.

"Never," I lie. The new(ish) Seth has his groove on. He's tanned to perfection, thanks to airbrushing. His hair is still chin-length, but product-heavy and I'm pretty sure it's highlighted. His clothes (Armani suit, Tom Ford tie, Prada shoes) are strictly from Fred Segal or Barneys. The only thing missing are Seth's trademark silver shades. Usually whether we're indoors or out, Seth has them glued to his face — along with his Bluetooth.

"Good," he says and his eyes, 20/20 thanks to Lasik eye surgery, bounce from one person to the next. "Let's get you in the conference room and pick your next project." Seth puts his arm around me and leads me down the hall.

The Creative Connections conference room always makes me feel like I'm in a fishbowl. One wall faces busy

Wilshire Boulevard and the other three walls are made of glass so everyone in the office can look in. The refreshment table along the back wall is fully stocked with three types of water, Coke and Diet Coke, and an assortment of flavored coffees. I grab a Smartwater and take a seat in the chair Seth has for me at the head of the table. Every seat has a pink folder with an embossed K on the front. At the opposite end of the table is a large flat-screen TV. Mom and Dad take seats on either side of me. (Laney has decided to wait in Seth's office and make some calls.)

"As you can see, we're excited to have you here." Seth stands next to the TV. "And we're committed to helping you take the next step in your career."

The lights dim and I dig my fingers into the chair. Oh no. I know what's coming. My mouth feels dry and I do my best to resist the urge to dive under the table. A Josh Grobin song plays as images of me on *Family Affair* flash across the screen.

"Even as a small child, Kaitlin Burke was destined for stardom." A voiceover that sounds like Seth narrates.

They highlight some of Sam's biggest moments — her first kiss, her first horseback riding championship, fights with Sara, the heroic moment when she saved her mom during the Buchanan Manor fire — and include this famous *FA* scene. I'm five and Sam is in the hospital because of one of the many bizarre illnesses she's developed over the years. Paige and Dennis are crying over my limp body and I sit up and say, "Stop crying! I'm not dying, you know." Tom thought I was so funny, he left the line in.

"As the years passed, Kaitlin's star shined brighter and the film world beckoned." Roles like *Off-Key* are shown and there's even footage from *PYA*.

"The public's appetite for everything Kaitlin is insatiable," Seth adds as several of my magazine covers, my Fever endorsement, Nickelodeon awards, TV appearances, and red carpet moments flash on the screen. "The question is, what is Kaitlin's next move?" The screen goes black. "The answer? Anything she wants." Images of Barbie dolls, Oscar winners, the VMAs, and other Hollywood commodities zoom by. "The choice is up to you, Kaitlin, and Creative Connections is ready to help you make it." Everyone applauds. When the lights come up I see that Mom and Dad are teary.

This. Is. So. Embarrassing.

"The film, TV, music, reality, and theater divisions are all here and they have a lot of exciting offers to go over with you," Seth continues. "It's time to leave the wholesome goodness of Sam behind and take on a new character and a new career path that will distinguish you from your work on *Family Affair*."

Why does everyone keep reminding me that I'm no longer playing Sam? For years all anyone would say was how lucky I was to play such a goodie-goodie who is adored by the public and the press. Now everyone wants to throw her under the bus.

The film division is first. There's a bizarre action flick shooting in Mexico that is based on a true story. I would play a missionary's daughter who single-handedly saves a whole village from extinction. It sounds intense. There's also a teen comedy from a well-known director whose films all make a truckload of cash. I'd play a high school party girl who takes over the principal's office and runs the school. Um, if I'm leaving Sam behind, I want something more mature. That's why the third film sounds so appealing. It's a chick-flick drama based on one of my favorite books, *Manolos Are Meant for Small Feet*. It's set in London and I would play a college freshman who unearths all this dirt about the television industry. None of the movies start shooting till the summer.

Next the television division pitches several pilots. Seth points out what I already know and dread — if I want to do another TV show, I have to pick a pilot right away. The first pilot is *I Would Hate You If I Didn't Love You*. Seth says they definitely want me to take a meeting. I feel uneasy, knowing this is Sky's number-one choice. The next one is about a group of college kids in Alaska and it's directed by a little-known filmmaker whose last movie I adored. It sounds quirky and irreverent and a total change of pace. The third pilot is an ensemble drama with a killer cast (Pam Sommers is the Meryl Streep of TV and she'd play my mom!) and a well-respected director who is known for giving his actors great scenery-chewing moments. The problem is I'd be playing the youngest daughter, who is giving the family trouble. I'm not sure how I feel about playing the daughter role again in a family drama. How could any family compare to the one on *FA*? I know I have to stop thinking like this, but I don't know if I'm ready to commit to another show — that could take up the next ten years of my life if it does well — just yet.

Seth's next pitch blows my mind. He wants me to star on Broadway. "Doing a play is very chic," he says. "Lots of stars are doing three-month turns and getting rave reviews. This kind of experience could catapult you to the adult roles I know you want."

Wow. Star on Broadway? "But I've got no stage experience," I remind him.

"You'd be a natural," Seth tells me. "The play we're thinking of just finished a sold-out run in London's West End. It's called *Meeting of the Minds*. The star, Meg Valentine, is coming to the States to reprise the role, but she has to drop out in May, which is perfect timing. They're dying to meet you."

"I did some plays back when I was in college," Dad tells us all proudly. "There's no thrill like live theater, Kate-Kate. Every night is a different show and you react off the crowd. I think you would really love it."

I've never heard Dad so excited. I'm about to tell Seth I want to read the script when Mom interrupts. "Has no one thought of Kaitlin doing her own CD?" she asks.

I can't help but glare at my mom. She's got to be kidding.

First she kidnaps me and now she wants me to be a rock star? I'm not recording an album no matter how much she begs.

The music division pounces and Broadway is forgotten. Apparently several music makers, including hotter-than-hot producer TJ, have asked to meet with me about an album. TJ has sculpted the music careers of several stars with great success, and he's only in his twenties.

HOLLYWOOD SECRET NUMBER FOUR: Ever wonder why so many movie stars cross over to the music world? In my opinion, it's because they can make major cash from a CD. If they've already established their name as an actor, then music companies think those fans will follow them to iTunes. And nowadays, anyone who can hum a tune can make a decent record. You wouldn't believe how they over-produce and synthesize things till you sound like a completely different person.

"There is one more pitch," pipes up a tiny agent at the far end of the table. "A Burke reality show. VH1 wants to follow Kaitlin as she makes her next acting choice. They'd introduce your mom, and then when you're tired of filming, they'd spin off the show and make it all about her management business."

I open my mouth to say no, but Mom speaks first.

"I love it!" she gushes. "Don't you think it's fabulous, Kaitlin? I mean, I always thought I was destined for TV. People have told me I have a natural gift of gab. I have to call

Fashionistas and tell them so they can add this to their story. *Fashionistas* is profiling me next month," Mom tells the room. "This is a great idea, I can feel it. We should do the show!"

"You would be good at this, sweetie," Dad tells Mom. "But Meg, I'm not sure a reality show is the route we should take with Kaitlin's career."

"Why not?" Mom demands. "Plenty of big names do reality shows, don't they?"

NO WAY, I want to yell. I may enjoy *Tori & Dean: Home Sweet Hollywood* as much as the next person, but the world already knows too much about me as it is. I'm not about to invite them into my house on a daily basis. And besides, this meeting was to give me options. I'm not expected to make a decision about them today, am I? I feel a throbbing at the back of my neck. I'm on the verge of having a major tension headache, I can feel it. I rub my neck deeply, but it does little to ease the mounting pressure.

I glance at Seth. Thankfully he's giving me his "Not-over-my-dead-agent-carcass" look that we've worked out for situations where Seth can't speak, but I need to know what he's thinking. "I want to thank you for giving me so many choices." I change the subject quickly, trying not to let my voice give away how anxious this meeting has made me. I need to sound professional right now even if I want to curl up in a corner with my pillow. "I like the sound of that film shooting in London and the TV show about college in Alaska sounds funny. I need time to read all the scripts first and then I can decide. There's no reason I should move too quickly, right?" I laugh nervously.

"I think we should pick one right now," Mom says stubbornly. "That reality show . . ."

WHAT? Mom has to be joking. I can't choose a career-making move on the spot. I just can't! My stomach growls in protest and I fear I may have to bolt for the bathroom. My neck is throbbing and my forehead starts to too.

Seth saves me. "Kaitlin needs time to mull things over. None of these offers are going to disappear overnight. We'll reconvene next week."

I start to rise from the table and my legs are shaking. I feel heavier than I did an hour ago, and not just because I drank two Smartwaters. This is a huge decision I have to make. I manage to thank everyone again and Seth walks us to the elevator to say goodbye.

"I'm going to be calling you a lot, Kaitlin," Seth sounds like he's warning me. "Until you pick your next big thing, I'm going to be on you like white on rice."

Mom smiles brightly and looks in my direction as Seth hands me a pile of scripts.

"I know you will, Seth," I say weakly. "Believe me."

Thankfully the elevator doors close before he can say anything else. I'm free — for the moment.

Wednesday, January 14
NOTE TO SELF:

Thurs. AM — FA cast shoot 9 AM. Shooting afterward.
2 PM — three phoners
4 PM — autograph signing @ studio w/Make a Wish
kids
Dinner w/A — Friday ☺
CALL LIZ! MUST GET TOGETHER.
Call Ava back!
Study *The SATs and You,* pages 48-62.
Nadine's SAT quiz on Friday and again on Monday!
Read scripts!

KAITLIN BURKE KIDNAPPED??   January 14

Yes, we've heard the alarming rumors and seen the photos too. At 4:14 PM PST, several Web sites posted pictures of *Family Affair* star **Kaitlin Burke** being forced into an unknown Escalade at the Santa Monica Pier while her assistant and bodyguard stood by in horror. Kaitlin had just finished shooting scenes for *Family Affair* on location at the Santa Monica Pier when the incident occurred. "Kaitlin was talking on her cell phone and laughing and all of a sudden this car screeched to a halt in front of her and her face froze," says one eyewitness. "She obviously didn't know the people in that car, but for some reason she went with them anyway. I was really worried for her."

Since Private Hollywood Eyes cares about Kaitlin's well-being too, we sprang into action, contacting *FA,* the police, and Kaitlin's publicist. Kaitlin's mouthpiece, Laney Peters, called back immediately. "This is such a ridiculous accusation that I shouldn't even justify it with a statement, but I will so that the rumors stop. Kaitlin Burke was NOT kidnapped. She was late for a last-minute meeting and her parents surprised her by picking her up at the Pier. She was thrilled to see them." Hmm . . . if that's true, then why did Kaitlin look so upset? And why was Kaitlin's bodyguard overheard saying, "They don't give that girl room to breathe"? Is there more to this story? We've all heard what a nightmare Kaitlin's momager, Meg Burke, can be. Don't worry, readers. Leave it to us at Private Hollywood Eyes to find out. Stay tuned . . .

8. EXT. SUMMERVILLE HIGH SCHOOL LOCKERS—DAY
SAMANTHA is stressed. She has three minutes to grab her
books for Chemistry and get to gym for yogalates. Her books
come tumbling out of her locker and she begins to cry.

RYAN
(dropping to his knees and putting a hand on her
shoulder) Rough day?

SAMANTHA
I'm fine. I'm just . . . overwhelmed. Too much homework.

RYAN
Sam, you've been acting weird. No offense, but
homework overload doesn't cause a person to totally
avoid her boyfriend.

SAMANTHA
I'm not avoiding you. I just have a lot on my mind.

RYAN
Tell me what's going on in that super-smart brain of
yours. I'll understand.

SAMANTHA
(Tears stream down her face.) I want to tell you, but

I don't know how.

                          RYAN

Sam, you're scaring me. Is this about . . . us?

                        SAMANTHA

No. I mean yes. I'm not sure.

                          RYAN

Are you breaking up with me?

                        SAMANTHA

No! (pauses) But you might want to dump me when you
hear what I have to say. (sees Ryan's face) I didn't
cheat, if that's what you're thinking. This has to do
with my family.

                          RYAN

Okay, that's a relief. Family stuff we can handle.
Sure, yours is a little more high-maintenance than
most, but Granddaddy Buchanan doesn't scare me.

                        SAMANTHA

I wish Granddaddy was the problem.

SARA approaches. She's sipping a smoothie from the
Summerville High coffee bar.

                              SARA

Hey, sis! Whoa. What's with the tears? Are you two
breaking up?

                         SAMANTHA AND RYAN

No!

                              SARA

(She makes a face.) Figures. You two are so into each
other, you'll probably date all through college and
get married.

                              RYAN

And what would be so wrong with that, Sara?

                              SARA

If that's what works for you. (to Sam) I guess he's up
for the long distance thing, huh?

                              RYAN

Long distance? Sam and I are applying to the same
college.

                              SARA

It's going to happen sooner than that, Ryan. (to Sam) I
can't believe you haven't told him yet.

                            SAMANTHA

I was trying to when you interrupted!

                    RYAN

Sam, what is your sister talking about?

                    SARA

(seeing her sister looks upset and can't speak) We're
moving to Miami, Ryan. My dad is the CEO of this new
company that makes stuff for the space shuttle and
we're moving in a few months, case closed.

                    RYAN

(looking at Sam) How long have you known about
this?

                  SAMANTHA

(quietly) A few weeks. I didn't know how to tell you.

                    RYAN

Were you waiting for the moving van to arrive? I
thought we were tighter than that, Sam. One of the
biggest tests of our relationship happens and you
can't find a way to let me know? I guess you want to
call our relationship off.

                  SAMANTHA

(crying) NO! Please understand, Ryan. I was going to
tell you. I want us to be together. I don't want to go.
I want to stay in California. (She reaches out for
him, but he pulls back.)

                              RYAN
Sam, you know your parents are never going to let you
do that. I can't do this.

                            SAMANTHA
Ryan!

(Ryan walks away.)

FIVE: *Life on Hold*

"That's a wrap!" Tom yells as Ryan (played by Trevor Wainright) walks away from Sam for the twelfth time. Any time we have to shoot a scene over and over, it's tiring, but this one was mentally exhausting. To make myself cry on command, I pretended this was the last *FA* scene I was ever going to film. That did the trick. Now I can't stop crying.

"Are you okay?" Sky says as we walk off the set. She's wearing a bold Michael Kors zebra print tunic and her black hair is tied in a side ponytail. I wish my hair was off my neck. Paul left it down because he said it looked good with the cute, pale yellow cotton peasant top by Bebe and the wide-leg navy trousers from the Gap I'm wearing, but I feel really hot. "You didn't overdose on Sudafed again, did you?" Sky says accusingly.

That only happened one time and Sky won't let me forget it. I had a bad cold at work and I took two Sudafed capsules, thinking the dosage was the same as Tylenol. I was wrong.

With Sudafed, you only need one pill. I panicked at first, but Nadine said I was fine. The only thing that happened was I acted a little loopy — and overly affectionate to Sky, which drove her nuts. "I'm just tired," I tell Sky, and wipe away my tears.

That's partially true. I met with Nadine on my lunch hour and she pressed me about those scripts I've been reading *and* scheduled another SAT practice test. Nadine has turned into a mini-Mom/Laney the way she hovers and it's starting to wear on me. Thank God I have a date with Austin later. First, I have to stop by my dressing room and do a quick phoner, call Liz, and grab my script pages for tomorrow. Then I'm out.

"You're lying." Sky eyes me suspiciously. "You look like hell. You've got nasty under-eye circles, your skin is blotchy, and you have a monster zit on your chin."

I gasp. "A zit? Where?" I touch my chin, but I don't feel anything.

"You're so easy to fool, K." Sky snorts. "But I wasn't lying about the blotchy skin and ugly circles. You need to get to the spa pronto. What's wrong? Are you sleeping?"

Not really, I want to say. I've been like this all week. I'm tired, but every time I close my eyes I can't stop thinking about *FA* or my meeting with Seth and my parents, and then all I do is toss and turn. "I'm fine," I insist. This is Sky's version of being concerned, which is really sweet, but if I tell her that, she'll just deny it.

"Whatever." Sky shrugs. "So did you take your driving test yet?"

My shoulders tense. Driving lessons have sort of been put on the back burner, which is a sore subject with me. I'm the only seventeen-year-old I know who doesn't have her license yet. But between work and all the other stuff I have going on, I haven't had a chance to have more than one or two lessons since the Wheel Helpers incident last fall. "No," I admit sheepishly.

Sky looks like she's about to make a comment, but then she spots Trevor. She walks up behind him and winds her body around his like a cat to a scratching post. "Hey, Trevvie! You were amazing in that scene. When you got teary, I got goosebumps."

"Thanks," Trevor says nonchalantly. "I've got some calls to make." He winks at me as he passes and Sky and I stare as he saunters off in his dark denim Levis and a gray Strokes concert tee. He runs a hand through his blond hair before letting his muscular arms swing as he walks.

I've been secretly coaching Trev on how to get Sky to fall all over him, and it appears to be working. The first time the two got together, Trev was Sky's plaything. Now that Sky's interested in him again, Trev is making it look like he's not that into her, which is driving Sky nuts. It's a lot of fun to watch.

"I don't get it." Sky is flabbergasted. "I'm wearing his favorite perfume and a push-up bra. How could he run off like that, K? I thought he'd *at least* offer to get me a latte from crafty."

I try not to laugh. "I wouldn't be offended. He said he had to make some calls."

"You're right." Sky doesn't look convinced. "Do you think it would be weird if I brought him a latte instead?"

She looks at me for approval and I nearly fall over. "I think he'd really like that." Sky strides off to craft services with a goofy grin on her face.

I head to my dressing room, keeping my eyes peeled for Nadine. I can't handle another work/life/Kaitlin's-well-being speech today. She's turning into Dr. Phil. Thankfully my dressing room is empty. The reporter calls on time and my phoner is done in fifteen minutes. I look at my Princess Leia watch. Liz should be on her way to kickboxing, so I might be able to reach her on her cell before class. Liz is the only one I can talk to about all these feelings I've been having. We haven't talked all week, which is unlike us. Liz never called me after the Cinch party to make plans, and I've only talked to her once since then. Today she picks up on the first ring.

"Hey, Kates," Liz says, sounding distracted.

"Hey, stranger," I joke. "Did you lose my number?"

She doesn't laugh. "I'm sorry. I've been so busy."

That's it? She's been busy? That's no excuse for not calling your best friend. We usually talk every day! "So have I." I'm a tad defensive. "But I've really missed you so now I'm stalking you."

This time she laughs a little. "I'm sorry," Liz says, sounding more like her old self. "I'm tired. You have no idea how much work I have. This NYU summer program application is taking so much out of me."

I have no idea what she's talking about. "What summer program?"

"It's a summer workshop for high school students interested in the arts," Liz tells me. "Mikayla thinks I'm a shoo-in if I do a killer application video. Thank God for her. I don't know what I'd do if she wasn't helping me with this."

So Liz is going away for the summer and she didn't think it was important to tell me? "That's great." I try hard to be supportive.

"I'll fill you in when I see you," Liz says. "I'd really, really love to have lunch. Can you do the Cheesecake Factory and shopping at the Grove on Saturday?"

I smile. Food and shopping. This is just what the two of us need. I can tell her what's been going on with my projects and she can tell me more about this NYU program. I look at my Sidekick schedule and breathe a sigh of relief. I'm actually free! "That sounds great. I've got so much to talk to you about. Work has been —"

"Kates, I'm sorry, I have to go," Liz interrupts. "Mikayla's here and we're late for kickboxing. I'll call you later." Click.

Did Liz really just cut me off? This day keeps getting worse.

I grab my things and rush out the door to meet Rodney at the car. I take a few deep breaths and remind myself that the car will be nice and quiet. In twenty minutes, I'll see Austin and I can forget about everything else.

I slide into the backseat and bump right into Matty and Nadine.

"What are you guys doing here?" I ask, alarmed. I thought Nadine left already.

"Don't worry," Matty tells me. "Rod is going to drop you off on your date first, and then take me home. I waited around because I had something I wanted to tell you: I got the part in the Scooby-Doo pilot!"

For a split second, I'm stunned. You mean, my younger brother already has another job lined up and I don't? I instantly feel worried, but then I remember that this is Matty's moment, not mine. My fear will have to wait. "That's awesome!" I hug him. For once, Matty actually lets me. He usually complains that I make him appear younger than he really is when I get all affectionate.

"I'm going to play Velma's boyfriend," Matty tells me. "He's new to the gang."

"If we could just get *you* to settle on something, the Burkes would be set," Nadine says to me.

I feel my skin bristle, but I smile. I'm already freaked out enough as it is; does Nadine have to make it worse? "I thought you had to go somewhere," I say.

"I went and came back," Nadine explains. "Seth had more scripts for you to read." She drops them in my lap. "Have you thought any more about that play in New York? Seth said they're dying to fly you out there to talk about the part. And they want to put you on the phone with Meg Valentine, the original star, to hear more about the show."

"I'm interested," I admit. "But I'm nervous because I've never done theater."

"You need to leave the Sam stigma behind and this would be one way to do it," Nadine says. "I still can't believe you didn't like *I Would Hate You If I Didn't Love You.*"

I do a double take. Is this Nadine talking or my mom? Sam stigma? I read the *I Love You* pilot that Sky likes and hated it. "Nadine, that show wanted me to do nudity!" I remind her.

"True," Nadine agrees. "There's other stuff to consider, right? You have more meetings and Seth has another offer for you. Chili's wants you to be the voiceover for their fall TV ads."

Matty and I both scream. I don't even have to think about this one. "Say YES!"

HOLLYWOOD SECRET NUMBER FIVE: Most big stars wouldn't be caught dead doing a television commercial — unless it's for a well-known charity. But voiceover work is different and lots of big stars from George Clooney to Julia Roberts are rumored to have done it. The reason is simple: You can make big bucks in as few as two or three hours. The best part? Most stars put it in their contract that the company will never confirm or deny it's you voicing a little green lizard or a singing bee. Commercials are the filet mignon of voiceovers.

"See how easy that was to say yes?" Nadine asks. "All you have to do now is pick a movie or a TV pilot and do the same thing."

My smile fades. I start to feel hot, then clammy. I can't take much more of everyone hounding me. Thankfully Rodney has stopped the car, which means we must be at Clark High School, where I'm meeting Austin after his lacrosse practice. "This is my stop," I say quickly. "See you guys later."

"Kates, wait," Nadine begs. "I just wanted to ask you a few more things —"

I pretend not to hear her, slam the door and walk as fast as I can over to the lacrosse field. My phone starts to ring immediately. That better not be Nadine. I fish through the mounds of stuff I threw in my Cinch bag this morning — Bubble Yum, my Coach journal, Altoids — and look at the screen. Voicemails. I have six messages in the last hour. Only in Los Angeles could you be driving and hit enough dead spots to miss that many calls.

The first two are from Seth. "Hey there, shooting star. Seth here. I hope you're enjoying this great January weather and spending some time in the backyard reading *Manolos Are Meant for Small Feet*. Talk to you soon." I thought he said I could have till next week. And then another one. "Kaitlin? Seth again. Maybe hold off on reading *Manolos* till you read *Meeting of the Minds*, okay? Have fun, shooting star!" Click.

I feel a little woozy when I hear Laney's voice. "KAITLIN. *SURE* WANTS YOU FOR A COVER TIMED TO THE END

OF *FA.* I SAY WE TAKE IT. WE CAN STILL GET *ALLURE* AND I THINK — WHAT? NO! I SAID LIMESTONE IN THE MASTER SHOWER. NOT MARBLE! DOES NO ONE LISTEN TO MY — " Click.

I feel like I'm being suffocated. I can't handle all of them badgering me. I begin to feel slightly dizzy and reach out for something to hold on to. I shake my head to clear it and almost miss my next message, which is from Mom. "Kaitlin, the editor at *Fashionistas* wants to talk to you about me being your mother. I know you're out with Austin, but I told her she can call you tonight. I didn't want to be rude. Make me sound good, sweetie!" Click.

"AAAAAHHHHHHH!" I scream and drop the phone. I step on it with my pointy heels and stomp around in a circle screaming. "They're driving me nuts!" I yell at the sky. "I can't take it anymore!" I scream again then stop and take a few deep breaths. I look down at my phone. The screen is cracked. Oops. Guess I won't be getting anymore calls on that tonight. For some reason, that actually makes me giggle.

"Burke?"

I turn around. Oh my.

When I chose to have a freak-out, I didn't realize I was standing in front of the lacrosse field. The entire Clark High team has stopped playing and is staring at me. My face feels hot.

Austin runs toward me. He has taken off his helmet and I can see his face covered in dirt. His blond hair is matted to his head. He looks worried. "What's the matter? Are you okay?"

"Um, yeah," I say, knowing all eyes are on me. "Just a momentary lapse in judgment." I wave to the team. "Hi guys! Sorry about that. Just blowing off some steam."

"Don't worry about it," yells Austin's good friend Rob Murray, who dates my friend Allison. I met Allison and Rob through Liz when I went to Clark last spring.

"We were finished anyway," Austin tells me. "Are you sure you're okay?"

The guys walking off the field stare at me, and I continue to blush. "You must be starving. We can talk about it later. I don't want to miss our reservation," I tell him. We're trying out this new restaurant called Helios. I hear it's totally romantic.

"If we miss it, we miss it," Austin tells me. "There are ten million restaurants in Los Angeles. I'm sure we'll find another one. I just saw you smash your cell phone to pieces." Austin smirks. "Tell me what is going on."

He is so sweet. I lean in to give him a kiss. His mouth tastes like sweat and Gatorade. Someone behind us whistles. Just being here with him, I feel better already. It's only been a little over a week since I've seen Austin, but it feels like a lot longer. My friend Gina says that's the problem with dating a non-celebrity. Actor types are unemployed on a regular basis (days off from taping a show, in between filming movies, etc.) so most actor boyfriends can hang out in your dressing room 24–7. Still, I like that Austin has his own life that is just as busy as mine. I wouldn't want it any other way.

We take a seat on the bleachers. "I'm just frustrated," I explain. It feels good to get this out. Lately, I feel like I'm in a bubble. Nadine has gone wacky, Liz is preoccupied, my friend Gina left last week to shoot a movie in Australia, and the only one I can talk to is Austin. Thank God I have him. "I'm having a harder time with *FA* ending than I thought," I admit, "and no one seems to notice or care. I feel like I'm graduating, but I don't deserve my diploma."

"You're just scared," Austin says. "That's normal. I kind of figured you'd have a bit of a freak-out after you met with Seth and heard all those offers." He grins. "No offense, but you do tend to fly off the handle sometimes."

It's hard to be offended when it's true.

"You just need time to digest everything," Austin adds, "and come to terms with the show's ending in your own way."

"That's the problem," I complain. "I don't have any time to do that. Everyone wants an answer from me immediately and I have no clue which project is the right one. The only thing I've gotten excited about so far is our invite to the *Vanity Fair* party."

Austin's face drops. "I was going to talk to you about that tonight. I have bad news. I can't go. Coach organized a lacrosse scrimmage for us in Phoenix and it's the night of the Oscars. I just found out this afternoon."

Half of me is disappointed by the news, but the other half is impressed that Austin cares more about his beloved lacrosse than he does about meeting Jessica Alba. I don't think I ever really realized how into lacrosse Austin was. Now that the season is coming up, he practices all the time. If I call him before school, his mom says he's working on his toss in the backyard. After school, whether there is an official group practice or not, he's out there. And on weekends, if he's not playing, he and Rob are critiquing their performance on a tape of a game they played last year. And guys say girls are obsessive. "I understand," I squeak.

"Why don't you ask Liz?" Austin suggests. "I'm sure she'd love to chat up Katie Holmes with you."

"I guess I could." It's not the same thing, though. The *Vanity Fair* party is like the Hollywood version of the prom. Everyone wants to take their boyfriend to the prom. But I guess if I can't take Austin, the next best thing is going with Liz. She's always wanted to go to the *Vanity Fair* party.

"I'll make it up to you. I promise." Austin kisses me. "Now let's get back to fixing you. Tell me about the scripts you're reading."

"Well, the first one is this —" I pause.

Austin's cell phone starts ringing and he reaches into his pocket and pulls it out. He looks at me curiously. "It's Nadine," he says and answers. "Hi. Yeah, she's right here." He holds out the phone.

For a moment I think I might throw it. "This better be important," I grumble instead of saying hello. I can't believe

Nadine of all people had the nerve to call Austin's phone to reach me. I could see Mom doing that, but not Nadine.

"I've been calling and calling you!" Nadine complains without an apology. "Your phone keeps going to voicemail so I had to call Austin."

I don't tell her about my broken phone because I'm already annoyed. What is so important that Nadine had to track me down on my date *through* my date? "What's going on?" I say.

"A lot," Nadine says. "Rodney is coming back with the car right now. You have to meet with the executive producer of that ensemble family drama TV pilot tonight. He's flying out to scout locations in Vancouver tomorrow and he needs to make his casting decisions right away. It's tonight or never. You have to go."

"You're kidding, right?" I complain. This was the show I was least interested in and now I'm being dragged out of here for a meeting without even being consulted first? This is crazy! I'm with the one person who actually cares about what I'm feeling and now I have to leave. I won't do it! "Forget the show," I say defiantly. "If it has to be tonight, I don't want to go."

"Don't make me call back your mother and Seth and tell them that," Nadine warns. "Be reasonable. You can have dinner with Austin afterward. If you even think you might want in on this show, the meeting has to be now."

I want to throw a fit again, but if I do that I might break

Austin's phone too. I cover his phone with my hand, stare at the sky, and scream. I turn to Austin and grumpily explain what's going on. "What do you think I should do?" I ask him.

"Dinner can wait," he insists. "Burke, what if this show is the one? Go to the meeting. I'll shower, Rod will pick me up, and then if it's not too late we'll have dinner afterward. You don't want to miss the chance just because we have a dinner reservation, do you?"

Part of me does. I feel so powerless. But I don't really have a choice about this meeting, do I? If I don't go, Mom will kill me. And so will Laney. And Seth. And, it seems, Nadine. If I do go, I lose out on my time with Austin. It's so unfair. Ava's right. When do I get to do what I want to do?

I uncover the phone and sigh heavily. "I'll be standing in the school parking lot in five," I say curtly to Nadine and then hang up without saying goodbye.

I'm about to put my personal life on hold. Again.

Wednesday, January 21

NOTE TO SELF:
Set up Jay Godfrey fitting 4 Vanity Fair dress!
Order car 4 VF party.
Choose Oscar gift suites 2 attend.
RSVP yes 2 Gucci dinner.
Call J.J. Abrams back.
Call back Seth. Break news about pilot gently.

HOLLYWOOD NATION'S

HOT TOPIC

Family Affair—What Your Favorite Family Members Are Doing Next
by Kathleen Pearl

They've made us laugh, they've made us cry, and now they're leaving us with an empty hole in our hearts and in our TV schedules on Sunday nights. Thankfully, there is life after the Buchanan clan skips town. You can still catch your favorite stars on the screen, both big and small, this coming year. Here's what the *Family Affair* stars have planned for an after-party.

Melli Ralton (Paige, Grandaddy Buchanan's daughter, mother of Sam and Sara, wife of Dennis)
After a summer-long hiatus, Melli will be seen on the big screen in the girl-power flick *Revenge*. Playing against type, Melli will star as the mother of two small kids who finds out her husband is actually wanted by the FBI.

Spencer Hirsch (Dennis, Paige's hot hubby and Sam and Sara's

pop—and the reason the gang is moving out of Summerville!)
He'll appear this summer on London's famed West End in a modern retelling of *As You Like It*. After that, he flies to Yugoslavia to shoot the thriller *Tell Me What Time I Die?*

Sky Mackenzie (Bad seed Sara, daughter of Paige and Dennis, and twin of Samantha)
Sky's got *Pretty Young Assassins* to promote with FA costar Kaitlin Burke (see below) and has had offers to do several pilots. We hear she's *this* close to choosing one for the CW about bratty girls who live in a Chicago hotel and make backstabbing their favorite sport. Guess our favorite bad seed will continue to be the bad girl in town. We love it!

Trevor Wainright (Samantha's boyfriend)

FA's resident hottie is upping his smoldering quotient with a shirtless star turn as a slacker surfer in *Beach Bum,* from can't-miss comedy director Jus Apple. "This is going to be the film that takes Trevor from sidekick to major movie star," Apple tells us.

Tom Pullman (*Family Affair*'s creator and executive producer)

Said to be in demand for several TV series offers, Tom has just signed on to do a pilot for the CW based on Scooby-Doo. The Buffy-esque plot, full of sarcasm and too-cool-for-school wit, follows the Scooby Gang and their comrades in monster-slaying. Don't be surprised if you see several *Affair* players pop up in this series should it get picked up for the fall. Matt Burke, Kaitlin's bro and *FA*'s newest cast member, just signed on to play Velma's boyfriend. Which brings us to….

Kaitlin Burke (Practically perfect Samantha, Paige and Dennis's daughter, Sara's twin)

This is where things get interesting. *Family Affair*'s stand-out teen and media darling hasn't signed on to do a single project! Her publicist, Laney Peters, says she's mulling over offers, but an insider tells us that Kaitlin has refused to commit to anything she's been given so far. The only Kaitlin news we've heard lately is this bizarre story about Kaitlin smashing her cellphone at her boyfriend's lacrosse practice. (Did you get bad news, Kates? Uh-oh.) That means other than promoting *Pretty Young Assassins* this summer, we'll be Kaitlin-less for a while. Make up your mind, Kaitlin! We miss you already. ●

SIX: *Kaitlin Burke — Music Star?*

"YES!" I scream after the car door closes behind me. I start bouncing up and down on the seat in excitement.

It's Saturday morning, and Seth, Mom, and I just came from a breakfast meeting with the director of *Manolos Are Meant for Small Feet.* I read the script and loved it. It was very *The Devil Wears Prada* meets *Legally Blonde.* What could be better than that? I told Seth I have to have the part. This is the only script I've flipped over so far. The family drama pilot I had a meeting about the night I was on a date with Austin turned out to be too similar to *Family Affair.* (At least the meeting was semi-short. Austin and I were still able to have dinner afterward.) I don't want to repeat what I've already done. That jungle flick would certainly be new territory, but when I met with the director yesterday, his vision — method acting with us actually living in the jungle during filming — seemed too much for me. *Manolos* might just be what I'm looking for. I feel safer picking a movie as my next project than a TV show. In my head, a movie is something I would do on hiatus anyway so I can pretend this is just another one. Even if it really isn't. "Dean was so funny and smart," I gush about the film's director. "I really liked what he said about this role being my chance to be seen as more than just a flighty teenager."

Seth nods. "He's right. This is exactly the type of project we need for you if you want to go to the next tier. I'm going to call him as soon as we get back to the office and find out what he thought of you, but I'm sure he loved you. We could have an answer by the end of next week."

I scream and Mom holds her ears.

"Stop that," she complains. "And to tell you both the truth, I didn't really like Dean all that much. Or his script."

"What?" Seth and I say at the same time, shocked.

Mom shrugs. "I thought he seemed cocky and his script was pompous."

"Meg, he's a well-respected director," Seth starts to say.

Mom waves her hand flippantly. "I don't think Kaitlin wants an offer for this movie. It's not right for her."

"MOM," I say a tad sharply. I'm growing tired of how dismissive Mom is of my opinion, especially when she does it in front of Seth. "I *do* want an offer. This is the first project I've liked the sound of. You have no idea how hard all this has been on me —"

"You *think* you like the sound of this project because you

haven't met with other directors yet," Mom cuts me off. "We have to meet with the network about those other pilots and the reality show. You have to make a decision and soon, Kaitlin. I will not have another article on our hands like that one in *Hollywood Nation*."

"Meg, that article was ridiculous," Seth tells her. "Kaitlin is doing the same thing everyone else on the show is doing, considering offers. We're not behind — yet. We just have to find a project she really likes. I already had Laney call *Nation* and tell them about the projects Kaitlin is currently considering."

I beam at Seth. I love how he has my back when it comes to Mom. Seth hasn't said it in so many words, but Nadine thinks Mom's managerial style really gets under his skin.

"Several of the projects Kaitlin is considering are very promising." Seth winks at me.

"I finished that TV pilot about the teens in Alaska and I thought it was remarkable," I tell them. The writer for the show is phenomenal. Even though the idea of a new TV show scares me, this script was so good I couldn't put it down.

"I'm trying to get you a meeting next week," Seth says. "Are you game?"

"I hated it," Mom interjects. "A show set in Alaska sounds boring. That's the only TV pilot I've read that I've hated."

Seth and I just look at her. If Mom tries to stop me from meeting with this director, I'll freak out. My mother, more than anyone, should know what kind of roles appeal to her daughter and what don't.

"I can't wait to hear what you think of the play when you're finished reading it," Seth tries to change the subject.

"I started reading it last night and it's really good," I admit. I'm still terrified of the idea of live theater, but I think being onstage could be very liberating. Dad's right. Every night your performance is different, and every night the audience reacts to it differently. It sounds like great thespian training. And a play is something that could help me transition from being just a teen actress to a more grown-up one.

When I think about it, I do have a lot of good choices. I just have to get past the idea of accepting one of them as my new job (if I'm offered one, of course). I can like the scripts all I want, but the idea of committing to something makes me want to breathe in a paper bag.

"I still think TV is the way to go," Mom says stubbornly. "It's much more stable."

"That's not true, Meg," Seth interjects again, sounding a wee bit strained. "Pilots are a gamble. Kaitlin could work with a brilliant director and a talented cast and the show could still not get picked up."

Seth knows HOLLYWOOD SECRET NUMBER SIX: Very early in the pilot season, the buzz always centers around pilots that have star quality of some sort. If the show has a big-name creator, is a popular current show's spin-off, is based on a popular book or movie, or has a star attached, then everyone gets all excited and writes about how the pilot is the next *Friends* or *Sex and the City* or *Gossip Girl*. Sadly, it rarely works out that way. At the end of the day it doesn't matter who wrote the pilot or who is attached to star or what book the pilot was based on — to get picked up, the show has to be good. It's that simple.

"Which is why I want to cover all our bases," Mom says stiffly. "That's why I made the next appointment."

"What appointment?" Seth and I say at the same time again.

"Mom, I have to meet Liz in an hour," I moan. "You knew that."

"Kate-Kate, I was not about to pass up a meeting with TJ from Jay Street Records because you're meeting Liz to go shopping," Mom tells me." Tell Liz you'll be there when you can."

"Mom, you have to stop booking things for me and not telling me!" I complain. I'm not sure what to freak out over first — the fact that Mom is ruining the first date I've had with Liz since before Christmas or the fact that I'm being forced to see a famed record producer, which I do not want to do.

I've never met TJ before, but I know all about him. He goes by just TJ. His first name is Troy, but no one seems to know what his last name is or if it even starts with the letter J. He's this musical whiz kid. He had his first triple-platinum album at seventeen, started his own label at nineteen, pillaged a rival label's clients at twenty and now at twenty-two has arguably one of the best music catalogs in town. He's also known for his hard-partying ways. How he gets any work done is beyond me. There's not a night that man isn't photographed on the town.

"Mom, I am not going to have a music career," I say, my voice rising. "I have no interest. None whatsoever. Tell TJ we're not coming."

"Give us one good reason you shouldn't be a crossover star?" Mom says calmly. "You have the look, you're the right age, and you've got a decent voice. With TJ behind you, your sound could be great."

"Kaitlin doesn't want to cut an album," Seth interjects angrily. "She's told us that on several occasions. And besides which, if she did want to do one, *I* would have set up the meeting, Meg, not you. How could you do this without telling me?"

"I am not making an album!" I say over their raised voices. "You can't make me do it!"

Why won't anyone listen to me? I feel like a caged animal being held against my will. My face feels hot, and not just because I'm angry, and I'm having a hard time breathing normally. I feel a knot in my neck start to scream again in protest. Not another headache! I reach into my bag for my diminishing bottle of Tylenol. "See what the stress is doing to me, Mom?" I want to yell.

My hands are shaking, but while Mom and Seth argue, I

quickly text Liz. When she doesn't respond right away, I call her phone and it goes straight to voicemail. "Liz, if you get this, I might be late. Mom is forcing me to go to a meeting that she never told me about. I'm so sorry. I'll tell you more when I see you. I'll get there as soon as I can."

Our car pulls up to a nondescript office building. "Oh look! We're here and there's a Starbucks!" Mom says happily. She seems to hit a Starbucks on every street corner. No wonder she's always so wired. Mom turns toward me. "Just meet with TJ, okay? He really likes your look."

Suddenly I feel very tired. Too tired to argue. Mom has won again and I don't have the energy to fight her. "Fine."

Mom grins. "Good. We have ten minutes before the appointment so I'm going to pop in Starbucks, get a double soy cap, and call the *Fashionistas* editor again. I thought of another quote I want to give her." Mom puts on her sunglasses and wraps her head in a scarf, then slides out of the car.

"I don't know how you do it, Kaitlin," Seth says quietly when Mom is gone. "Your mom is a tough negotiator."

I close my eyes to keep the car from spinning. "I know."

"I guess if we're here, you should meet with TJ," Seth says with a sigh. "He hates being stood up. Even if you don't want to do an album, you want to stay on his good side." I nod. "But I'm not sending you in there alone. He can be quite a shark and I don't want you signing on to let your mom produce your debut album without my consent."

"Okay." Somehow I feel better knowing Seth is with me.

Ten minutes later, I'm standing face-to-face with TJ himself.

"Kaitlin Burke." TJ shakes my hand warmly and takes a seat across from me in his large office, with almost 360-degree views of Los Angeles. TJ is shorter than I imagined, but in every other way, he is exactly how I pictured him. He reminds me of Kanye West. He's short, never takes his sunglasses off even when he's indoors, and he talks in a soft, smooth tone. "I was wondering when we'd finally get you in here. Meg and I have been talking for weeks about this." Mom clears her throat.

Weeks, huh? "I appreciate you waiting to see me," I tell him politely. "I've been swamped with work."

TJ stares at me as he lounges in the other chair. "Not for long though, huh? That show is history!" He laughs and the sound shoots right through me. If TJ wasn't so important, I would snap back that my show is as long for the world as his weak new artist, Rocco, is for the top-ten chart.

"Anyway, the reason I called you in here is because, as I told Meg, I think you have talent that's untapped and if we can harness it, you could be a major music star," TJ says. "You'd have it all in this town. Not many can do that."

You can say that again. Do you know how many music stars have tried to break into Hollywood and vice versa? Now is probably not the time to bring that up.

"I've already got a whole game plan in mind for you if

you're up for it," TJ tells us. "We'd cut several tracks for your album right away, and the rest we'd do after the show stops taping. You'd have to finish things up at night or on weekends and we'd have to get going on cover art for your album ASAP. We're thinking a vampy look. The anti-Sam. Fishnets, a bustier or a corset. Something like that."

Fishnets? A corset? I wouldn't even wear that on Halloween!

"That's a pretty radical change for Kaitlin," Seth pipes up. "She's idolized by a lot of young girls and we don't want her to lose her fan base."

TJ laughs. "Kaitlin doesn't seem too worried about that," he says, looking at me. "You're the master at press, if you ask me. First you vacation with the party set, next you stage your own kidnapping. I've seen all those pictures of you with Lauren Cobb and Ava Hayden too. Those two are not exactly tween-friendly, if you know what I mean."

"I wasn't actually kidnapped," I tell TJ. "And Lauren, Ava, and I just started hanging out. It's not what it appears to be in the papers." I can't believe how off-base the press has been about my whereabouts and partying. It just goes to show that you can't believe everything you read.

"I've had some good times with Lauren and Ava," TJ reminisces. "When you see them, tell them I said holla. And ask them if they remember that night in Cabo." I glance at Seth out of the corner of my eye. "I think it's great that you guys are hanging out. I like the new you," TJ adds. "We're thinking of some really sexy songs that show the world how grown-up you are. We want them to see you're nothing like that little sweet pea you've played all these years. This is a grown-up Kaitlin and she's ready to rock out. We're talking songs about boys wanting more, driving cars, dealing with bad breakups, and guys leading you on. We want angst, anger, sexed-up energy."

"Wow." Seriously, that's all I can muster right now.

"I'm sure Meg would agree with me that anger, angst, and sexed-up energy is not the way we want to go with Kaitlin," Seth says, looking at Mom, who looks ready to pass out. I think she's just realized she's in over her head.

So have I. I feel like the walls are closing in. Sexed-up Sam is not me. I picture myself with big hair and a whip on my CD cover. "That's not really me," I tell TJ.

He shrugs. "We can talk about playing with your look. One thing we won't compromise on is the tour. We're talking some arenas, tons of radio shows. We'll send you to the opening of a Wal-Mart if we think it will get you fans." TJ laughs. "But who am I kidding? Wal-Mart won't even carry your CD because of the content. This baby is going to be too hot to handle."

I smile weakly. Too hot to handle? I look at Mom. She looks nervous too. At least she's finally paying attention, even if it has nothing to do with something I said. I wonder if Mom actually talked to TJ about any of this beforehand or if she was so excited about Kaitlin Burke, music star, that she just wanted to get me in here? I glance at the door. What would happen if I bolted?

"Of course, we'd build up your album with tons of pre-publicity," TJ adds. "We rock at that. We'll leak the most offensive, or hottest, song first and see what the public thinks before we commit to a first single."

"Thanks for your time, TJ," Seth says, putting his hand on my shoulder and helping me stand. Mom quickly moves to Seth's side. "We'll think about it and call you."

I look at the clock. I still have fifteen minutes to get to the Grove. If Rodney takes the side streets I might make it on time. I sneak a peek at my Sidekick. I have no new messages. I hope Liz heard my voicemail.

"Whoa, whoa," TJ holds up his hands in surrender. "This offer is only good if I can hear her sing. Meg said she has a killer voice and I want to hear those pipes."

My chest begins to constrict. "Here? Now? I don't have anything prepared," I blurt out. I look at Seth and Mom. Mom is actually perspiring, something I've never seen happen to her before.

TJ hands me a sheet of paper. "That's okay. We already wrote you a song. Our mixing room is on this floor. I've got a group waiting to lay it down. Once we hear you sing it, we can move forward."

Okay, this is moving too fast for me. I glance down at the paper. The song is titled "Paparazzi Princess."

"TJ, I don't think Kaitlin is prepared to sing for you today," Mom tells him. "Maybe we could come back another time."

"Who comes to a record meeting about an album without being ready to sing?" TJ laughs. "You said she'd sing and I cleared my schedule so that she could do that."

The room is quiet. TJ has us. Seth pulls at the collar of his pressed white shirt, which he's wearing under a smart navy suit that I'm sure is Ralph Lauren. Mom fans herself with the sheet music.

"It's just . . . Kaitlin's vocal cords are kind of strained," Mom starts to say. Then she sees TJ's face. It could melt rubber. "But I guess she could do a quick take. We can't make time for a studio session. Kaitlin could sing a few bars for you right here if you want. Do you have a tape recorder?"

"Mom," I hiss.

"This will only take a few minutes," Mom says dismissively as TJ reaches into his desk and pulls out a tiny pocket recorder.

I read over the words to the song and am not sure if I should laugh or cry.

You think you know me,
but can't you see?
I'm tired of being the princess. I don't want to win your heart,
that was fine to start,
but the truth is:

(Chorus)
This Daddy's girl is ready to fly,
watch me, world, with a close eye.
I've got a new way of doing things.
This time, I'm the one pulling the strings.
Lights! Camera! Action!
You've never seen anything like the new me before.
And you probably never will again, you bores.

I'm a bad girl stuck in a good-girl role,
but now that the show is over, I've got a new goal.
I want to be your paparazzi princess. I want to have your attention.
Keep your eye on my ascension.
When you're not looking, I'm a different girl.
I'm not Sam. I'm ready to take the bad new me out for a whirl.
DJ, hit it!

(Chorus)
This Daddy's girl is ready to fly,
watch me, world, with a close eye.
I've got a new way of doing things.
This time, I'm the one pulling the strings.
Lights! Camera! Action!
You've never seen anything like the new me before.
And you probably never will again, you bores.

There's more to it, but I can't read another line. TJ has *got* to be kidding.

I'm being Punk'd, right? This is definitely part of some celebrity nightmare show for sure. But then I look at TJ. His face is smooth and calm. Mom is staring at me nervously and Seth is sweating.

I'm your paparazzi princess? You've never seen anything like the new me before, and you probably never will again, you bores? Eww. I want to rip this piece of paper to shreds and stuff them down TJ's throat. I glare at Mom. Mad doesn't describe how I'm feeling right now.

"Pretty solid, huh?" TJ asks. "We thought you'd like that."

"Words cannot express what I'm feeling," I tell him calmly.

TJ's phone rings and he excuses himself. That's when the three of us pounce on each other.

"Meg, I've had it," Seth whispers heatedly. "You need to back off and give me room to do my job. What were you thinking?"

Whoa. I've never heard Seth talk to Mom like that. If anyone else talked to her that way, she'd fire them on the spot.

"I see now that this was a mistake," Mom says, sounding hoarse. Her face is flushed. "But I don't know how to get Kate-Kate out of this." She looks at me. "I promised you'd sing, and TJ knows too many people for you to disrespect him by not doing this. You don't have to make the CD. I promise. Just sing the song once and we'll leave."

"I just want to get out of here," I tell them both. "I feel completely humiliated! Did you read the lyrics? Paparazzi princess? Who wants to be the princess of the paparazzi? That's not me! I want this song burned after I sing it."

"Kaitlin's right." Seth is calmer. "We need to get that tape from TJ after Kaitlin sings for him. He's legit, so I know he won't use it against her when we tell them she's not doing an album, but I'd still feel better if I had the tape in my hands."

"I'll sing and then you get the tape," I say wearily. "Then I'm out of here. I don't want to hear about meetings or work for the rest of the weekend," I tell my mom.

"And all future meetings should be cleared by me before we make them, okay?" Seth says, looking at Mom.

Mom is aghast. "I know I screwed up on this one, but my heart was in the right place," Mom says. "Kate-Kate needs me!"

"I need Seth, Mom," I say quietly. "This is his area of expertise."

"She's right, Meg," Seth says. "This is why you hired me. You have to trust that I know what Kaitlin needs."

"I know what Kaitlin needs," Mom says defiantly. "I'm her mother!"

"Yes, you're her mother," Seth repeats. "You're not an agent!"

Double whoa. I'm just as angry as Seth is, and probably more on his side than I am on Mom's, but if I don't rein them both in, TJ is going to walk in and freak out. I feel sort of dizzy and I have to sit down. My chest feels tight, but I have to get this out. "Everyone calm down," I say. "I'll sing, Seth will get the tape, and Mom will leave me alone for the weekend. We'll discuss the future after that."

"Okay," Mom agrees. "Whatever you want, sweetie. I know you're going to the Grove. You can take my black AmEx." I glare at her. Even retail therapy won't make up for the way I'm feeling right now. I'm tired of being bullied.

The door opens and TJ walks over with the tape recorder. He holds it out for me.

"Ready to sing it for me?" TJ asks. "Or should I say rap? We thought it would sound better if you were angry."

I take the cold tape recorder from his sweaty hands. "That won't be a problem," I say sweetly.

Saturday, January 31
PRINCESSLEIA25: Liz, where R U? If U get this, I'm on my way!

seven: *Tell Me How You Really Feel*

"Rodney, can't you go any faster?" I beg, looking at my Movado watch for the hundredth time in minutes. Mom felt so guilty after hearing me sing that awful song that she let me go ahead with Rodney while she waited for another car for her and Seth. The two of them still weren't speaking when I left them standing in front of TJ's building. Seth was livid about me having to sing that song. (He said it was bad business to turn TJ down on the spot so he planned on calling him tomorrow to let him down gently — and insist on getting my demo back.)

"Kates, Liz will understand," Rodney assures me. "You had meetings."

One awful meeting and one great meeting. I really liked the director of *Manolos*. That movie would be a great stepping stone for me, but I feel guilty thinking about it too much. I know it sounds silly, but part of me still feels like picking a new role is cheating on Sam. On the other hand, there's Mom, who thinks the project is all wrong for me. How could the two of us disagree that strongly on what's right for my future? I'm so confused. Maybe I'll feel better after I talk it out with Liz. I can't wait to tell her about the *Vanity Fair* party!

My cell phone rings and I pick up before even checking the caller ID. "Liz?"

"Kates! Where are you?" It's Liz, and she sounds a little annoyed. "I thought we said eleven-thirty."

"I know. I'm so sorry! I've been calling and calling," I tell her. "Didn't you get my text or message? Mom sprung this stupid meeting on me and it took longer than I thought. It was dreadful, Liz."

"Tell her we're going to lose our spot if she's not here soon," I hear someone in the background complain.

"Who is that?" I ask.

"It's Mikayla," Liz says awkwardly. "We were studying earlier and she heard my dad say I was coming to Cheesecake." She sounds almost apologetic. Almost.

"Oh." My heart sinks. "I just thought . . ." Today was supposed to be about us, I want to say. It's not that I don't want to meet Mikayla, but I was looking forward to having Liz to myself today. I thought Liz was looking forward to having some "us time" as much as I was.

"I know," Liz says even though I haven't finished the sentence. She sighs. "Look, don't worry about being late. I'll tell the hostess you're on your way. How long do you think you'll be?"

I look out my window. We're getting off the freeway. "Ten minutes."

"Okay. Meet us upstairs."

Rodney pulls into the Grove and drops me off near the restaurant so that he can go and park. I hit the ground running, stopping only twice to scribble a quick autograph, and then I race to the Cheesecake Factory. I'm looking down at my leopard Cinch bag, trying to find my Sidekick and that's when I run smack into a girl standing in front of me. "I'm sorry!" I apologize. "Are you okay?" We both look up at the same time and say, "Hey!"

It's Lauren. "What are you doing here?" she squeals. "Ava, come here!"

Ava is yakking on her cell phone, but she hangs up midsentence and rushes over to hug me. "I thought you had meetings," she says accusingly.

"I did all morning," I tell them. "Now I'm meeting my best friend Liz for lunch. I haven't seen her since before Christmas."

"Some best friend," Lauren snorts. She is wearing a killer green sweater and black leggings with thigh-high boots. She looks like she just stepped out of *InStyle*. She eyes my outfit and hones in on my bag. "You're using the Cinch bag! Did we tell you it was hot or what? What did your mom say?"

I blush. "I haven't told her how much it cost yet," I admit.

"Thatta girl," Ava says admiringly. Ava is in an oversized beige sweater, a Dolce tank and wide-leg jeans that look just like the ones I have on. Mine are paired with a black Tahari turtleneck and Chloé heels. Over it I'm wearing a lightweight North Face vest in creamy white with a fur trim hood. Not exactly Los Angeles appropriate, but since I'm not going to Sundance this year to ski, I might as well wear it now.

"So do you have to do lunch with your friend?" Ava whines. "We're more fun."

"Ditch her!" Lauren seconds. We all laugh. "Seriously though, when are we getting together? We'd have so much fun."

"I know," I lament. Hanging with these two really does seem like a great escape. "Maybe this week?"

Click. Click. Click.

I turn around and see Gary, Ava and Lauren's favorite paparazzo. That guy is everywhere! Ava turns me to face him. "Smile!" she says. The two of them hold up their loot from Barneys.

"What'd you get?" I say in between grins.

"A few sweaters, a cute necklace," Ava tells me. "It's rotten when you have to pay full price."

HOLLYWOOD SECRET NUMBER SEVEN: I've already told you that celebrities get a lot of their clothing for free, but when we shop retail we pay for things just like everyone else. Yes, many companies like the Gap send me clothes, but when I'm trying on jeans at the Grove, no employee comes over and says, "You can have those for free." Freebies come directly from corporate. Smaller shops like Becky in Bloom give discount cards to their preferred customers (i.e., the celebrity quotient), but others go one step further. If I bring an armload of clothes up to the counter at a boutique and the designer is there, they'll often tell me they're on the house. I'm usually so embarrassed that I insist on paying for a few items.

When Gary is done taking pictures, I turn to Ava and Lauren. I can hear the seconds tick away in my head. "Guys, I have to go."

They both groan. "Cancel!" Lauren moans.

"I'll call you!" I promise them. I look at my watch. I'm now half an hour late. Yikes. I push through the restaurant doors and scan the room for Liz. The hostess sees me and smiles. "Kaitlin Burke, right? I'll show you where your friends are sitting," she says.

Sometimes it really does help when strangers know who you are.

Liz and Mikayla are at a booth in the back of the restaurant. Liz sees me and waves. She's wearing one of her trademark head scarves over her long, dark hair and her olive skin looks great in a peach Chanel sweater that we got at Fred Segal right before she left for Hawaii. Mikayla is sitting next to her.

I can't deny Mikayla's pretty. She's got long, curly red hair, and porcelain-white skin that reminds me of a China doll. Her slightly round face is dotted with freckles. I can't see her whole outfit, but she looks very J.Crew from where I'm standing. Her green cable-knit sweater and pleated khaki skirt stand out in a sea of J. Brands and Stella McCartneys that usually dot the patrons at the Grove. I look at Mikayla and smile. "You must be Mikayla," I say as warmly as possible. "It's nice to meet you."

"That's me," she says, and shakes my hand. I notice her give me a complete once-over as I take my seat. "How were your meetings?"

I blush. "I'm really sorry I'm late." I quickly fill them in on my two meetings and Liz roars when I tell her about the song TJ had me sing. My bad mood vanishes. It feels good to see Liz, even if we do have company.

"Oh, Kates, that's priceless! You must be ready to kill your mom."

"I was, but she feels pretty guilty," I admit. "She even gave me her credit card to go shopping."

"Then she definitely feels guilty." Liz laughs.

I glance at Mikayla. I probably shouldn't say too much more about my mom or about work in front of her. I know Liz likes Mikayla, but I don't know this girl. I've learned the hard way that I need to be careful who I say things in front of. "I guess the card will come in handy," I say. "I have to get a new clutch for the *Vanity Fair* Oscar party."

Liz's jaw drops. "You're joking! How did you score an invitation?"

"Laney got me in," I say giddily. "Austin has a scrimmage out of town so I was hoping you'd be my plus-one. What do you say?"

Liz grimaces. "Oh, Kates, I can't. I'm going to be on the east coast. Daddy is taking me to look at a few backup schools. He doesn't want me to pin all my hopes on NYU. Mikayla offered to check them out with me since she'll be back at NYU by then."

"I know finding backup schools are important," I say gingerly, trying not to be too self-conscious, even though I know Mikayla's eyes are on me, "but isn't there plenty of time for that? Do you have to go to New York that weekend? Lizzie, we've wanted to go to the *Vanity Fair* party since we were twelve!"

"I know," Liz says regretfully, "but Dad already took the weekend off to go with me and Mikayla cleared her schedule. I can't cancel. I'll go with you next year." She gives me a small smile.

"Sure." I try not to look too upset. If there was one thing I thought Liz would say yes to, it was this party. Suddenly I feel like the girl I'm sitting across from is a stranger. We hardly talk anymore and she's planning trips and making summer plans without me. What's happened to us?

The silence is awkward. I decide to change the subject. "So tell me more about how you two met."

Mikayla's face lights up and she and Liz look at each other

and giggle. "I was windsurfing and Liz walked over and said she'd never windsurfed before and she wanted to try it. The resort only had one board, so we had to take turns." Mikayla's green eyes are wide. "I didn't tell Liz I learned how to wind-surf that morning so I was just as bad as she was."

Liz laughs. "The two of us kept falling off and bashing our knees. We were so bruised up after an hour that we gave up and went to the spa instead."

"After that, we were inseparable," Mikayla tells me, grabbing Liz's arm and giving her a bright smile.

"Liz tells me your family just moved here from New York," I mention.

"My dad took a new job this spring at the University of Southern California, which is great for him, but my broth-ers, sister, and I were upset." Mikayla shakes her head. "Los Angeles is nice and all, but why would anyone want to leave New York City? It's the best city in the world. No offense." She smiles. "Anyway, my dad felt bad and took us on a trip to Maui while our stuff was being moved from New York."

"I'm a native Los Angelean and I adore it," Liz tells her. "You will too. I promise. Los Angeles is amazing."

"Yeah," I pipe up. "Think of the weather. You'll always be tan, your lawn will always be green. You don't have to deal with snow. We have sunshine almost year-round. You can swim in January!"

"You also have mud slides, earthquakes, and wildfires," Mikayla points out. "Not to mention a major obsession with all things Hollywood and who has the most money or the best car. It's pathetic how people worship stars out here." Her cheeks redden when she looks at me, as though she just remembered who she's talking to.

Yep, that would include me, Mikayla. I don't call her on it, though.

"Anyway, I can't wait to get back to New York," she adds.

"Mikayla is a freshman at NYU," Liz tells me for the ump-teenth time.

"You'll be one in two years," Mikayla says confidently. "Your SAT scores were really good and with the summer pro-gram, you'll be a shoo-in." She looks at me. "What about you, Kaitlin? Where do you want to go to college?"

I open my mouth, hoping something clever and smart will come out, when Liz answers for me. "Oh, Kates isn't sure she's going to college yet. She might get another show or do some films."

"Instead of college?" Mikayla looks surprised. "I thought your show got canceled."

"It wasn't canceled," I bristle. "We're *choosing* to go off the air."

"Either way, it sounds like a good time to consider college," Mikayla says. "My parents and I have been talking about col-lege since the day I turned twelve. If you want some help look-ing at schools, I'd be happy to guide you the way I am Liz."

The offer is nice, but if anyone is going to help me in that area, it would be Nadine. "Thanks, but —"

"How did you do on your SATs?" Mikayla interrupts. "A good score is crucial."

I blush. "I haven't taken them yet. I'm taking them for the first time in March."

"You haven't taken them yet?" Mikayla looks like her head is going to pop off. "But how will you have time to take them three times before sending out your college applications?"

"I don't know," I admit. "I'm not sure what I'm doing yet. I may take classes part-time or put college on hold."

"That's crazy!" Mikayla tells me. "What if your career washes up? Don't you want something to fall back on?" Liz nudges her and Mikayla seems to snap out of her rant. She takes a deep breath. "Look, you seem like a smart girl. Take it from someone who knows, good SATs are important. I know you're a celebrity and all, and I'm sure plenty of schools would like you for that reason alone, but you shouldn't rely on their charity."

Ouch. My shoulders tighten. "My career is *not* going to wash up," I say stiffly, feeling the anger bubble up inside me. "I know you don't know anything about Hollywood, but the truth is, if I go to college full-time, *then* I'm at risk of my career washing up. I appreciate your help, but I know what I'm doing." Study for the SATs! Pick a movie! Pick a TV show! I'm so sick of everyone thinking they know what's best for me. I need time to make the right decision on my own and I need people to stop badgering me about it.

Liz and Mikayla just look at me. Our waitress hovers near the table with our drinks, but seems afraid to approach. I feel my cheeks burn. I can't believe I just snapped at Liz's friend like that. "I'm sorry." I look downward. "The future is sort of a sore subject with me at the moment."

"It's fine," Mikayla says, sounding anything but fine. "I just think it's good to have a backup plan." She turns to Liz. "I'm going to go to the bathroom."

"Geez, Kates, what's with you?" Liz asks when Mikayla's out of earshot.

"Me?" I'm shocked.

"She can come on a little strong, but she's really nice," Liz insists. "Mikayla's really helped me with the college thing. She's got her whole life mapped out. And she loves NYU even more than I do. She practically grew up on campus."

"And you grew up near Beverly Hills. That's way better," I joke, trying to lighten the mood.

"This is serious," Liz sounds agitated. "College is important to me. If you were around more, you'd know that."

"You're the one that's been MIA lately," I point out. "You never return my calls. We haven't seen each other since before Christmas."

"And that's my fault?" Liz asks, sounding angry. "You're the one who has had meeting after meeting and couldn't hang out till February 1st. I've been dying to talk to you, but you're unreachable! You have no idea what's going on in my life."

I feel like the room is closing in on me. "And you have no idea what's going on in mine," I complain. "I am under so much stress. Every time I do talk to you, you cut me off. You don't tell me anything anymore and you certainly don't listen."

"That's because I can't find you to talk to you!" Liz accuses. "Mikayla's been there for me. She knows what I'm going through. You and I both know that college is not your first priority. My next move is college. I want to get into NYU. *You* have no idea how stressful it is thinking about colleges and the pressure *I'm* under this year to do well. We have different priorities now. I can't party all the time like you and Lauren and Ava."

I feel like I've been punched in the stomach. "I don't party all the time," I say. "And you know those stories are bogus! Even if I was going to events more often, having different priorities never bothered you before." I choke, trying hard to fight back the tears. What exactly is going on here? How did this conversation turn sour so quickly? "What's happened to us?" I ask, afraid of the answer. "I feel like we're worlds apart."

"Maybe we are," Liz says quietly. She doesn't look at me. "Things don't feel the same. Maybe we're just . . . growing apart."

The words hang there and the thought knocks the wind out of me. I blink several times, willing the tears away. "I thought we could talk to each other about anything," I whisper.

"Hey," Mikayla says happily as she slides back into the booth and interrupts our fight. She sees our faces. "Is every-thing okay?"

"Fine," Liz and I say at the exact same time. The silence at our table, in the middle of the crowded restaurant, just sticks there like the restaurant's pea soup.

One of my tears falls on my wrist and I wipe my eyes quickly with my napkin. This is all wrong. How did I lose my job, my best friend, and my ability to choose all in a matter of a month? I have to get out of here. "I have to go," I say, not looking at Liz. "I forgot I have an interview with *Self* this af-ternoon about *PYA* and *FA*."

"Eff Ay?" Mikayla asks, looking confused.

"It's what everyone calls *Family Affair*," Liz explains stiffly.

"Oh, I don't watch network television." Mikayla shrugs. "Just the History Channel, Bill Maher, and some CNN."

"Anyway," I interrupt, "It was supposed to be at four thirty, but Laney just left me a message saying they moved it up and I have to be there in forty-five minutes."

"Kates, wait," Liz looks tentative. I can't look at her di-rectly or I'll burst into tears. "Are you sure you have to go? Let me at least walk you out," she says. She has a weird look on her face.

"No thanks," I tell her and sling my Cinch bag over my shoulder. "I think I can take it from here. It was nice meeting you, Mikayla."

And then I turn to leave through the crowded restaurant, my eyes brimming with tears. I don't even give Mikayla a chance to say goodbye.

Saturday, January 31
NOTE TO SELF:

Call Laney. C if I can get an article in *Self*.
Study 4 SATs.
VF party — Sunday, February 8
Final Jay Godfrey fitting — Tues. @ 7
Gift suites: Sat. all day.
Date w/A: Sat. night B4 he leaves 4 scrimmage.
Sun. — Tina coming @ noon, Paul styling @ 2, Shelly coming @ 2:30.

Find date 4 *VF* party. ☹

EIGHT: *All's Fair in Friends and* Vanity Fair

Tonight is the night. I'm about to go to the most talked-about event of the year, which some might call an award in itself.

I'm not talking about the Oscars, silly. Who wants to sit for four-plus hours in a stuffy auditorium as part of a live audience? Can you say booooring? I'm talking about the *Vanity Fair* party at Morton's in West Hollywood. And this year I have my own invite, which means I can share the dish as it unfolds in front of me. Here we go . . .

"We're minutes from talking to George Clooney!" Matty sounds hoarse. "Julia Roberts! Maybe Robert Redford. I can't breathe."

I fan his neck with my small clutch.

"Matty, you've got to calm down," I tell my brother as our limo inches closer to the *Vanity Fair* party. Yes, Matty is my date tonight. With Austin and Liz out of town, Matty seemed like the next best option. Needless to say he was really excited. Mom was a bit unsure, though. She and Laney seemed concerned about me bringing my brother as my date to the biggest party of the year. They went over the pluses and minuses of taking Matty for an hour, until finally Matty and I broke in and told them that we were going together whether they liked it or not. Geez. It's not like they had to worry about us going all Angelina Jolie and her brother on them. Eww.

It's been a week since my fight with Liz at the Cheesecake Factory and thankfully all the Oscar parties and preparations have kept my mind off the fact that my best friend and I aren't speaking. I want to call, but I'm still so hurt. How could she say I haven't been there for her? She hasn't been there for me either. My life is one big stress ball. I'm still not sleeping that well, and I haven't told anyone this yet, but I think I've developed some sort of hearing problem. Whenever I think about all I have on my plate — Seth hasn't heard back from the *Manolos* director, Mom and Dad are grilling me about choosing a different project, the SATs are in a few weeks, I'm freaking out about my future without *FA* — I feel like I'm going to hyperventilate and I hear a whooshing sound in my ears.

"I don't know if I'm ready for this," Matty tells me. Now he's hyperventilating. "Rodney, turn the car around! I can't go through with this!" The invite says black tie, so Matty is wearing a black Armani tux. His shirt, tie, and jacket look crisp, but his face is a mess. He's red and sweating and if he doesn't stop it soon, his perfectly gelled hair is going to frizz. "Kates, I can't," he tells me, breathing heavily. "David Beckham is here! And Clooney! And Angelina! Kates, Angelina's here. I can't make small talk with Angelina and Clooney. I'm not even sure where Darfur is."

I shake him. "Get it together," I practically shout. "You can do this." I've never seen Matty this vulnerable. Usually he's Mr. Suave (or at least trying to be), but today, he's all worked up. Mom and Dad didn't help matters. They were so nervous for us, they didn't eat all day. Mom just followed us around the house as Tina styled our outfits and Paul and Shelley did our hair and my makeup. It's been twenty-four hours of primping — Mom made me hit the sauna and get a facial yesterday, and then we went airbrush tanning together at our usual place with our girl, Eva.

I think the primping was worth it. This Jay Godfrey gown makes me feel like Cinderella.

HOLLYWOOD SECRET NUMBER EIGHT: It is no coincidence that the dress a star wears to an award show fits her like a glove. Almost every celebrity I know works with a stylist, but some go one step further — they collaborate on their dresses with the designer of a gown. When you do that, you're almost guaranteed a one-of-a-kind creation that will wow the crowd and the tabloids. Many designers sent over dresses for me to wear for tonight, and some even designed things with me in mind, but Jay was the first designer to create the dress of my dreams. This is how it was done: First I visited Jay's office and discussed exactly what I envisioned wearing. I flipped through some of Jay's design books for ideas. A week later Jay presented me with sketches based on the silhouettes and colors I liked. He picked materials for the gown and after we agreed on them, Jay's team hand sewed the dress for me to try on. The minute I slipped it on, I knew it was the one.

The navy dress is tight through the hips and then flows with several light layers that fall into a short train that can be bustled for dancing. The dress is so pretty that Jay said I didn't need a necklace. I just borrowed a ten-carat diamond bangle and three-carat dangling sparklers from Harry Winston. (Security will be waiting for me at the end of the *VF* party to take back the baubles.) I'm pretty excited about my hair too. We ironed it flat and Paul cut a few wispy bangs. Shelly gave me smoky eyes, nude lips, and blush.

Mom loved how Matty and I looked so much that she took a ton of pictures as if we were off to the prom. Except if I was going to the prom, I'd be with Austin. I wish he could be here instead of seeing it all in pictures tomorrow.

"Ready, kids?" Rodney asks as we pull up to Morton's Steakhouse.

Matty and I look at each other. "Are you ready?" I ask.

"Yeah." He blots the sweat from his brow. "Just don't leave me, okay?"

Aww. "I won't. We'll stick together."

I don't tell Matty this, but I need him as much as he needs

me tonight. As exciting as all this is, and as much as I've been looking forward to it, I also feel strangely alone in this world. My costars are at different parties, and my TV star pal Gina is in Europe. Lauren and Ava are going to be here, but we're not close enough that I felt comfortable suggesting we go together.

The car door opens and Rodney is there to help us out. I hear the click of the cameras and photographers yelling things like "Look over here!" Now I'm getting nervous.

Matty steps out first and I'm right behind him. Morton's restaurant has been transformed into a *Vanity Fair* ad. The magazine's logo is up in yellow lights above the white building and there is also a thirty-foot high myrtle topiary sculpture. People dressed in black are everywhere, and I can see the magazine's editor-in-chief, Graydon Carter, way up ahead near the door, situated next to someone with a clipboard checking off names. Before we can even get to the door, we have to do the long red carpet.

"KAITLIN! KAITLIN, LOOK OVER HERE!"

"HEY, KAITLIN, IS THAT YOUR BOYFRIEND?"

"THAT'S HER BROTHER!"

"IS THAT KAITLIN'S BRO? YO, LOOK THIS WAY!"

"KAITLIN BURKE! TURN THIS WAY! NOW OVER HERE!"

"LET'S GET ONE OF YOU TOGETHER!"

"NOW KAITLIN ALONE!"

"Wow, that was intense," Matty whispers after we've made

it through the line, greeted *Vanity Fair*'s editor-in-chief and the magazine's owner, and slipped inside.

Morton's in West Hollywood has been home to the *Vanity Fair* party for over a decade now (well, except for that year there was a writer's strike, but there was no bash that year anyway). Matty and I are attending the dinner party, which about 150 people are invited to and starts at 5 PM. It takes place during the awards, which you can watch on large screens. After the show wraps, the major mingling begins. The after-party is in a large tent behind the restaurant. It can hold up to 800 revelers. With a Hollywood crowd that big, I'm told you can run into almost anyone your heart can imagine — from old Hollywood, like Martin Landau, to politicians, athletes, and rock stars. You might find Kid Rock in a corner talking to Larry King. How weird is that?

A cluster of tables is set up with table numbers and Matty and I nervously make our way to ours. I know the guests have been carefully arranged to avoid any major drama. In years past, there have been a few scuffles, drinks thrown, and people tossed. The last thing I want is to get into a me-lee and get bounced from *VF* on my first year in. I've heard there's actually a list of major stars that have never been asked back to the party because they've behaved badly or been rude to the wait staff. Yikes.

I look around. The tables are sparsely decorated with white cloths, tiny lamps, and cherry brandy roses. Cookies stenciled with the image of *VF*'s annual Young Hollywood cover are on the table, as well as covers dating back to the 1920s. My one publicity goal is to make the Young Hollywood cover. It's a who's who of hotness. They've had the occasional TV star, but it's usually girls with major up-and-coming film careers that are featured.

With *FA* ending, now might be my chance to do just that. That is, if I stop feeling guilty and panicked long enough to pick a project and stick with it. But what happens if *Manolos* doesn't work out? What if I don't like any of the other pilots? What if the people from that play hate me? Could I be washed up at seventeen? Could my first year at the *VF* party also be my last?

"Check out the lighters," Matty interrupts my thoughts. I pick one up. They're custom-made Zippos engraved with the quote, *I've been to a marvelous party*. "I've got to take one of those," he adds. I give him a look. I'm not sure if we get to swipe these.

Dinner itself and the four-plus-hour award ceremony go by in a blip. It doesn't hurt that each course, prepared by Morton's chef, is more delicious than the last — burrata with a red and yellow tomato salad, New York strip steak with spinach and French fries, thyme-encrusted tuna with a fondue of leeks and rice, butternut squash ravioli with sage sauce, and apple tart with caramel sauce and vanilla ice cream.

The company is even better. Whoever did this seating chart must have read one of my interviews — I just spent four hours sitting next to Carrie Fisher. THE Princess Leia!

I'm sure she thought I was crazy because I kept staring at her. I wanted to ask her to say a line from *Star Wars* or something, but I was too embarrassed. I couldn't wait to steal away from the table and tell Austin. I even took a picture of us together with my Canon Sure Shot (the perfect camera for a tiny metallic purse). I'm going to have to blow it up wall-size for my room.

But you know what was even better than getting that photo? Carrie Fisher knew who I was! She loves *Family Affair*. My show! I could have died right then and there. The two of us started chatting about storylines and the next thing I knew she said the ten little words that make my heart start beating like an athlete after four Red Bulls:

"I can't believe *Family Affair* is going off the air."

And even worse:

"What are you planning to do when the show ends?"

Even on Oscar night, when everyone is focused on someone else's body of work and who's going to win the little gold man, I can't escape my career anxieties. Even sitting next to Princess Leia can't make me forget about that. I give her my stock answer that I've perfected by now: "I'm excited about the future and am exploring my options."

"Kates, can I talk to you?" Matty asks me after dessert, when everyone has moved to the 7,000 square foot tent for the after-party. It looks like a giant living room. It's quiet now, but it won't be for long. Throngs of famous faces are filing in behind us, air-kissing, congratulating one another on films recently released and quietly making business deals. I'm in awe of the string of A-listers walking past me. I keep a smile plastered on my face the whole time. I've never seen so many of my favorite stars in one room before. Matty's right — this is kind of nerve-wracking. Thank God I'm not alone.

"Hang on to my arm so we don't get separated," I whisper.

"Um, that's the thing," Matty explains. "I was kind of wondering if you'd be all right on your own for a while."

"What?" I'm surprised. "Where are you going?"

"A few actors from the Scooby-Doo pilot are here and they asked me to sit with them." Matty looks desperate. "I really want to make a good impression since we're shooting it next week." Tom is the show's director and he and Matty have cleared part of their days to shoot the other show. Since Scooby is all about monster-chasing, they're shooting a large part of the pilot at night anyway.

"I'll come with you," I tell him. I don't want to say I don't want to be left alone, but I'm starting to get freaked out. Orlando Bloom just winked at me. And, yes, I've met Rihanna, who is standing two feet away, but we've never said more than three words to each other. What would we talk about?

"I guess so," Matty says, but his face tells a different story. "It's just that if you come over, all anyone will want to talk about is you and *Family Affair* ending. If I go alone, I won't be Kaitlin Burke's little brother, you know?" His eyes plead with me.

I know.

"You go," I reassure him. "I'll mingle and we can meet up when you're done."

Matt kisses my check. "I won't be more than ten minutes."

*   *   *

Forty-five minutes later, I've met Shakira, had chicken skewers with Kelly Clarkson, and begged Hayden Panettiere to give me the scoop on what's going to happen on *Heroes*. I haven't seen Sky yet, who was invited to the after-party ("I didn't want to go to their dinner anyway. Who wants to eat in front of other people?" she told me), but that doesn't mean she's not here. This tent is packed and it's so dark in here, I can barely see past the next Cream-of-Wheat-colored sofa. The room is softly lit and really pretty. The tent's walls are made up of two layers of jute that have lighting in between them. Two-foot-long triangles are suspended from the ceiling high above the sofas and ottomans sitting on the bamboo-covered floor.

I glance at the crowded table where Matty is holding court and stare at it longingly. If I thought I felt lonely before, now I feel ten times worse. If things were different, Austin would be on my arm or Liz would be standing next to me.

Liz and I would have had the best time daring each other to approach Pam Anderson or Bono. She'd be the one telling me to ignore all the people talking about *Family Affair's* ending and just focus on tonight. We would have cooed over everyone's dresses and worried whether we'd been photo-graphed eating. Suddenly, I really miss my best friend. This is silly. So we had a little spat. We've been friends forever! I'm going to call her.

I make my way through the crowd to the bathrooms and move to a quiet(er) corner outside the entrance. The line is long, but I don't think anyone is paying attention to my call. I dial Liz's number. She picks up on the second ring.

"Hello?" The phone is full of static and I can't tell if it's my connection or hers.

"Liz, it's me," I tell her. "Listen, I'm at the *Vanity Fair* party and you'll never guess who I just met." The static is getting louder. "I really wish . . ."

"Can't. Hear." Liz's words are all jumbled and she hangs up.

". . . you were here," I finish the sentence out loud to my-self and wait for her to call me back. I'm sure my number came up on her caller ID so she knows it was me. If she's out of range she'll just find someplace with good reception to call me from. She knows where I am tonight so I'm sure she'll call me back. Suddenly I wish I could call Austin but he's in the middle of his scrimmage. I'd give anything to hear his voice right now; I miss him so much. But instead I wait for Liz to call me. And I wait. And wait.

But Liz doesn't call. I stand there for fifteen minutes, but my phone doesn't ring at all and I have four bars so I know I have a full signal.

I try to fight back my tears. I cannot cry in front of all these people. But that's all I want to do: cry. I want to forget about my fight with Lizzie. Forget about *Family Affair* ending. Forget about Mom and Dad and Laney and Nadine and Seth putting pressure on me to find my next big thing. I'm sick of hearing it all. And now I'm not just stressed, I'm getting angry. I don't know how much more of this I can take.

"Kaitlin? Are you okay?"

I look up. Ava is standing in front of me clutching a gold purse. She looks pretty in a turquoise Dina Bar-El gown that is fitted to her tiny frame. Her long blond hair is super curly and she's got on so much bling my eyes hurt staring at it. Lauren is with her, and she looks incredible in a short gold mini dress with her hair piled high on her head.

"What happened?" Lauren asks and puts an arm around me. "We've been looking for you everywhere."

"I have a headache and I just want to go home," I say tearfully.

"Hey," Ava says sternly. "Be real. You said yourself you've been dying to get an invite to this party. You're not going home. What gives?"

"You can talk to us," Lauren says gently. "We're your friends."

Friends. I like the sound of that. I really need friends right now. "Do you really want to know what's going on?" I ask doubtfully. This is usually the point where everyone else I know cuts me off.

"We wouldn't ask if we didn't," Ava says simply.

Click. Click. Click.

I look up. Gary and Larry the Liar are taking pictures of us.

"Get away from here!" Ava shrieks.

Gary looks alarmed. "But you said you wanted us to take your picture."

"Can't you see our friend is upset?" Lauren complains. "Go away. We'll see you on the dance floor."

I smile gratefully at Lauren as she hands me a crumpled tissue. "I'm really glad you two are here." I can feel my cellphone buzzing in my purse, but I don't stop to look. If it's Matty, we'll find each other eventually.

"Let's find a quiet table so we can talk," Ava suggests. She and Lauren both put an arm around me and we make our way to a small, candlelit booth in the back. People try to stop us along the way, but Ava and Lauren actually ignore them. "Tell us what's going on," Ava says once we're settled.

Once I start talking, I can't stop. Ava and Lauren really listen. They don't interrupt me at all except for an occasional "shut up!" or "they're crazy!" I vent about my parents, Seth, Nadine's nagging, my fight with Liz, how much I miss my boyfriend, and my equal fear and procrastination about finding another project. I don't hold anything back. It feels good to get it all out on the table. When I'm finished, Ava is the first to speak.

"You have to get rid of these people!" she declares. "They're dragging you down. Well, except for that hottie boyfriend of yours. He sounds okay."

I smirk. "He's a keeper, for sure, but, well, I can't disown my parents. But it's good to know whose side you're on."

"Of course we're on yours," Lauren says. "I think everyone is bullying you around. Who cares if you have a new show or movie to do this spring? Ava and I haven't shot anything since last year and the press still adores us. You don't have to toil away at work to get the perks of being a celebrity, you know."

I nod. But I don't want to be a celebrity. I want to be an actress. And the truth is, I like working. I think I'd be pretty bored if I was sitting home every day. I used to fantasize about time off, but a few months during hiatus is all I really seem to need. "I'm glad you guys understand. No one else seems to get what I'm going through," I complain.

"You know what you need?" Ava asks. "You need to take control of your own destiny. It's like I keep telling you — no one is going to give you the respect you deserve unless you take it for yourself. I can't believe they made you do a music demo! Stop letting them boss you around and make you do stupid things. You have to make the decisions. What do they know anyway?"

"Well, Seth is a well-respected agent," I admit. "And Laney is one of the best publicists around."

Lauren coughs. "You could get a publicist for half the

price who would do the same thing. I don't even have a publicist right now and look at me. I'm doing okay."

"Your last publicist dropped you," Ava reminds her. They both giggle. "For good reason."

"Why?" I ask.

"It doesn't matter," Ava says dismissively. "Right now we're worried about you. You're a mess! It's time for Kaitlin Burke to take some me time. Stop letting everyone else call the shots."

I feel the anger start to bubble over. "You're right!" I tell them. "I do deserve me time." I feel stronger just saying the words out loud.

"Thatta girl," Lauren commends me. "Be free." Suddenly she gasps and grabs my hand. "I love this song!"

It's a Ne-Yo tune and I know the lyrics by heart. The three of us start singing at the top of our lungs and I don't care if people are staring. It feels good to let loose.

"Ooh! Let's go dance," Ava suggests. "We can dance and make fun of people at the same time."

Lauren giggles. "Seriously, this is one of our favorite pastimes," she says conspiratorially. "Did you see what some of these people are wearing?" My face must look surprised because then she adds, "We do it all in good fun. We're not really being mean, you know. Everyone does it." I nod.

The two of them drag me away from our small corner after nearly an hour of chatting and we go dance. The party has an awesome DJ. We shimmy in a little circle, holding hands and singing to all the lyrics. We stop every so often so that Ava or Lauren can drool over some star that tries to break into our little group. I swear they must know everyone here. I'm having such a good time, I don't look at the time. It's not until Matty joins us that I realize how late it is.

"Rodney is waiting out front with the car," Matty yells over the thumping music. "It's one thirty."

One thirty? "Guys, I have to go," I tell Ava and Lauren sadly. They both groan.

"Nooooooo," Ava whines. "Do you have to go now? There's this awesome after-after-party happening in the Valley after this."

"I have to be at work tomorrow at seven," I tell them apologetically.

"Call in sick," Lauren suggests. "Fight the power!"

I laugh. "I can't call in tomorrow. Thanks again for tonight though. It felt good to vent."

"We're glad you did," Ava says as Matty begins tugging me. "We'll call you tomorrow."

It's not till we're finally in the car and I'm looking at Carrie Fisher's number on my Sidekick that I see I missed a call on my cellphone. It was from Liz. She called about twenty minutes ago. For a moment, I'm excited. If she's on the east coast it's not too late to call her and tell her all about tonight. But then again, why should I call? Liz didn't try too hard to reach me earlier. She could have left me a voicemail, but she didn't. Liz wasn't there for me when I needed her. Ava and Lauren were. I turn off the phone and replay my magical first *VF* party in my mind.

Sunday, February 8
NOTE TO SELF:

Monday calltime: 7 AM

BLOGS SIGHTINGS BIOS ARCHIVE

Oscar Night Sightings Continued . . .   February 9

Sky Mackenzie talking **Elton John's** ear off at the *In Style* bash. Guess Sky didn't have much company to keep. Her object of affection, **Trevor Wainright,** basically ignored her. Instead, he spent the night nestled between two unidentified blondes. Was Sky mad. Tee hee . . .

Rejected *Family Affair* costar **Alexis Holden** being turned away at the door to the *Entertainment Weekly* party. We're sure the bad buzz on her upcoming film, *Paris Is Burning* (which had already been recast once), had a lot to do with it . . .

Drew Thomas, holding court with the latest Hollywood "It" Girl, Piper Long, at the Governor's Ball. Hmm . . . was Drew actually into Piper, or just on her arm for the publicity? He was all love and affection in front of the cameras, but when the glare was off the pair, he looked beyond bored to us . . .

Mac Murdoch and his celebrity band taking the stage at the *Hollywood Nation* party. The guys were so awful that the room cleared in minutes. Do us a favor and stick to rockin' action films, Mac. Mwah!

Spotted at the *Vanity Fair* party in a delicious navy Jay Godfrey gown—none other than our favorite good girl, **Kaitlin Burke**. But were our eyes deceiving us or did she really spend the evening with notorious party animal heiresses **Ava Hayden** and **Lauren Cobb**? Those three seem to be spending an awful lot of time together. Better watch yourself with those two, Kaitlin. Unless you're gunning to be a daily fixture in this column for bad behavior, steer clear . . .

7. INT. BUCHANAN MANOR— SAM'S BEDROOM
SAMANTHA is at her bedroom window looking over the
Buchanan Estate. She's wearing sweats, her hair is uncombed,
and her face is free of any makeup. She opens her window
and waves to someone below. From underneath her bed she
pulls out a rope and flings it over the side of the window.
She starts to climb over when the door opens.

                    PAIGE
(alarmed) Samantha! What do you think you're doing?
(grabs her daughter's arm)

                    SAMANTHA
Going out. Get off.

                    PAIGE
You're not going anywhere. You're grounded, young
lady! (looks out the window) And you're certainly not
going anywhere with Nick Masters. He's a con artist.

                    SAMANTHA
Nick is the only one who understands me.

                    PAIGE
Understands what, Sam? That you don't want to move?
This is no way to make a case for staying. You're not
with Ryan anymore. Your teachers keep calling about

missing assignments. You got detention last week for
mouthing off to the principal. This isn't you, Sam.

                    SAMANTHA
Maybe it's the new me, Mom. Did you ever think of
that?

                    PAIGE
Sam, I know you've been having a hard time adjusting
to the news that we're moving, but that doesn't give
you license to act out like this. Fighting what's
happening won't change things.

                    SAMANTHA
Maybe, but seeing the grief it causes you certainly
makes me feel better.

Paige starts to cry and Sara enters the room.

                    SARA
Whoa. Sam, way to dress casual. Why is Mom crying?

                    SAMANTHA
I'm done with this drama. I'm out of here and I'm not
coming back. Enjoy Miami!

Sam shimmies down the rope and runs to Nick's car. The two
tear off with the engine roaring as Paige and Sara look on
from the bedroom window.

nine: *Someone's in Denial and It Feels So Good*

"Thanks, Pete," I mumble sleepily as he hands me my second iced double espresso latte of the day. "You're a life-saver."

Did I mention it's only ten thirty AM?

If we didn't have craft services at work, some days I don't know how I'd survive. Pete keeps crafty stocked with everything you could possibly need for a good jolt (frozen coffee concoctions included) or a major meltdown (M&Ms and brownies at your service). He's a pro at knowing exactly what we need when we need it — like the morning after the Oscars, when almost everyone on set is overtired and cranky. Calling in sick won't fly. Tom knows we were out partying last night. He's got the paparazzi pictures in every major magazine and on every Web site to prove it.

Things are moving slower than usual, though. We've only shot a three-minute scene inside Summerville Breads (a school hangout) and we still have to get through the scene where Sam runs away from home. (Tom promises Sam will get her act together before the last episode. In the meantime, the bad Sam is fun to play.) I don't know if we're going to get to that scene today. We're all tripping over our lines. Thankfully Tom was out last night too, so he can't get too mad.

Sky snatches her own latte from Pete's outstretched hands. "There better be an extra shot of espresso in mine."

"That's Sky's way of saying thank you," Trevor tells Pete. Instead of coffee, he takes another Red Bull.

"How would you know what I meant?" Sky asks, sounding upset. "People have to spend time with other people if they want to know those people's thoughts. You can't ignore people and then expect those people to pay attention to you." Her voice is rising and Pete steps back to avoid the fire. "Isn't that right, K?"

Sky looks at me helplessly. Her under-eye circles are huge, as I'm sure are mine. The whole set has them and I'm sure the makeup staff will go through at least a dozen tubes of concealer today trying to cover them up.

"Yes?" I say, even though I'm not sure what Sky is so worked up over.

"So you're saying people need people?" Trevor starts singing the old Barbara Streisand song as he walks away and I can't help but giggle.

Sky's chest is rising and falling like she's just run a marathon. She grunts loudly in exasperation. "I don't get him," Sky complains to me. "He asked me if I was going to the *In*

Style party and I said yes. And then when he got there he ignored me all night. I skipped the *Vanity Fair* party because of him and he still didn't talk to me!" She looks so upset that I actually feel bad for her. Maybe I should tell Trevor to tone down the cold shoulder act a bit. It could backfire.

"Did you ever think that Trevor was just trying to make you jealous?" I ask.

Sky's face brightens. "Did he say that?" she asks hopefully.

"No," I lie. I can't sell Trevor out completely. "But maybe that's what he's doing to get you back for the way you treated him last summer."

Sky rolls her eyes. "He's not over that yet?"

"Not all of us bounce back from humiliation as quickly as you do," I remind her. "Maybe if you just keep being nice to him, and don't fall all over him, he'll pay more attention to you. Give him time."

"Okay," Sky mumbles. "Now enough of you giving me advice. It's making me itchy. How was your night?"

I take a sip of my latte. "Fun. I hung out with Ava Hayden and Lauren Cobb."

Sky's eyes darken. "Again? What is with you three and the paparazzi?"

"We've hung out a few times," I say. Being with Ava and Lauren is the most relaxed I've felt in a while. "They're nice."

Sky makes an unidentifiable noise. "You wouldn't say that if you really knew them."

It's all coming back to me now as the sleep fog lifts. Lauren mentioned Sky! Apparently they were a tight threesome up until last year when they all had a major falling out over some guy. They hate each other now.

"Have you guys talked to Melli?" Matty interrupts us as he approaches crafty. He takes a granola bar and an apple from the table. "She dropped out of that *Revenge* movie."

"Are you serious?" I'm shocked. Melli couldn't stop talking about the part all last week in between takes. "She loved that role!"

"It's in this morning's *Variety*," Matt says.

"You went to the *Vanity Fair* party and still woke up early enough to read *Variety*?" Sky asks.

Matty shrugs. "Anway, I just passed Melli talking to Tom and she said she realized she didn't want to take on another role so soon. She wanted time with her family."

"What did *Variety* give as the official reason?" I ask.

Matty smirks. "Creative differences."

Ah. That's always a good one.

HOLLYWOOD SECRET NUMBER NINE: Even after a celebrity has made it public knowledge that they intend to do a film, it doesn't mean it's actually going to happen. I've already told you about stars that are dropped like hot potatoes because the director realized their golden child was not so golden after all. But what happens when it's the stars, not the director or studio, who want to pull out of a role they've already committed to? You could probably pull out when you get a new draft of the script and hate it or if the film switches directors, but what if neither of those things happen? If you don't want to wind up slapped with a multi-million dollar lawsuit for delaying filming, then you have to be careful. Most stars who do this sort of thing veto the project somewhere between the original verbal agreement and the date they sign the official contract a few weeks later. Sure, it upsets the studio, but they can't actually sue you over that. And if the studio has already announced or leaked that you were starring in their summer must-see, it's their mess to clean up.

"So Melli's got no project lined up after *Family Affair?*" Sky looks stunned. "What is she thinking? People will forget about her!"

"I highly doubt anyone is going to forget about Melli," I tell her patiently. "She's a huge star."

Sky shrugs. "That's today, but a few months or a year without anyone seeing her face on TV or in theaters and she'll start getting passed over for Hallmark movies. You know how this town works — one bad role and you're yesterday's news." Sky shakes her head sadly. "I know Melli's made money on this show, but it won't last forever. She won't be able to keep affording that house if she doesn't sign on to new movies."

"You're wrong," I tell her. I'm shaking and I fold my arms across my chest. It's kind of cold in the studio when all you have on is a Juicy tank and sweats. Sky is in a green skirt by Zac Posen, with ankle high boots and a belly-baring fitted dress shirt that screams tacky. "Not everyone has to have project after project lined up," I remind Sky. "Maybe Melli wants to take time before she makes her decision. Maybe she's tired of everyone bossing her around! Or maybe the project she really wants just hasn't gotten back to her yet." I think of the *Manolos* movie. The director has been out of town for two weeks and Seth hasn't reached him. I'm beginning to lose hope.

Matty shifts uncomfortably in his Nike track pants and the Summerville High sweatshirt he had on for the previous scene.

"Are you sure we're talking about Melli, K?" Sky asks lightly. "Stop getting so stressed out. It's ruining your complexion." She takes a loud sip of her coffee, smiles at Matty, and practically skips off to her dressing room to get ready for the next scene.

"HEY!" Nadine's voice is so loud and bubbly; I practically fall backward into the craft services table. Pete, who was in the middle of making a smoothie for Matty, drops the top of the blender and it clanks onto the floor.

"What are you doing? Are you done with the scene?" she asks. She's clutching an oversized paperback book to the bible, which can only mean she wants to . . .

"Run," Matty whispers in my ear.

"I was hoping we could do another SAT test," Nadine says. "I wasn't thrilled with your last score."

I groan. "Nadine, I've been studying every day," I complain.

"I don't think I can handle another practice test. Not today. I'm exhausted."

"What are you going to do if you have to work late the night before the test?" Nadine asks me. "You'll have to trudge on. This is good practice!" Her beaded bracelets dangle on her wrist. She's wearing a cute brown sweater with khaki pants. The look is dressed up for Nadine.

"Are you going somewhere after work?" I ask.

She looks at me like I'm crazy. "We'll be on set till at least ten PM."

"Then why are you dressed up?" I ask.

Nadine looks down at her outfit. "I'm trying to dress more professionally," she says. "But that's not important. What is important are the SATs. The test is —"

"In a few weeks," Matty and I finish in unison, our voices as flat as a supermodel's stomach.

"Exactly." Nadine nods, oblivious to our tone. "We should really get in one extra test a day until then. Oh! And I talked to Seth again." She begins flipping through her binder and hands a few loose papers to Matty.

"Since when does she talk to Seth?" Matty asks me quietly.

"Ever since she started morphing into Laney and Mom," I whisper. I love Nadine to death, but I don't know how much more of these cheerleader SAT/career pep rallies I can take. I want my real Nadine back. I don't understand what happened. Nadine went home for the holidays and came back a task-master monster.

"It looks like the director of *Manolos* is still out of town."
Nadine frowns. "I think Seth sounds a little worried you're
not going to get this part, but that's just my opinion. The
folks from that play are flying out this week to talk to you.
But that won't work. You have to study for the SATs. I'll have
to reschedule that." She begins dialing her phone.

"Nadine, wait!" I beg. "If they're flying out to meet with
me, I can't reschedule."

"We'll have to keep the meeting short then," Nadine
stresses. "Your mom doesn't want you to do the play anyway.
She said it's not enough exposure."

I throw my head back and groan. What alternate universe
have I fallen into? That's the only explanation I can come up
with to explain how Nadine could be brainwashed by Mom.
I roll my neck like Austin taught me. He thinks it will help
the tension I seem to carry in my neck and shoulders. My
pocket starts to vibrate and I reach in for my phone. Finally
some good news — it's Austin!

"Hey!" I turn away from Nadine and Matty, who is talking
to Pete about a second smoothie to take back to his dressing
room. "How was the scrimmage? I tried calling — "

"I know, I'm sorry. We won and coach took us out for dinner to celebrate." I hear a lot of noise in the background and
realize Austin must be on the bus heading back to school.
The scrimmage wasn't till 8 PM last night and the game was
two hours away so the team stayed overnight.

"That's great!" I tell him. "Were there any scouts?"

"Actually one knew my name and said he'd be calling me," Austin says. "And I met one of the coaches from that camp Rob and I want to go to in Texas."

"Sounds like you had a good night." I smile. Just talking to Austin lifts my mood. I wish he were here now. I really miss him.

"You too, Miss *Vanity Fair*," Austin teases. "Partying all night like a rock star, posing with Jay-Z and Ava Hayden. It looks like you had a ball."

"How do you know that?" I ask.

"Rob brought his laptop," Austin says. "They had Wi-Fi in the hotel. I checked out the pictures this morning. It made me madder than ever that I had to miss taking you. You looked gorgeous."

I blush. "Thanks."

"KAITLIN, YOU'RE HOT!" I hear someone yell. "WE LOVE YOU!"

"Guys, enough." Austin laughs. "Let's just say your red carpet pictures were rated a ten."

"I'm glad they approve." I giggle. "Even if your opinion is the only one that matters."

"I didn't know you knew Ava Hayden," he says. "There were a ton of pictures of you two with some girl named Lauren."

"Cobb," I tell him. "She's really nice. I think we're going shopping together later this week."

"Cool," Austin says. "So, I hate to bring this up, but have you talked to Liz yet?"

I take a deep breath. "I tried her last night, but we got disconnected. Then she called me back, but I missed her call."

"So try her again," Austin pushes. "I'm still not sure what happened at your lunch, but Josh said Liz has been really upset about the fight you guys had and I know you are too."

"I am," I admit, "but I'm not sure how to fix things. I know we've both been busy, but I didn't think we'd grown apart. Liz feels differently. She said I can't understand what she's going through."

"She said that?" Austin sounds surprised.

"Basically," I say quietly. "I guess I feel the same way. She's so busy with Mikayla and NYU stuff that she has no time for me either." A wave of sadness washes over me again, but before I get upset, I think about Lauren and Ava and how supportive they were last night. "Look, if that's the way Liz feels, she's entitled to her opinion. I don't know where we go from here and to be honest, I have too many other things stressing me out at the moment to deal with this too." Okay, that's sort of a lie. I can't stop thinking about Liz, but I'm choosing to ignore the situation till I figure out how to deal with it. How do you make up with your best friend when she's said things that really bother you?

"I don't understand girl fights," Austin says. "I swear, guys have a disagreement and it's over in two minutes. Girls, they drag it out for weeks or months."

"We're sensitive," I sniff.

"Can we talk about it more when I see you?" Austin pauses. "When am I seeing you anyway, Burke? I miss you."

I smile. "How about Friday?"

"Friday it is. I hope I can make it that long."

Aww.

"I'll call you after work," I promise.

"You better," he says and hangs up. I'm in such a daze after that, I don't see Tom standing right in front of me.

"Hey, sport," Tom says with a smile. His face looks haggard and his skin is almost yellow. "Did you have fun last night? Great shot of you dancing on a couch at the *Vanity Fair* party."

"How come everyone has seen these pictures except me?" I complain.

"They're on Private Hollywood Eyes," Matty says as he drinks his strawberry smoothie.

"Anyway, I was wondering what you're doing now," Tom asks.

I'm confused. "I think the next scene, right?"

Tom shakes his head. "We're shooting one with Melli and Spencer right now. You don't have another one till around two."

"You mean I'm off till two?" I can barely handle my excitement. This means I can sleep!

"Oh good! You have time to study," Nadine jumps in. I ignore her.

"Actually, I was hoping Kaitlin could do her *FA* retrospective interview," Tom says. "I don't know if you've heard, but we're doing one that will air in May. Everyone is shooting individual interviews. You'll be asked about your first memories of the show, your biggest fashion faux pas, what your favorite episode was. It's simple. You'll be done in under an hour and still have time for lunch."

I can feel my palms begin to sweat and the whooshing noise in my ears. Shoot the retrospective show? Is it time to do that already? That means we're really nearing the end now. "I don't know, Tom," I say nervously. "I have such under-eye circles today. I don't know if Shelly has enough concealer to retouch me."

"You look fine," Tom insists. "Kaitlin, I know it's hard to say goodbye, but —"

"I don't have a problem saying goodbye," I lie. "I'm just tired."

"You'll be fine," Tom assures me. "I'll come find you in fifteen minutes and see if you're up for it." He walks off.

"I'd say no," Nadine tells me. "He sprung it on you! You can do that later. Right now we should do a test." Her phone rings. "Oh hi, Laney. Meg. What's up? What? No I haven't seen the pictures. Who are Lauren and Ava?"

I'm not even paying attention to what Nadine is saying and that's because across the soundstage I see a group of grips tearing down the Summerville Breads set. At first I think they're just redressing it, but then I see them taking down the back wall board by board and someone carrying away the booth Sam and Sara always sit at.

"What are they doing?" I ask Matty in alarm. "Why are they taking my booth?"

"Kates, weren't you listening?" Matty asks, looking at me like I'm nuts. "That was the last scene we're shooting there. They're getting rid of that set. There's only a few weeks left of filming, you know."

I hold Matty's wrist firmly as I watch two men carry the jukebox out of the way. Do you know how many quarters Sam has dropped in that thing? How many times Sam and Ryan danced slowly to Robin Thicke? Summerville Breads is where the Jonas Brothers played last season and Joe gave me one of his guitar picks. And now the place is gone. One of the grips has powered up a small chain saw and is cutting down the door Sam ran through when she found out she was a finalist for the Summerville Golden Apple, this writing contest she entered. I blink back tears.

"Kates, are you okay?" Matty sounds worried. "You don't look good."

I have to get out of here. Suddenly I feel very hot. I can't breathe. I'm about to panic when I hear my phone ring.

"Hello?" My voice sounds teary.

"It's us!" Ava squeals.

I take a deep breath. "Hey."

"Where are you? We just got up and we're driving around looking for a place to park it for lunch," Ava adds. "Join us and we'll shop after. You in?"

"I can't," I tell them, wincing as I notice the popcorn machine is the next thing to be carted away. "I'm at work."

"Do you have to be there?" Ava moans. "Are you filming like right now?"

"Not exactly," I tell her. "My next scene is at two."

"Your mom wants to talk to you," Nadine mouths to me.

"Kaitlin! Come on then!" Ava is begging. "Get out of that dark soundstage and come meet us. Take back the power! You promised. We'll pick you up and whisk you back to set before your call time."

The chain saw sounds louder and louder. Nadine is still yakking in the background. Whenever I glance her way she holds up the SAT book and points to it. Nadine writes something on a piece of paper and hands it to me. It says, *Your mom is mad. Wants you to ditch* Manolos *idea. Thinks the reality show is the way to go.*

I feel like I can't breathe. My chest is tight. Matty is looking at me strangely. I've got to get out of here.

"Can you be here in ten?" I whisper quickly.

"You've got it," Ava says. "She's in," I hear her tell Lauren, who cheers. "Just give me directions."

I give Ava directions as I bolt from the room. The sound of the workers dismantling Summerville Breads rings in my ears.

"Kaitlin? Where are you going?" I hear Nadine yell over the chain saw. But I ignore her.

I'm out of here.

Monday, February 9
NOTE TO SELF:

B back @ 2.

ten: *Playing Hooky*

Being with Ava and Lauren is so much fun. They don't care whether I'm taking meetings with Paramount or Universal. They have no clue how much my asking price should be for my next film. And they're not at all interested in whether or not I'm taking the SATs. The only thing these two want to talk about is clothes and boys, in that order.

"You have to buy those!" Ava coos when I walk out of Belladonna's dressing room wearing a khaki Juicy Couture Chunky Sweater ($300) and trouser-cut Citizens of Humanity Birkin jeans ($188).

We've just come from having lunch at The Blvd restaurant in the Beverly Wilshire, and even though I only have an hour and a half to spare, Lauren and Ava said I deserved a shopping spree after walking off set the way I did. That's how we wound up at Belladonna, which is owned by *Celebrity Insider* correspondent Taylor Ryan. She owns this small chain of California chic clothing stores and you can always count on finding something unique here.

HOLLYWOOD SECRET NUMBER TEN: You know how I said a lot of stars don't do hands-on work in their restaurants? When it comes to stars owning clothing boutiques or having their own clothing label, the story is usually different. Several of my celebrity pals have their own labels and they oversee everything from first sketches and fabric and color choices to fittings, sitting in on meetings and doing runway shows. If I had my own label, I think I'd want to make clothes that are reasonably priced and fashionably cute. Maybe I'll have my own line at Target. Just because I spend a ton on clothes, doesn't mean I don't wince at the sales receipt sometimes.

"Tell me you're buying that outfit," Ava insists. She's wearing a Joie Sugar black sheer blouse that looks great against her pale blond hair. She has on the same jeans I do, but you wouldn't know it because they look completely different on her.

"You really like it?" I ask and bite my lower lip. I've already decided I have to have the Scoop Metallic Ballet Flats in silver (cost: $165) and the Rachel Pally Sweetheart Dress in graphite ($248) and if I buy this outfit too, I'll break the one thousand dollar mark. That's way over my limit. (Mom caps me at $300 a month max and I still haven't told her how much the Cinch bag cost.) I guess I'm getting a little carried away, but it's so easy with these girls. They carry boatloads of clothes into the fitting room, not restricting themselves to an outfit or two like Liz and I usually do. (Liz may have no limit on her AmEx, but she tries to curtail her dad's griping by keeping transactions on the low side.) Lauren and Ava also think everything looks superb and never glance at a price tag. This shopping spree will get me in a lot of trouble. But . . . I feel the sweater against my chin and it's so soft and woolly I could fall asleep. What the heck. I'm buying it!

Click. Click. Click.

I whirl around clutching my bag to my chest. I'm fully clothed, but whenever I get snapped inside a store, I feel naked. Most stores don't allow the paparazzi to shoot inside, but Ava's and Lauren's sidekick Gary is standing right in front of me and he has Larry the Liar with him. Larry gives me this weird little smile and I shudder.

"What are they doing here?" I complain.

"Relax," Ava says. "We invited them."

"Shopping?" I protest. "I don't want pictures of me on my lunch hour." Larry takes another photo of me anyway and I glare at him. That just makes him take more.

Ava pulls me aside. "Lau and I have this agreement with the store. We give them publicity; they give us loads of free stuff. I'm sure they'll gift you some stuff too if you stop whining. What's the big deal anyway? If they weren't in here, they'd be taking your picture through the window. Then it would come out blurry, and blurry pictures make people look fat."

I don't like the sound of this. I know there are some stars who invite the paparazzi everywhere they go, but I'm not one of those people. I don't need any more exposure than I already have and I certainly don't want to use publicity to get free stuff. Still, I don't want to be a pill. Ava is looking at me like I'm trying to spoil the party and I don't want to do that, especially after they've been so great. I guess the pictures are okay just this once. "Fine, they can stay."

Click. Click. Click. Gary and Larry start shooting again right away.

Lauren screams from the other side of the store. "We all have to get this!" Lauren catwalks out, throws her brown hair around and does a full circle in a black Tibi mini dress that has a white daisy pattern and ruffles. Gary snaps away. The outfit is really cute and Ava and I applaud. "We can wear them to LAX nightclub this weekend for Simon Barter's party!" Lauren suggests. "This is only three hundred dollars."

"Kaitlin, you're going to Simon's party in Vegas, aren't you?" Ava asks.

I want to say I've never met Simon and that my mom will probably never let me go to Las Vegas again after what happened when *FA* had their disastrous cast trip there last fall, but I know what Ava will have to say about that. So instead I say, "When is it?"

"Friday night," Lauren tells me as she piles another group of jeans over her arm.

"Friday night I have a date with Austin," I say. I would *never* miss a date with Austin for a party.

"Boo," they whine in unison. Boo seems to be one of their favorite words.

"I hate that she has a boyfriend and we don't," pouts Ava, hiding her head in a fur-lined Juicy hoodie she's still debating. "It's only fun if we all have boyfriends together."

That's a weird thing to say. Liz and I never cared if one of us didn't have a boyfriend and the other did. We've never let the situation affect our friendship.

"Well if you're not coming to the party on Friday night, then you have to go to Shelter with us on Thursday night," Lauren says. "We get there around ten. We can wear the dresses! The press will love it!" Lauren pulls Ava and me in for a tight shot and Gary and Larry oblige.

I don't want to say anything, but by ten on weeknights, if I'm not still on the set, I'm usually in my pajamas watching a TiVo'd episode of *Grey's Anatomy*. "Um . . ." My phone rings and saves me. I look at the screen and practically drop it. "Guys, I have to take this outside. It's, um, my agent." I motion to the store clerk about the phone and she nods. I guess she doesn't think I'm about to run off without paying.

I take a deep breath. Then I answer the phone. "Hello?" I use my cheeriest voice.

"Kates? It's Liz." Her voice sounds small and shaky.

Maybe that means she's as bothered by us not talking as I am. But then I remember everything she said. Even if she is upset, she still thinks we've grown apart. "Hi. How are you?" I say stiffly.

"Good," she says. "You?"

"Good," I lie.

"Great," Liz says, sounding nervous. Then there's a long pause.

That has never happened before. Usually it's a case of us talking so much that Nadine has to pull the phone from my ear so that I'm not late for wherever I'm going. Suddenly, even the Scoop shoes and cute Juicy sweater don't thrill me. Thinking of Liz and our fight makes me sad.

"I feel bad about what happened at lunch," Liz says.

Really? "Me too," I admit. And just like that I feel hopeful. Maybe this was all a misunderstanding.

"I didn't mean to upset you, but I thought you should know how I was feeling. You've been so distant lately and it really upset me."

The hope bubble bursts just like that. "You haven't been around either," I say lightly. I'm afraid to make things worse, but I'm not going to lie either. I take a deep breath. I have to say this. "I don't know why us growing apart — as you call it — should be all my fault." When Liz doesn't say anything, I start to babble. "I'm not saying we *have* grown apart. I mean, maybe we have, but I didn't see it that way. I just thought we were both busy and —"

"That's what I've been trying to tell you, but I just don't know how to explain myself," Liz says, sounding as awkward as I do. My babbling seems to have rubbed off on her. "I'm not used to us . . . and . . . I mean . . ."

Liz can't seem to find the words and for a moment, I want to wait and listen. I want to tell her it's okay. We both messed up. I'm thinking about saying just that when —

"CHICKY, what are you doing out here?" Lauren pokes her head out of the store and yells at me. "We have to try on more shoes and we can't do it without you," Lauren adds. "Gary is waiting!" She sees my phone and looks at me suspiciously. "Who are you talking to?"

"Liz," I mouth and motion for her to give me two seconds.

"UGH! Hang up already! She's not worth the minutes," Lauren complains.

My face flushes and I'm mortified. I hope Liz didn't hear that.

"Who are you talking to?" Liz wants to know.

"My friend Lauren," I say slowly. "I'm actually out shopping with some friends."

"I thought you were at work," Liz says. Her voice sounds strange.

"I was, but I'm on break. Lauren and Ava picked me up for lunch."

"Kaitlin," Lauren whines. "Come on! I told you Gary is waiting. He just got another call and he has to leave. We've got to get the last shot. Hang up with that loser. She doesn't deserve you!"

My jaw drops. I know Lauren is just trying to defend me, but Liz is not a loser. Liz had to have heard Lauren. I know it. And now I have a feeling the conversation we just had made things worse between us. I'm too tired to be upset. I just want this fight to be over.

Before I can say anything, Liz says stiffly, "I can see you're busy with your new friends. I'll try you another time."

"I'm sorry. Can we talk soon?" I ask awkwardly and try not to sound too sad when Liz hangs up without saying when.

I push open the doors to Belladonna and my phone rings again before I even have time to take in what's just happened. Liz tried to make up, I think, and I started rambling and then Lauren interrupted us and I let her. Why did I put Lauren before Liz? Why didn't I tell her I had to take care of this first? This conversation was important and I think I just blew it. What if I ruined my only chance at fixing our friendship? I think I'm going to throw up. What's wrong with me? My phone rings again. Is that Liz calling back? I look at the screen and see "restricted" on the caller ID.

Oh God. Who could that be? My breath gets tight and short. Someone other than Matty and Nadine knows I'm not at work, don't they? I've been avoiding all of Nadine's calls, but I don't know who this is from. Tom? Should I just let it go to voicemail? I take a deep breath and answer.

"Kaitlin speaking." I try to sound super professional. If it's Mom or Tom I can try to say I had a dentist appointment. If it's Nadine, I'm in big trouble.

"Hey, gorgeous," I hear Austin say.

I exhale. "Austin, hi!" I walk back into the store and forget all about what just happened. "Your number came up funny."

"My cell phone died. I forgot to ask you something before so I'm on Rob's phone," he explains. "Where are you?" I'm sure he can hear all the commotion in the background. Lauren just found a pair of Scoop shoes she had been looking for and she and Ava are jumping up and down and screaming while Gary and Larry take more pictures even though Lauren claimed they were getting ready to leave.

"Shopping," I admit guiltily. I mouth the word "Austin" to Ava and she grins.

"On a workday?" He laughs. "I don't know how you squeeze everything in."

"Well, I had a break so I'm out with Ava and Lauren. Those are the girls in the pictures with me from the *Vanity Fair* party —"

"Hi, Austin!" Lauren grabs the phone from my ear and Ava snuggles up next to her so she can hear too. "This is Lauren."

"And Ava!" Ava winks at me.

"I've seen your picture and I have to say you're really cute." Lauren giggles.

"Way hot. You're not a dork though, are you?" Ava asks.

"Ava!" I scold.

They fire off a few embarrassing questions before I wrestle the phone back. "It's me," I say, shooing the girls away by pointing out a cool bag I just spotted.

"So that's Lauren and Ava." He sounds amused. "They sound . . . interesting." I'm not sure if that's a compliment, but I'm too afraid to ask.

"They are," I promise, "and they're dying to meet you."

"So when are you due back at work?" Austin asks. "I've never heard of you shopping on your lunch hour before."

"Yeah, well." I can't lie to him. "Tom wanted me to film my interview for the retrospective and Nadine was driving me up a wall so I bailed."

"Burke, that's not like you," Austin scolds.

"I know," I say guiltily.

"What time are you due back?" Austin asks.

I look at my watch. It's 2:15 PM. 2:15! I was due back at work fifteen minutes ago! "I'm late," I shriek. "I'll call you later."

"Get back there," Austin says. "Miss you."

"Miss you too," I murmur. I wish I could say more, but the "I love you" thing can't be said over the phone. Especially with Larry the Liar nearby.

"Guys, I've got to go!" I wave down Lauren and Ava before they can head back in the dressing room with another pile of clothes. "I'm late."

Lauren looks up. "No biggie. I'm sure they'll be cool with

it. We'll leave in a few." She pulls me close for another picture.

The sales woman walks over and offers to take my stuff from me and turns to Ava. "I just talked to Taylor. We can give you a thirty percent discount today, but I can't give you anything gratis. We've had a light month. I hope you understand."

"Sure. No problem," Ava says with a tight smile. Then she pulls Lauren and me into the dressing room and makes a face. "Great. I was sure she'd comp half our stuff for sure when we brought Gary! She always does!"

"What a pill," Lauren moans.

"I'm going to sort through my stuff and go pay," I tell them as they continue to complain. As I walk up to the register, I can still hear Ava and Lauren whispering in the dressing room. Hmm . . . how much do I have here? I start pulling things apart and making two piles as Gary and Larry take more pictures. When are they leaving?

"What are you doing?" Ava asks as she makes her way out behind me. "You loved all this stuff."

"I know, but it's more than I should spend." I hold up the beloved Scoop ballet flats and frown.

Ava coughs. "Hello? If you don't treat yourself well, who will?"

I stare again at the pile. Part of me feels guilty, but the other part of me agrees. I do deserve this stuff. I pull my credit card from my Chanel wallet and bang it hard on the counter. Ha! That feels good.

I feel so free spending like this. No one is here to stop me, or question my color choice (green) for that Alice and Olivia dress. I made every decision on my own. I have the power!

The clerk hands me the credit card slip to sign and smiles politely.

My total is $1,584.58.

GULP.

That is a *bit* more than I thought it would be. When I added the items up in my head it was only around a thousand dollars. I guess I added one or two things, or maybe four, but . . . I start to hyperventilate. Larry and Gary keep taking my picture and I'm so annoyed I put my hand up in front of Larry's camera.

"Trust me." Lauren pulls my hand down. "When your mom sees the great loot you got, she's not going to care what it cost. Tell her she can borrow some. Your mom has a good body. She can pull it off."

Lauren's bill is way over two thousand dollars. Ava is next and her bill is equally steep. Neither of them seems worried. Maybe I shouldn't be either. How often do I splurge like this?

"Okay," says Ava, pulling out her keys. "Let's get you back to work."

Outside the store, a crowd has grown. A girl our own age taps Ava on her shoulder. Her friends are standing behind her. They all look nervous. "Hi," the girl says. Her hands are shaking. "You're Ava Hayden, right? And Lauren Cobb and Kaitlin Burke? Could we get your autographs?"

I smile and put my hand out to take her piece of paper. Ava pushes it away. "Can't you see we're busy?" she barks at the girl. "God." Ava looks at me and rolls her eyes. "It's like these people don't appreciate that we have our own lives and we don't want to be bothered every second of the day! Can't we just shop in peace?"

I want to tell Ava that she just spent an hour posing for the paparazzi while she shopped and she didn't consider that an invasion of privacy. "I'll sign it for you," I tell the girl kindly. Her friends file behind her.

"You're such a pushover." Lauren giggles. "We'll meet you at the car." The two of them walk away and I can see them whispering to each other.

"Is she always like that?" one of the girls asks me.

"She's really nice," I tell her even though I'm completely rattled by what just happened. How could Lauren and Ava have been so rude? Signing autographs is part of being a celebrity. Sure, I don't want someone to stick a pen and paper under the bathroom stall, but when I'm out shopping, I don't mind.

"She doesn't look it," complains another girl.

Ava honks her horn and I can see that her candy apple–colored BMW convertible is idling. "Come on! You said you had to go!" Ava's right. I apologize to those I didn't get to and rush to the car. Gary and Larry take a few parting shots of us as we drive off.

"Let's hit Fred Segal in Santa Monica," Lauren pleads as Ava peels away. "I need to get a jacket to match this cute skirt I lifted." She unzips her slouchy bag and pulls out a plaid pencil skirt. Several more items are crammed inside. "What?" Lauren asks me when she sees my freaked-out expression. "What was I supposed to do? She wouldn't give us the discount."

"They won't even know it's missing," Ava adds. "We do it all the time and no one cares. I got stuff for you too. Show her, Lau."

Lauren pulls out a black fitted top I really liked. "This is for you," Lauren says and holds the shirt out to me.

I stare at it and try not to freak out. "I can't take it," I blurt out and clutch my bag of actual purchases to my chest. "I don't feel right. You guys keep it."

I see Ava roll her eyes in the rearview mirror. "Suit yourself. You're lucky you and I are the same size."

I don't get it. Ava and Lauren have boatloads of money. Why would they steal stuff? Wouldn't they be mortified if they were caught and the story was all over the news? I know I would be. I'd even be embarrassed if I was with them when they were caught. I don't want to be associated with this sort of thing. I picture my young fans. I've done some irresponsible things over the years, but I've never broken the law.

Between this, the way Lauren reacted when I was on the phone with Liz, and the way they treated those fans, I'm starting to see Ava and Lauren in a new light. And I don't mean the bright, shiny, happy one I saw before. I hate to say this, but maybe Sky was right.

"So what do you say, Kaitlin?" Lauren asks again. "Want to go to Santa Monica?"

"This was a lot of fun, but I don't want to get myself fired. I have to get back," I tell them.

"You're not wimping out on us because we took that stuff, are you?" Ava asks. "Because it's nothing. We just do it for kicks. That stuff is way overpriced."

"We don't do it that much," Lauren adds. I nod.

"Look, we won't do it when you're with us, okay?" Ava says, sounding annoyed. "I can see it makes you uncomfortable." She looks at Lauren. "And we were going to stop doing it soon anyway, right Lau?" Lauren nods.

Well, I guess if they were going to stop anyway, they're not that bad. And they have been pretty great to me these last few weeks when no one else (other than Austin, of course) has. "I'm not mad," I say. "You do what you want." Ava smiles.

"Are you free tomorrow night? We're doing dinner at Mr. Chow." Lauren squeals. "You have to wear the dress. We'll all wear it. It will look so cute."

Ugh. I hate matching outfits. It's so babyish. But Lauren and Ava are looking at me hopefully, and I feel guilty saying no. I do like Mr. Chow. They have the best fried rice with shrimp. Besides, what's the alternative? Going home and being grilled by Mom and Dad or Nadine? Listening to Mom pace the halls as she waits for the DHL guy to bring an advance copy of her *Fashionistas* issue, which is due any day now? No, I need to get out. Even if it is a work night, it's not like I'm going to bed early. I can hardly sleep anymore. "Okay," I agree.

They both let out an ear-piercing squeal.

I look at my watch. It's now 2:30. I'm already thirty minutes late and by the time I get back to the set it will be forty-five. That's pushing it.

My Sidekick hums and I groan. It's Nadine.

FUTUREPREZ: Where R U????????????

ℱashionistas

Mommy Dearest

Being a mother and manager to one of young Hollywood's hottest stars—Family Affair's Kaitlin Burke—is a juggling act, but Meg Burke says it's all in a day's work. "If you want to keep your kid on top, you've got to push them hard. Even if they hate you for it." Looking out for your superstar daughter's interests are one thing, but critics say Meg's bullying is not only alienating her daughter, it's turning off the whole town.

By Andrew Pullichi

It's almost eighty degrees on this January morning in Los Angeles, but Meg Burke looks cool as a cucumber. Dressed in a dazzling Michael Kors pant suit and Jimmy Choo heels, the mother of *Family Affair*'s Kaitlin Burke says she doesn't perspire. "I will myself not to," she declares. "It's so uncivilized. I tell Kaitlin if she just concentrates, she can do it too."

Just another nugget of advice from a woman whom some have nicknamed a momager—a mother whom pushes, pulls, and micromanages her child's Hollywood career to the point of making them almost not want one. "Some days Kaitlin looks like she just wants to cry," admits a friend of the young star. "She enjoys acting, but her mom puts so much pressure on her that sometimes I think she'd walk away from the whole business if she could." Not so, says Meg, who claims her daughter gets to make her own career decisions. "Kaitlin has to work hard if she wants to succeed," says Meg, sipping an unsweetened ice tea poolside at the family's multi-million dollar abode (which was paid for with earnings from her daughter's career). "She's one of the least stressed teenagers I know. She has a great job. She has an amazing career. Girls her age would kill for that attention. Is there anything wrong with making sure she ups that drive? Kaitlin knows what we do is for her own good."

What Meg thinks is good business, others see as a real problem. "Kaitlin could be the next Reese Witherspoon," says one studio executive. Others interviewed echo that sentiment. With Kaitlin's show *Family Affair* going off the air in May, now is the time for the young star to really carve a niche for herself. "What could hold her back is her mother," adds the source. "There are studios who don't want to work with Kaitlin because her mom always has to put in her two cents. Meg's always making Kaitlin's deals more complicated," admits one studio executive. "She feels the need to be part of every decision, even though she knows so little about the business.

"Kaitlin could be the next Reese Witherspoon. What could hold her back is her mother."

All she cares about is profit and what she can get from the deal." Those who know Meg best claim she's even driving Kaitlin's beloved agent, Seth Meyers, up a wall with her excessive calling and her overblown ideas. "This woman wants to live her life through Kaitlin," says another friend. "She's going to ride that girl's fame to the bank."

The whole family seems to have the same idea. A former secretary, Meg left her job to manage Kaitlin after she scored a part as one of the Paige's and Dennis's twins on *Family Affair* when she was four. Kaitlin's father, a former car salesman, followed suit and started producing movies his daughter would star in during hiatus. After a while their son, Matt, now thirteen, wanted to get in the business too. "They drove studio executives crazy with their demands to get Matt hired for Kaitlin's movies," says a studio source. "The kid was cute, but he certainly didn't have the same potential that Kaitlin did right off the bat." Matt currently has a role on — what else? — Kaitlin's show, *Family Affair.*

Over the course of the few weeks we spent with Meg, we heard about her own love of stardom at least a dozen times. "I always thought I would be great in front of a camera," Meg tells us one afternoon. "I could be the next Diane Sawyer if I had the chance." She's currently pushing her daughter to do a family reality show that would eventually be spun off and just follow Meg and her management duties. "Of course, Kaitlin would pop up from time to time," she adds.

So what does Kaitlin herself think of all the drama? "My mom is very organized," says Kaitlin cautiously, when asked to comment on her mother's momager nickname. "She is on top of everything and usually knows who the hottest up-and-coming star is before I do. I always tell her if she was my age, she'd be a star ten times bigger than I am."

Meg Burke would love to believe that.

Retail Therapy   February 14

BFFs Kaitlin Burke, Lauren Cobb, and Ava Hayden forgo food for footwear during a one-hour shopping spree at Belladonna
By Kayla Steven

Who needs Cobb salad? Not Kaitlin Burke. Friends of the *Family Affair* star say she normally relaxes in her dressing room or hits the studio cafeteria on her work lunch hour, indulging in a salad or her favorite Subway sandwich and a TivO'd episode of *American Idol*.

But that was before she started hanging with socialites turned reality stars Ava Hayden and Lauren Cobb. During a break from shooting her hit show on Monday, Kaitlin and the girls went shopping at hipster store Belladonna and blew a ton of money. "Kaitlin was trying on dozens of outfits," says a source on the scene. "I've never seen her spend so much in one day before. Her bill was over a thousand dollars. She looked nervous about spending so much."

Belladonna sales clerk Prue Hammon says that Kaitlin was sweet and easy to deal with. "She's welcome to shop at Belladonna anytime," says Prue. (For a look at exactly what Kaitlin bought, click here.)

Kaitlin's friends hope the excessive shopping and partying (Click here for a story about Kaitlin's hectic week!) aren't turning America's sweetheart into a paparazzi princess for all the wrong reasons. "Ever since she started hanging out with those girls, Kaitlin has been acting weird," says one close confidante. Buying cute Scoop shoes doesn't seem that weird to us, but if anything changes, you know *Hollywood Nation Online* will be the first to find out!

eleven: *We Interrupt This Party to Bring You an Important Message*

"Stop right there!"

I have my hand on the front door when Nadine's angry voice echoes through my home's two-story foyer. I sigh and turn around.

"Where do you think you're going?" Nadine wants to know as she winds around me and blocks my exit out the door, sounding and looking a lot like a mom should. But Nadine's not my mom. She's my assistant, and what she's still doing here at eight thirty, I don't know. All I know is she's going to make me late.

"I'm going out," I tell her. Isn't it obvious? I'm wearing my new Birkin jeans and Juicy sweater.

"You have to be on set tomorrow morning at seven!" Nadine reminds me. "And the SATs are in three weeks. You should be studying. You should be getting beauty rest so you look refreshed for your meetings and shoots. What's going on, Kaitlin?"

"Nothing," I say calmly.

Well, nothing may be pushing it.

I have been a *teensy* bit off my game lately. Nothing major, I swear. Just um, late back from lunch a few times, the first time being the day after the *Vanity Fair* party when I skipped out to go shopping with Lauren and Ava. When I got back to the studio late, Nadine was waiting outside, red-faced and looking like her head was about to explode. Not only did I leave without telling her and ignore her text, but I was late, something I never am for anything *FA*-related. Even though Nadine was mad, she still covered for me with Tom — she told him I had a dermatologist appointment I had forgotten about — and promised I would shoot my retrospective interview in the next few days.

I didn't. I've, um, kind of made excuses ever since.

And that's not the only thing I've put off. I know I need to call Liz back after what happened when we last talked. I'm just so embarrassed that I don't know how to start the conversation. Lauren and Ava think I'm crazy to even make up with Liz. Not that I completely trust their opinion after what I saw them pull that afternoon at Belladonna and with those fans. I actually talked to them about what happened and Ava said she was having a rough day and didn't mean to be so rude. That made me feel a little better, but I still can't push the stealing out of my mind. I've turned down all their offers to go shopping ever since. I can't seem to get out of our dinners, though. I already promised I'd go to events with them this week before that all happened and now I'm so busy that I've had to turn down a few work appointments. Seth has been trying to set up a meeting with the people for that TV pilot set in Alaska — one I actually like — but I've been putting him off too.

I know I should feel bad about avoiding everyone, but you know what?

I've *liked* playing hooky.

Yep, that's right. I'll admit it. The girl who plays practically perfect Samantha, the one who pretty much does everything her parents, manager, assistant, and publicist tell her to do, who stops to sign every autograph that is asked of her, has actually enjoyed being out from under everyone's thumb for once.

"This is not nothing," Nadine tells me, throwing her arms up in exasperation. "I never thought I'd see the day when you'd be this irresponsible."

"What good is being responsible anyway?" I question bitterly.

Being responsible hasn't saved my beloved job. Or made me hear back from the *Manolos* director yet (he's still out of town). It hasn't gotten me an offer for that Broadway show, *Meeting of the Minds*, either (even if the show's producers said I nailed my audition). So why shouldn't I blow off a little steam? As Ava says, everyone needs to party.

Nadine glares at me and I glare back. We're still glaring when Mom sweeps through the hallway on her way back from her Pilates workout on her new Pilates machine she bought to reduce the stress that's been brought on by her *Fashionistas* article. (She hasn't left the house in days she's so upset over it.) "Hi, girls," Mom says as she picks up the phone in the hall. "On your way out?"

"Kaitlin is," Nadine says, her eyes never leaving my face. "Not that I think it's a good idea."

"What did you say, Nadine?" Mom asks. She has the phone to her ear. "I couldn't hear you. I'm leaving another message for my lawyer." Mom is threatening to sue *Fashionistas* for defamation of character.

My stomach tightens. I don't want Nadine giving me a hard time in front of Mom. If it wasn't for the *Fashionistas* article taking up all of Mom and Dad's attention, Mom would be flipping out over all the stupid articles being written about me. Every day this week there's been another picture of me with Lauren and Ava or an article about my supposed "reckless" behavior. How is shopping and going out for dinner or dancing with friends reckless? (There was one article about my nice Valentine's Day dinner with Austin, but still.)

The press is so over-the-top sometimes. They've written so many false stories about me lately, including the kidnapping and my vacation BFs, that I'm not worried about what they're writing now. It's not like I'm driving without a license and getting into fender benders or shaving my head.

Nadine looks incredulous. "Haven't you been reading the tabloids this week?"

"Nadine, I've been a bit preoccupied," Mom snaps. "I have a lot on my plate with this *Fashionistas* fiasco. I don't have time to read all of Kaitlin's clippings."

Thank God.

"But —" Nadine tries again.

"Nadine, seriously, if something is wrong, Laney will tell me," Mom says.

Laney *has* been annoyed, but she's only yelled at me twice so far. She's also been busy. One of her other clients got into a huge fight in Vegas and caused massive damage to one of the casinos. Luckily, Laney has experience putting out Vegas fires!

"I know Kaitlin has been going out lately, but there's nothing wrong with that," Mom continues. "I've been begging Kaitlin to be seen at events for years. I'm just glad she finally listened."

"Wow, Mom, thanks," I say and shoot Nadine a triumphant look.

Nadine rolls her eyes. "Being seen out is fine, but I'm not sure the company Kaitlin is keeping is the best. Controversy follows Lauren and Ava wherever they go."

"I don't know," Mom says, looking pensive. "Lauren's mom is on a few committees with me and she is a doll."

Nadine's face darkens. This is one argument I don't think she can win.

"Kaitlin, by the way," Mom adds. "They have a date for the *Pretty Young Assassins* press junket. It's going to be Saturday, February twenty-eighth."

Wow. I can't believe it's time for that already.

"Oh and I saw Liz's dad today," Mom says. "Are you two fighting?"

Nadine gives me a look and I turn away. "No," I squeak.

"I didn't think so," Mom says. "I told him if you two weren't speaking, I would know." She heads to the kitchen. "Have fun tonight!"

Nadine and I are alone again. Awkwardly, uncomfortably alone. I sidestep Nadine and reach for the doorknob.

"I don't care what your mom thinks, Lauren and Ava *are* a bad influence," Nadine says quietly.

I whirl around. "I don't care what *you* think," I say boldly. "I don't care how many articles you leave me, I'm not going to stop hanging out with them just because *you* say so."

Nadine genuinely looks confused. "I haven't been leaving you any articles."

Someone has. They've been leaving them under my dressing room door.

"Kaitlin, I just want what's best for you," Nadine stresses.

"I thought you wanted what's best for *you*," I point out. "Maybe if you'd stop pushing me around so much and blabbering on about the SATs all the time, I wouldn't have to go out on a work night to blow off some steam. Just because you haven't done anything with your life other than be an assistant is no reason to take it out on me! You've become a real pain, Nadine."

As soon as I say the words I want to take them back.

Nadine's face is ashen. I didn't mean it like that. I was just angry, I want to say. But I don't.

"I didn't realize I was being a *pain*," Nadine says, looking hurt as she emphasizes the word *pain*. "I'm just trying to be your friend. Friends tell each other when they're about to fall off the edge of a cliff, and that's what I think you're doing. Lauren and Ava aren't going to do that because they like watching people fall. They only care about themselves. Once you've driven your career into the ground, they'll move on to some other starlet. Just like they did when they were friends with Sky. You know that's what happened, don't you? As soon as Sky stopped buying them expensive presents and taking them on vacation with her, they dropped her."

"You don't know what you're talking about," I say uncertainly. I know they're not friends anymore, but Ava and Lauren said it was because they had a fight. A car horn beeps outside and I jump. That's got to be Ava and Lauren. "I have to go," I say simply and then I disappear into the warm Los Angeles night air while Nadine watches me from the doorway.

*   *   *

On the car ride to the club Shelter, I'm quiet. Ava and Lauren don't seem to notice because they're singing at the top of their lungs to Rihanna. I feel too guilty to join them.

I can't stop thinking about what I said to Nadine. Even if she has been going overboard, I shouldn't have been so cruel.

She may be pushy lately, but I'm lucky Nadine hasn't left me to pursue business school, like she always said she would. For the first time in a while, I feel very tired. But we're at the valet and I have to go inside.

No matter where we go, my nightlife routine with Ava and Lauren always works the same way: pose for the paparazzi outside the club, schmooze the club owner and take a few more photos, go in and grab a table in the VIP section, spend twenty minutes talking to whatever celebrities happen to also be there that night, pose for pictures with them (if any paparazzi happen to be inside), and then hit the dance floor. Tonight I sit the first few songs out. After fifteen minutes, Ava and Lauren slide back into our booth.

"Kates, how could you not join us for that song?" Ava wants to know. "It's the new Layla and the CD won't be out for three weeks! DJ O is going to get it for playing that."

"Why?" Lauren asks. "It was on Ryan Seacrest's show this morning already."

HOLLYWOOD SECRET NUMBER ELEVEN: You know how songs from an upcoming album sometimes get leaked to radio stations or on the Internet before a CD release and the star screams "I'LL SUE?" Well, that's pretty much bogus. Most songs that are leaked to the Web are on there because the label wants to test the waters and build up buzz for an album before it drops. Sure, sometimes songs get leaked by disgruntled employees, or vengeful assistants that have been treated badly, but for the most part, when stars say how "hurt, upset, and betrayed" they are to find out their hotter-than-hot new single was leaked ahead of time, they're usually stretching the truth.

"I didn't realize it was Layla," I admit as I absentmindedly stir my seltzer with my straw. "I wasn't really listening."

Ava and Lauren look at each other. "Listen, Kates, we have to tell you something," Lauren says. "The poor-little-sweet-Kaitlin-I'm-so-depressed act is getting old."

I feel like I've been slapped. "Excuse me?"

"It worked for Britney for a while, but then people got tired of her too," Ava adds. "We thought you'd brighten up after we let you tell your sob story, and you did for a few nights, but now you're all sully again and it's keeping the cute guys at bay."

She's got to be kidding. "You mean *sullen*," I clarify. "You said *sully*." It's an SAT word so I should know.

"Whatever," Ava says. "The point is you're bringing everyone down. We just saw Lauren, Lo, and Audrina and they didn't want to come over to take a photo because you looked so miserable."

"Oh look! There's Paris!" Lauren shrieks. "Let's go say hi."

The two of them leave and I find myself relieved that they're gone. The fog has definitely lifted. Maybe Nadine was right. When I think back over the last few weeks, I can't make excuses for the girls anymore. Yes, they were there for me when I needed them, but that doesn't mean they're the best people to hang around with. Lauren and Ava are awfully obsessed with having their face in the paper. They talk about everyone we see behind their backs. They're mean to their fans. Their stealing is going to catch up with them eventually and I don't want to be there when that happens. And going out all the time is overrated.

I've got to admit the truth to myself if no one else. At first the nightly dinners and dancing were a great escape. But after two weeks of it, I have to admit I'm bored and exhausted. Spending all this time at the big celeb hangouts only reminds me of why I never go in the first place — it's not fun to be photographed all night and hang out with stars that only care about being a star.

I miss Liz. I miss the old Nadine. And even if I don't make up with either of them, I'm starting to think I can't spend all my time with Lauren and Ava either.

"Hey, Kaitlin." Diane Byler approaches the table and smiles at me.

I know Diane because we're both on the same network. Or I should say *were* since Diane's show was canceled two seasons ago. *Spaces Between Us* had a long run. Her show was on for six seasons, which is better than most. Diane and I sometimes used to eat lunch together and I was bummed when her show ended and we didn't get to do that anymore. She's really sweet and very quiet.

"Hey, Diane," I say, happy to see a friendly face. "What have you been up to?"

She shyly sits down. "Auditioning for pilots," Diane tells

me with a grim face. "Same thing I did last year, but the one I had last time didn't get picked up."

"I'm sorry to hear that," I say.

"I'm tired of being offered the same role over and over," Diane complains. "Everyone wants me to play a character like the one I had on *Spaces*. It's so hard breaking out of that typecast. I guess it's hard finding something great when you had great once before. Nothing compares, you know?"

"I know what you mean," I tell her and mean it.

"I was stupid when the show ended." Diane shakes her head sadly. "I passed on a few great movies. I thought the work would always be there, but it gets harder the longer your face isn't seen on camera."

That could be me in a few months if I'm not careful! My heart starts thumping to the beat of a Kanye West song. And not in a good way. "I'm sure things will turn around," I say and put a hand on hers. She smiles at me gratefully.

"Hey, Kates." Lauren and Ava are standing over our table staring at us.

"You guys know Diane, right?" I ask.

Lauren and Ava barely nod. "Kates, we need you for a second," Ava says and tugs on my arm. "Can you come with?"

Diane looks uncomfortable. "That's okay, I should go," she tells me. "It was great seeing you. Keep me in mind if you hear of anything, okay?"

"I will," I tell her.

When Diane is far enough away, Ava and Lauren burst out laughing. "What a loser, asking you for career help," Ava says.

"She doesn't need my help," I say defensively. "Diane's career is fine. She's just hit a rough patch."

"Some rough patch. That girl has sunk so low she'll never float again," Lauren says. "Especially since she packed on those ten pounds."

I can't believe they're being so cruel.

Then again, is it so hard to believe?

"She looks like a sausage in those white jeans," Ava adds and laughs so hard the table shakes. Lauren's drink spills onto her jeans.

"Idiot!" Lauren says and grabs a napkin to blot her pants. "I just stole these jeans from Blue Moon yesterday!"

"Whatev," Ava says. "We'll just go back and get another pair tomorrow. Maybe we should pick one up for Diane too. She could use some sprucing up. Too bad she couldn't fit in any of their sizes!" The two of them roar with laughter.

If it wasn't clear enough before, it is now. The three of us are too different to be close friends. Ava and Lauren don't have rules or listen to anyone else's. They're fun, yes, but they're also mean, and disrespectful to anyone who doesn't do things their way. I feel whooshing in my ears and suddenly I'm very hot. Being here with Lauren and Ava doesn't feel right. Tossing and turning at home over my future and the end of *FA* doesn't feel good either. Even in a packed club of people, I feel very lost. I have to leave. "I think I had some bad sushi for dinner," I lie. "I'm going to call Rodney to pick me up."

Lauren pouts. "You're lame! We just got here."

"I know, but I just remembered I have an early call time tomorrow and an early photo shoot on Saturday. I need to get my beauty rest," I say, repeating Nadine's words.

At the word photo shoot, Ava's frown turns into a smile. Her whole face lights up. "Who do you have a shoot with?"

I have an overwhelming feeling I shouldn't tell them who it's for, but I'm sure they could find out if they really wanted to. "I'm doing a cover shoot for *Sure*." They both squeal.

"We love that magazine. We should come with," Lauren tells me.

"We'll be your personal stylists," Ava adds and puts her arm around me. "Just tell us where and when."

I grab my Cinch leopard-print bag, the one Lauren and Ava convinced me was so "me." Looking at it now, it doesn't feel so me anymore. "I'll call you," I say even though I don't think I mean it.

"Okay, hon," Ava says. "Feel better. Love ya!"

Then I walk away from the table, sure of one thing: The minute I'm gone, Ava and Lauren are going to talk about me behind my back, just like they've done to a dozen other people tonight.

Thursday, February 19
NOTE TO SELF:

Apologize 2 Nadine.
Call Liz.
Check on *Manolos* & *Meeting of the Minds*
Read remaining scripts.
Study 4 SATs!

IN THE KNOW

Is Kaitlin Burke headed for disaster?

by **Nicki Nuro**

America's sweet-faced teen star is hanging with some questionable new pals—party girls Lauren Cobb and Ava Hayden—and friends worry it could lead to her downfall.

On a recent night out at Mr. Chow, the appetizers looked yummy, the laughs were fast and furious, and Lauren Cobb and Ava Hayden seemed to be having a good time. The only one didn't look like she was enjoying herself was Kaitlin Burke. Could it be that Kaitlin has finally caught on to Ava's and Lauren's ways and is questioning their friendship? That's what one friend of the star thinks. "When Kaitlin first started hanging out with them, no one in her entourage really cared, but as her personality slowly began to change, everyone became worried. Those girls are a bad influence on Kaitlin and Kaitlin knows it."

"Kaitlin has been having a rough time lately," another source confirms. "With *Family Affair* ending and the intense pressure to find a new project, she seems really stressed. Plus she's fighting with her best friend so the world just seems against her at the moment."

Enter Ava and Lauren. When the two first appeared at Kaitlin's side, the trio seemed to be all about fun and games. The newly formed threesome have been inseparable ever since they vacationed together in Turks and Caicos over the holidays and hung at the Cinch for a Cause luncheon. Their datebook has been full ever since. They've been spotted shopping at hot spots Belladonna, Belle Gray, Kitson, and Bleu, eating at Oasis, Koi, and the Ivy, and dancing the night away at Parc. They've also taken to wearing matching dresses.

Kaitlin certainly smiled for the camera when we approached the girls outside Mr. Chow, but looks can be deceiving.

"Kaitlin definitely seems to be out of her element," says a source. "I'm worried that she's in over her head."

> "I'm really upset about her. She's going to ruin her career if she is not careful. I'm asking the public to pray that Kaitlin gets the help she needs before it's too late."

Lauren and Ava are known for mischief and controversy, the kind that can get a respected star like Kaitlin in trouble. Kaitlin's already witnessed their dark side first hand—the group's night at Parc ended when Lauren and Ava started a fight with arch nemesis Blake Porter and got thrown out of the club. That's probably the first time Kaitlin, known as a sweet girl who always does what she's told, has been thrown out of any establishment. But when asked to comment on her new friendship, while shopping at Bleu, Kaitlin said, "I'm doing great!" That's what Lauren and Ava think too. "We adore Kaitlin," said Lauren. "She's such a great girl and we love hanging out with her."

But Kaitlin's friends at *Family Affair* hope the star is not courting disaster. "Kaitlin is a teen and she's allowed to be flighty," says a show source. "But hopefully these two don't influence her too much. I'd hate to see a promising career like Kaitlin's fall apart because she loses her head."

Kaitlin's certainly seen her share of less than glittering press the past few weeks—her night life, lack of a future project, and her mom's scathing interview in Fashionistas have caused some to worry about Kaitlin's post-*FA* career. "I'm really upset about her," sobbed former costar Alexis Holden, who claims she's seen this meltdown coming for a while. "She's going to ruin her career if she is not careful. I'm asking the public to pray that Kaitlin gets the help she needs before it's too late." ●

TWELVE: *Kaitlin Isn't* Sure *of Anything Anymore*

Austin slides into the backseat next to me and looks around the empty car. "Where is everyone?"

It's Saturday morning and Rodney and I have just picked up Austin on our way to my *Sure* photo shoot. Normally I'd have a huge entourage with me for this sort of thing, but Mom had a date with, um, a collagen injection (shhhh!), and Nadine had to fly to San Francisco to be a bridesmaid in her cousin's wedding. I've been so preoccupied with my social life that I forgot Nadine was even going out of town. I didn't realize she was gone till I got to my dressing room on Friday morning and I found a detailed itinerary for my shoot and my weekend plans. For once there was no personal note attached saying something like, *Miss you! Have a great time!* Nadine always leaves me notes. But that was before I lashed out at her the way I did.

I feel guiltier than ever about the way I've been behaving lately. Seeing how Lauren and Ava treat others has made me realize how important it is to have people around you that you trust. I can do that with Liz and Nadine. A fight shouldn't get in the way of our friendship. I know now I have to fix things with both of them before it's too late.

"My dad and Matty are going to meet us at the shoot," I tell Austin. "They had an early tee time this morning so they were going home to shower first. Laney is coming from a press conference so she's got her own car."

Austin moves closer and snuggles my neck. "I'm glad we're alone. I've missed you," he says. "You've been so busy I've barely talked to you this week."

Austin smells so good I think I may pass out. He doesn't look so bad either in his American Eagle jeans and a button-down striped shirt that is open over a navy blue tee.

"I've been with Lauren and Ava a lot," I admit, "but I think I'm sort of done with all that partying."

Austin smiles. "It's not really your style, is it?"

Austin hasn't come right out and told me what he thinks of Lauren and Ava, probably because he's still never met them, but he's talked to them on the phone, and he never sounds too jazzed when he gets off. Instead he's been making little comments, like that one, that lead me to believe he's not their biggest fan.

I fill Austin in on how Lauren and Ava have been behaving and what a jerk I've been to Nadine. I tell him what happened the day Liz called me and how I've been too embarrassed and unsure of what to say to her about everything to call her back. The great thing about Austin is that he listens, but he doesn't pass judgment. Instead he says: "You'll fix things with Nadine and Liz, but I guess Lauren and Ava aren't the people you thought they were."

"Lauren and Ava were a great escape from all these major changes in my life," I admit. "They have no responsibilities and all they seem to do is shop or party. Being with them was fun for a while, but it wasn't real." I look out the window. Our car is driving higher and higher in the Hollywood Hills and I know we must be minutes from our destination, a private home *Sure* borrowed for our shoot. Apparently it has magnificent views of the city. "I'm going to fix things with Nadine and Liz right after this photo shoot is over. It's the first time in days that I'll have a good, quiet moment to dedicate to them, and that's my first priority." I'm not sure what I'm going to do about Lauren and Ava though. They called me yesterday, but I haven't called them back yet.

Austin leans in and kisses me again. "This is what I love about you," he whispers in my ear, shooting hot breath onto my neck. I feel electricity pulse through my veins. It's the L-word again! "You always do the right thing in the end."

"You've taught me well," I joke. I'm not sure how to react. Do I say, "This is what I love about you too?" I'm still a little unsure about when to use the L-word and when it's overkill. Like, when we're eating ice cream, is it too much to say, "I *love* that you *love* black cherries on your sundae too"?

"Have you figured out what you're going to do about work?" Austin asks.

I shake my head. I know I screwed up with the friend thing, but when it comes to everything else, I'm still at a loss. The more I think about my future, and hear Laney's, Seth's, and Mom's voices in my head, the more freaked out I become. My dizzy spells and constricted breathing attacks are getting more frequent and I'm starting to think that something is seriously wrong with my health, but I'm too scared to tell anyone what is going on. I can't even concentrate on my SATs, which are around the corner.

"Try not to stress about that this morning," Austin says. "You need to look good for the camera, which shouldn't be too hard." He kisses me. "How could they not get a great picture of you? You're gorgeous."

He's making me blush. Again. Austin has a way of doing that.

"We're here," Rodney announces and takes a sip of his protein shake. "We're fifteen minutes early, just like Laney and Nadine wanted." In the rearview mirror, I can see him frown. "Since this is a private road, I can't park on the street. I can't fit in the driveway either because they have so many vans. I might have to go all the way back to the bottom of the hill and that could take a while. Will you be okay going in alone? I'll be back as soon as I can."

"I'll be fine, Rod," I promise.

When I open the car door, Christy Connor is waiting. She's *Sure*'s senior writer, and she's in charge of my story. "Hi, Christy. How are you?" I say, extending my hand.

"Great! Everyone inside is really pumped for today's shoot," she tells me.

Christy reminds me of those overly exuberant tour guides you usually have at a museum. Her voice is high and every word is perfectly enunciated. She's shorter than I pictured her, but very tiny, like a little wind-up doll, and she has short brown hair and really amazing gray eyes that have wandered over to meet Austin's.

"This must be Austin Meyers," she says. "We know all about you. Or, should I say, we wish we knew more. Any chance you'd like to sit down for a secondary interview to add to Kaitlin's story?"

"Today is all about Kaitlin." Austin winks at me. "But maybe next time."

Wow, Laney has really taught him well. One fifteen-minute tutorial with her, and he's a media pro!

"I understand," Christy says, even though she looks disappointed. "Should we head inside?" She turns and walks up the stone stairway and opens the double doors.

The house they've rented is gorgeous. Every stitch of the floors, ceiling and furniture are a shade of white. I'm afraid to touch anything! The living room we've walked into is expansive. It only looks smaller because rows and rows of designer clothes are hanging on rolling clothing racks, waiting for me to look at them. There is a large team of people standing by to dress and primp me for the shoot, which will probably take place outside. On either side of the living room fireplace are sets of French doors leading onto what looks like a large patio and infinity pool. They have a killer view of the city, which you can see really well now that the smog has lifted. I notice the photographer is already setting up on the patio. I breathe deeply. To my left must be the kitchen and from the smell of things, I'm thinking some sort of quiche, or possibly chicken and veggies, are on the catering menu for today.

"Wow," Austin whispers.

Wow is right. It looks like the *Sure* crew went all out.

"Has Laney Peters or my dad gotten here yet?" I ask. It's not like Laney to be late for anything.

Christy shakes her head. "I'm sure they'll be here soon. In the meantime, we were thinking we'd get you styled and made up, take some test shots, and then maybe break for lunch. If you don't mind, I can interview you then," Christy tells me.

As I head off to makeup and to get my hair done, Austin settles into one of the comfy-looking white couches and picks up the latest issue of *Sure*. A magazine assistant quickly hurries over with smoothies for each of us. Someone hooks up their iPod to the sound system and blasts the latest John Mayer CD. I begin to relax when my phone rings.

"KAITLIN?" It's Laney. "THIS FREAKIN' TRAFFIC ON THE 101 IS A MONSTER. I DON'T KNOW WHAT IS GOING ON. MY CAR HASN'T INCHED IN AN HOUR.

IF SOMETHING ISN'T ENGULFED IN FLAMES WHEN I FINALLY GET PAST THIS JAM, I'M CALLING SCHWARZENEGGER TO COMPLAIN!"

"It's okay," I tell her. "I'm just doing hair and makeup right now."

"THAT'S FINE, BUT DON'T DO YOUR INTERVIEW TILL I GET THERE," Laney barks. "I'LL CHECK IN WITH YOU — *beep* — TER." Someone else is calling me. I look at the ID. It's Dad and Matty.

"Okay, Laney," I tell her. "Call me soon." I click over to Dad and Matty. "Where are you guys?"

Dad moans. "A tractor trailer fire on the 101 has blocked off all but one lane of traffic," he laments. "We haven't moved in almost an hour."

"Laney is stuck too," I tell him.

"We'll be there — *beep* — as we can," Dad says.

I look at my caller ID again. It's Mom now. "Dad, Mom is calling. I have to go." I click over again. "Mom? I thought you had a procedure."

"I'm going in, sweetie, but I just heard fantastic news," Mom says. "E! wants to carry our reality show!"

"I thought we nixed the show idea," I say discreetly. I can feel my anxiety level rising by the second.

"Not completely," Mom says lightly. "I've been exploring it and I think it could be a great way to redeem our character after that horrid *Fashionistas* article. The exposure from that show could get you a TV show ten times better than that silly Alaska one."

My skin starts to prickle. I'm tired of Mom ignoring what I want. This is my career and she has to let me have a say. When I fix things with Nadine and Liz, maybe it's time for me to sit down and talk frankly with Mom too. "Mom, I like that show."

"Kaitlin, don't pretend to care about it that much," Mom snaps. "Seth told me you've been too busy this week to even take a meeting with them."

I've put off everything lately, but after what happened Thursday night with Lauren and Ava, I realized that had to change. I'm taking control of my future. That Alaska show, the play, *Manolos* — I'm going to make it a priority to try to get one of those projects even if I am terrified of moving on. Seth was out of town on Friday, but he's back today. As soon as I hang up, I'm calling him. "Mom, I have to go," I tell her.

"They're calling me in too," Mom says. "Give Daddy and Matty my love!"

I scroll through my numbers for Seth's and dial, but I hear someone clear their throat and I look up. The stylist is standing in front of me, waiting. Oops. I guess my new assertiveness will have to wait till after I'm primped and I pick out my wardrobe.

Choosing something glamorous to wear isn't tough. I adore a navy Stella McCartney dress, salivate over a Jay Godfrey one that is similar to the one I wore to *Vanity Fair*'s party, and can't get enough of a pair of Rock and Republic's wide-leg jeans and an Alice and Olivia wrap sweater. Since there will probably be three outfit changes (you need at least one look for the cover and sometimes two for the inside photos), the stylist tells me I can use them all.

I'm so glad I listened to Laney and took this cover offer. I was a little hesitant about doing *Sure* because a lot of people whisper that it's not true journalism.

HOLLYWOOD SECRET NUMBER TWELVE: *Sure*, like many British tabloids, actually — shhh! — sometimes pay for editorial interviews, and many stars like to do them. Not only are you paid, you get to control the content of the interview. You can state up front what you won't talk about — whether it's your crazy religion, your nasty recent breakup, or your hush-hush rumored lipo.

Laney's only ground rule for mine was that we not discuss Austin at length (my request, not hers).

My prep time flies by, but Dad, Matty, and Laney still aren't here so we move to taking the test shots. They come out really nice. The photographer even lets Austin keep one of the Polaroids (photographers always use Polaroids for test pictures). As we break for lunch, I'm in a really good mood. I change back into the Gap jeans and navy-and-white striped tee I came in (I'd die if I got food on one of those thousand-dollar dresses I had on!) and Austin and I sit down to eat. Christy quickly joins us after we've taken a few bites. She lays her tiny tape recorder ominously in front of us and then pulls out a second one. That's funny. I've never seen a reporter carry two recorders before.

"Do you mind if I ask you some questions while you eat?" Christy asks. Her own plate is practically empty except for a few small pieces of melon.

"Laney wanted me to wait till she got here to do the interview," I apologize.

Christy looks at her watch. "I'm sure she'll be here soon. We'll start off with a few easy questions until she gets here."

"Okay." I quickly swallow my last bite and wipe my mouth. "Austin is going to sit in, if you don't mind."

"I don't if you don't," Christy says.

The first ten minutes of questions are easy — my favorite things to do on a day off, what I wear when I'm home, what my last vacation was like — and then they get progressively more difficult — Austin and me (I answer briefly without too many details so that some part of our relationship is kept private), what my hopes for my career are, and what possessed me to do such things as fight with Alexis Holden in public or hide out in high school disguised as someone else. (Let's be honest, I saw those questions coming. Interviewers ask them every time.) Laney's still not here, but I feel comfortable enough to keep going. I get a little nervous when she asks about my mom's bad interview in *Fashionistas*, and why I don't have another project lined up yet, but then the *FA* questions begin. Talking about working with Matty is easy, but I still can't seem to swallow the topic of *FA* ending.

"Can we do those last?" I ask.

"Sure." Christy smiles. "Let's go back to career then. Where do you see yourself a year from now?"

I take a breath. "I hope I'll be working. I want to continue making movies and I wouldn't rule out another TV show."

"Do you think you'll make an album?" Christy asks me.

An album? "I don't think so." I laugh. "I don't have a great voice."

"Your voice is adorable!" Christy insists. "And the 'Paparazzi Princess' song is just a riot. Whatever made you come up with something so tongue-in-cheek?"

"The 'Paparazzi Princess' song?" I say slowly. My hands go numb. How does she know about that?

"I don't think I've heard the 'Paparazzi Princess' song." Austin looks amused. "Kaitlin's been hiding her singing talent from me." I grip Austin's hand tightly. I never told him about my music meeting because I thought it would all go away. Seth was supposed to get the tape from TJ ages ago!

"It's been on KROQ twice already this morning," Christy tells us.

"WHAT?" I practically shriek. I try to calm down, but I feel like I can't breathe. I try taking deep breaths, but I feel like I'm gasping for air. I wipe my hands on my jeans. They feel cold and clammy. "I mean, that was never meant to be released." I steady myself. "I only recorded it for a meeting. That was not for the public. When my lawyer finds out about this, I'm sure he's going to come down on whoever leaked it." I know I said some stars leak their tunes early on purpose, but this isn't one of those times. I never wanted anyone to hear that demo. How could this have happened? TJ may be a player, but he wouldn't do this to me. It's bad business.

"Burke, what is this song she's talking about?" Austin looks confused.

"I have a copy right here if you want to hear it," Christy says and she pushes play on the recorder before I can stop her.

My heartbeat speeds up the minute I hear my warbled voice. I place my hands over my ears. Oh God, this is awful . . .

You think you know me,
but can't you see?
I'm tired of being the princess. I don't want to win your heart,
that was fine to start,
but the truth is:

(Chorus)
This Daddy's girl is ready to fly,
watch me, world, with a close eye.
I've got a new way of doing things.
This time, I'm the one pulling the strings.
Lights! Camera! Action!
You've never seen anything like the new me before.
And you probably never will again, you bores.

I'm a bad girl stuck in a good-girl role,
but now that the show is over, I've got a new goal.
I want to be your paparazzi princess. I want to have your attention.
Keep you eye on my ascension.
When you're not looking, I'm a different girl.
I'm not Sam. I'm ready to take the new bad me out for a whirl.
DJ, hit it!

(Chorus)
This Daddy's girl is ready to fly,
watch me, world, with a close eye.
I've got a new way of doing things.
This time, I'm the one pulling the strings.
Lights! Camera! Action!
You've never seen anything like the new me before.
And you probably never will again, you bores.

"It's so cute," Christy coos when the song is over. I glance at Austin. He's trying his hardest not to laugh. I don't blame him.

"Listen, Christy," I start to say, but there is a loud bang and the front doors clang open.

"KATIE!" Lauren and Ava shriek. They're both disheveled, their hair is a bit messed up, and they're wearing dark sunglasses, jeans, and rumpled tees.

"What are you guys doing here?" I try to sound calm, but I start to wheeze. I can't breathe.

"We've been looking for you everywhere," Ava says, walking right in, grabbing a carrot stick from an assistant's plate and plopping down on the couch across from ours. She has her Pomeranian, Calou, with her and she puts the dog down and lets her run around the room. She's so wound up she starts doing laps around the coffee table. "You never told us where your photo shoot was today, but we called Gary — he's outside with Larry — and they said they followed you here. So here we are! Oh, by the way, Rod-o is in hot water."

That's what they've started calling Rodney. It drives him nuts.

"Why?" I ask. And how the heck were we followed? I didn't see anyone tailing us.

"Rod-o saw Gary and Larry trying to sneak up the private road and he tried to block them from coming up the street. Gary's car *accidentally* hit yours and now Rod is waiting for a tow truck." Ava giggles.

"Oh my God," I blurt out. This is not good. Ava and Lauren are crashing my shoot, the paparazzi are outside and my bodyguard is tied up. Laney isn't here to save me either. Is it hot in here? I grab a napkin off the table and begin fanning myself. Christy looks on in confusion.

"He's fine," Lauren enthuses. "He said to tell you not to let Gary and Larry in and that he'd be here in a jif. Gary wanted to know if you'd come outside and take pictures when you were done," she adds and then she spots Austin. "Hey, A! What's up? I'm Lauren."

"Hi." Austin's voice sounds like steel.

An ear-piercing shriek disrupts the awkward moment. "Lau, Lau, come here and look at these clothes!" Ava is standing at a rack; with sticky fingers from the donut she just grabbed off one of the trays, and is flipping through dresses. I see Christy cringe.

"Excuse me," an assistant says. "Could you be careful with those clothes? They're borrowed and we can't get any stains on them."

Ava ignores her. Instead she gasps. "KATIE, you've got to wear this!" She holds up a one-shoulder Grecian gown that would make me look like a potato sack.

"I have my wardrobe choices all picked out," I say cheerfully, but inside I'm starting to feel sick. I'm sweating. Maybe I've just developed a fever? My breathing is heavy, as if I've just run a marathon. Austin looks at me strangely and I smile weakly. I have to get Ava and Lauren out of here. They'll ruin the shoot. "Could I talk to you for a second?" Ava ignores me.

"OH MY GOD, look at this!" Lauren coos. She's holding up a sheer Rebecca Taylor top and leather skirt. "Ava, I have to try this on! Where is the bathroom?"

"Those clothes are for Kaitlin," a harried assistant insists.

"This will just take a second," Lauren says dismissively. She grabs the outfit, and a donut, the glaze oozing onto the top.

"Lauren, watch that donut!" I yell. My heart is doing double-time. My breathing is even worse. I'm starting to feel dizzy.

She laughs. "This is why they invented dry cleaning. Don't worry about it."

"I'll pay for that," I croak quickly to the stylist.

I get up from the couch and walk over to Ava. I feel dizzy, but I still manage to grab her arm. "You guys are embarrassing me," I tell Ava, embracing the power she always thought I needed. "I think you should leave." I'm proud of myself, but I feel like I'm having a heart attack or like I'm going to faint. Is a person's heartbeat supposed to sound this loud?

Ava rolls her eyes. "Is this any way to treat your friends? Geez, we're there for you time and again when you go loco and now you want to push us out because you have a cover shoot to do? That's rude."

I try to speak, but my throat feels like it's closing. Something is seriously wrong with me. I'm so dizzy, I'm sure I'm going to fall. I reach out and grab the couch for support before my knees buckle under me. This can't be happening. Where is Rodney? Where is Laney or Dad? I do not want *Sure* to think this is the way I roll. I try taking deep breaths to calm myself, but it's not working. I can't get enough air.

"By the way, Katie," Ava says. "We heard your song this morning on KROQ. How come you didn't tell us about it?"

My song. Everyone must have heard it. I'm going to be the laughingstock of the whole town. Suddenly the spacious living room begins to shrink. I feel like the walls are closing in on me. I have to get out of here.

"That dog!" the stylist screeches. "He's peeing on the Jay Godfrey!"

Calou has his little leg lifted and he's relieving himself all over my cover shoot dress. Then he squats and does number two.

Oh. My. God.

Ava scoops him up. "Bad doggy." She giggles. "His pee is tiny. You won't even know it's there when it dries."

"Pick that up," the stylist yells and points to the poop. "Pick that up now."

Lauren comes out of the bathroom wearing the Rebecca Taylor outfit and glares at the stylist. "Geez. Chill. Don't yell at the dog like that."

"Guys, you have to leave," I say more sternly, but quietly, so that I don't make an even bigger scene than there already is. It takes all my energy to get the sentence out. I feel like everyone is far away and I'm in some sort of bubble. Their voices are muffled and I can hear a whooshing sound in my ears. Even if I did assert myself, the girls are still ignoring me.

I hear something shatter and one of the assistants scream. The whizzing in my ears grows louder and I stumble. Austin grabs my arm. I feel so feverish I don't think I can stand on my own.

"Kaitlin, you've got to get Lauren and Ava out of here," he says to me, but he sounds so far away I can barely hear him. I hear him say my name though. Austin never calls me Kaitlin. Ever. That means things must be really bad.

Christy turns to me. "I want your friends out of here now," she says angrily.

"I'm trying," I wheeze. Air. I need air. Someone open a window! I need help. I need Rodney.

"Oooh, are you the reporter?" Ava asks a freaked-out Christy. "Let me tell you everything I know about Katie. We're so tight. We're inseparable. It's like we share the same soul, you know?"

Oh no. "I need ice," I tell Austin, as my body continues to heat up.

"You don't look so good." Austin says.

I feel so sweaty. "They're here," I think I hear him say, but I'm not even sure what that means. The room is starting to fade to black and I can barely make out Austin's face. All I can think about is the disaster in front of me. About that stupid song being on the radio. Christy's questions about *Family Affair* and my future replay in my head. My chest suddenly feels tighter than ever. I try to take a deep breath, but I'm having trouble. I can't breathe. I really can't breathe.

"Something's wrong," I whisper as I start to panic.

The sound of my heartbeat is so loud that I can't hear Austin at all even though he's talking to me. Christy is saying something too. Their faces start to blur. I try to take a deep breath, but I can't. I try grabbing Austin's arm again. He feels so far away. Calou's barking is getting louder. The last thing I think I see are Laney and Rodney running toward me.

Then everything fades to black.

BREAKING NEWS: February 21

Kaitlin Burke is rushed to the hospital

Family Affair star Kaitlin Burke has been admitted to Cedars-Sinai Medical Center this afternoon after collapsing at a cover shoot for *Sure* magazine that was taking place in the Hollywood Hills. "You could hear people screaming," a witness on the scene said. "Ten minutes later, an ambulance and the police arrived and things got chaotic." A caravan of paparazzi and Kaitlin's family and friends—including her distraught boyfriend Austin Meyers and publicist Laney Peters—followed the ambulance to the hospital, where only family members were admitted entrance. While details are still sparse, hospital sources say Kaitlin's condition is not life-threatening. There has yet to be a statement from Kaitlin's camp.

This latest incident caps off an out-of-character few weeks for Kaitlin. Just this morning, KROQ began playing a rough demo of a song supposedly sung by Kaitlin called "Paparazzi Princess." The good girl has also been hitting the club scene and hanging out with notorious party pals Ava Hayden and Lauren Cobb. Both friends were at the shoot with Kaitlin when the incident happened, but neither was allowed into the hospital to see her. (Laney Peters refused their entrance at the door.) "We don't know what happened," said a tearful Ava during an impromptu press conference she gave in front of the hospital. "One minute Kaitlin was laughing and happy, the next she was lying on the floor. All we can do now is pray she's okay."

While *Sure* has yet to comment on what happened, insiders tell us that Kaitlin was upset after Ava and Lauren showed up unannounced and disrupted the shoot. "Those two are terrors and Kaitlin was having a hard time making them leave," said a source. "A few minutes later, Kaitlin collapsed."

Hollywood Nation Online will continue to update you on the situation as more details become available.

THIRTEEN: *A Clean Slate*

I came to a few minutes later, but by that point Laney, Rodney, Austin, and the *Sure* crew were so freaked out that they'd already called an ambulance and were insisting I go to the hospital to be checked out. A few hours later, I'm lying in a bed surrounded by my family and friends. I must have fallen asleep after the battery of tests the doctors ordered, because when I wake up Mom is crying and Dad and Matty are wringing their hands. Nadine is pacing the room in a bridesmaid dress. Rodney is sitting with his head in his hands and Laney and Seth are bickering. Austin is the only one close enough to touch. He's sitting at the edge of my bed watching the commotion around him.

I grab his hand. "Hey." My voice sounds froggy.

Nadine gasps. "She's awake again!"

Mom rushes across the room and knocks Austin out of the way. "How are you, sweetie?" she asks. "I came as soon as I heard." She lets out a little sob. "We were so scared."

"Have the doctors said anything about what happened to me?" I ask nervously. "Did I have a heart attack?" It certainly felt like one. Well, what I would imagine one felt like.

"We don't know," admits Dad. "The doctors haven't told us anything yet. They should be in soon."

"You had us really worried," Austin tells me. Even though Mom pushed him, he's still holding my hand. I don't want him to let go.

"Has anyone told the editors at *Sure* that I'm okay? I don't want them to be mad that I ruined their shoot," I say. I feel like I'm going to cry.

"Mad?" Laney repeats. "We're the ones who should be mad. I can't believe Christy interviewed you without me there after I told her she couldn't! Then she let those morons into the shoot! I am never working with that magazine again." She pauses. "That is, unless they apologize for what happened and make it up to you in a major way with an offer for several well-timed covers."

"Even if they were upset, the ambulance and police arriving wiped away any ill feelings, I'm sure," Mom adds. "The press is usually very sympathetic about hospital visits — as long as it's for a good reason and not drugs."

Seth rolls his eyes. "Not everything has to be a publicity stunt."

"I'm not using my daughter for publicity!" Mom snaps.

The two of them start to bicker, but they are interrupted

by a light knock on the door. A young doctor in a white lab coat walks in and everyone gets quiet.

"Hi, Kaitlin," he says. "I'm Doctor Callahan. Would you like to talk in private?"

I shake my head. "Anything you have to say, you can say in front of them." I'm so nervous, I feel like I'm going to throw up.

Doctor Callahan nods. "The good news is you're fine," he tells me.

Thank God! I can't die before I get my driver's license. Or my first Oscar.

"We ran a few tests and everything came back normal," he adds.

"Then what's wrong with me?" I ask shakily. "This afternoon I felt like I couldn't breathe, my heartbeat was out of control, I felt woozy, and everything looked blurry." I glance at my starched, white hospital sheets. "Some of this has, um, happened to me before, but never this bad."

"It has?" Dad asks. "How come you didn't say anything?" I look away.

Doctor Callahan smiles gently. "What you had, Kaitlin, was a panic attack. They're extremely frightening, especially if you don't know what one is. But strange as it might sound, a panic attack is actually your body's way of protecting you from harm."

A panic attack? That's all it was? What I felt was so scary. "What causes a panic attack?" I want to know.

"Well, they can be brought on by a number of things," says Dr. Callahan thoughtfully. "They usually occur around periods of sudden stress or fear, moments where you sense a loss of control, life transitions, avoidance of panic-provoking situations or environments. Have you been experiencing more anxiety, or has anything stressed you out lately?" he asks.

"Don't look at me!" Mom freaks out on everyone before I can answer. "I didn't know the demo would be stolen. Seth promised to get it back."

"How am I going to tell the press she's in the hospital because of a panic attack?" Laney wonders out loud. "A panic attack makes her sound like she doesn't have her act together."

Laney has a point. How am I going to face everyone at work and tell him or her I was hospitalized for a panic attack? Doesn't it make me sound weak? I'm sure pictures of me being rushed to the hospital are all over the Web already. I'm completely embarrassed.

Everyone in the room starts talking at once. They're yelling at each other and the noise is deafening. Nadine is yelling at herself. Seth is yelling at Mom about my demo tape. (From what I can make out, a disgruntled assistant, mad at TJ, released it to radio. She's since been fired.) Laney and Dad are screaming about who is responsible for my partying and how they're going to handle the situation in the press. I hear Mom say something like, "I had my own tabloid nightmare to attend to!" Matty, Austin, and Rodney are just looking on in bewilderment.

Before things get any uglier, I've got to get control of the room.

"GUYS, STOP!" I yell and they actually listen.

"I'll give you all a few minutes," Doctor Callahan says. He looks freaked out. "But I ask that you not upset Kaitlin. She needs rest."

"You have to calm down," I say sternly when Doctor Callahan has shut the door behind him. "You can't blame each other. This whole thing is my fault."

"That is true," Mom sniffles. "It's not like *we* caused you to have a panic attack."

Ouch! "You certainly added to the problem," I say defensively. "I've been feeling all of the things Doctor Callahan mentioned for a while now." That gets their attention so I keep going. "*FA* is ending and I guess I just wanted to mourn the loss before I moved on to something new, but the minute we got back from vacation, everything started happening so fast I couldn't get a grip on things. All of you wanted me to pick a new project and had your own ideas of where my career should go next. I was studying for the SATs, doing all these interviews, hearing how important my paycheck was to this family, and not once did anyone ask me what *I* wanted to do, or give me a choice. You even kidnapped me for my meeting with Seth!" I remind them, staring at Mom and Dad, who look away guiltily. "All I wanted was a little breathing room. *FA* has been my second home since before I could ride a bike," I say quietly. "It's not so easy to wrap your head around leaving that."

"You should have said something," Nadine whispers.

"I didn't think I had to," I point out. "So when no one noticed, or cared that I was upset, I took out my anger on my credit card. I was so tired of being bullied that I did the only thing I could do without any of your say — I shopped and partied."

"Shopped is an understatement," Mom says and raises her right eyebrow. "I got your credit card statement this morning. Your bill was over four thousand dollars!"

Yikes. Is it really that high? "I'll pay you back," I promise.

"Couldn't you have found a different way to take out your anger with us?" Laney wants to know. "Lauren and Ava are bad news! The press has been all over this story. No one can understand why a good girl like you would hang out with the likes of them."

"I wasn't thinking clearly, I know, but at the time, I felt like Lauren and Ava were the only ones who were listening to me." My eyes glaze with tears. "You were all so busy, that the only ones I could turn to were Austin and the girls. I needed you and you all disappeared."

Mom starts to cry. "Maybe I was wrong," she says. "This whole thing *is* my fault. I should have been monitoring what you've been up to, but I was so busy dealing with my own fallout that I didn't pay attention. *Fashionistas* is right. I am a momager."

"You're not a momager," I tell her gently. "I know you're just looking out for me," I hesitate, "but sometimes you get a little one-track-minded."

"That's an understatement," Seth says, and then feeling guilty he puts his arm around Mom. She smiles.

"This is our fault too," Dad says, sounding upset. "I can see now that we put too much pressure on you. I guess at the end of the day some of us were worried about the end of *FA* too and what it meant for all of our futures. You've supported this family for a long time, and I feel guilty that a weight like that has been on your shoulders."

"I don't want you guys to blame yourselves," I tell Dad and the others. "Yes, I've been angry, but I should have been angry with myself. I know I've made a mess of things by not telling you all the truth. I just hope it isn't too late to fix things." I thumb at the hospital sheet nervously. "I *do* want to take my career to the next level. I just don't want to go full speed ahead and forget everything that's gotten me this far. You guys have to give me a little room to breathe." I laugh bitterly. "But who am I kidding? This isn't what I want. This is about what directors and casting agents want. I'm not sure I'm good at anything other than playing Sam."

"What are you talking about?" Laney demands. "You do movies all the time and none of them pigeonholed you!"

"Directors have wanted me to play roles opposite of Sam

because Sam still existed on *Family Affair*," I point out. "Now that Sam's gone, everyone will want me to re-create her. I'm going to be typecast as Sam for life. She's what I'm good at."

"You're kidding, right?" Matty asks. "Kates, I would kill to have your problems. You have a big TV show, you're a huge star and now your show is being cancelled and you're afraid no one will let you play anyone other than Sam. Boo hoo."

Ouch.

"Matthew," Dad says sternly. "That's not nice to say to your sister. She's upset."

"This happens all the time in Hollywood," Matty explains to my dad. "Shows end, good films bomb at the theater. But people move on, and Kaitlin has to too. No matter how scared she is."

My hands begin to sweat. My pulse races again. I do not want to have another panic attack. "I'm not . . . scared," I lie. "I just want time to grieve."

"You're scared," Matty says firmly. "You're scared to embrace anything other than Sam. Well, you have no choice, do you? But that's okay. You can do it, Kates. You're a great actress. We've always believed in you." He smiles. "It's about time you believed in yourself."

Aww, Matty! I never thought of it that way. Maybe I have been hiding behind my fears for too long. "Matt, I feel like I should pay you for a therapy session," I say with a small grin. "That was a great pep talk."

Matty blushes. "I've wanted to say that to you for a week, but I didn't have the guts. That's why I've been leaving all those articles under your door."

No way! I was sure it was Nadine! "That was you?"

He nods. "Even if you didn't want to see what was really going on, I did and I wanted you to know someone was watching."

"I'm sorry if you thought we were pushing you," says Seth. "We only want what's best for you. As hard as you think it is to move on emotionally, it's even harder to find another great project. We wanted to give you as many options as we could."

"I know, Seth," I tell him.

"Image is everything in this town, Kaitlin, and I'm not going to lie to you," Seth says. "Your behavior the past few weeks has been a problem."

I have a sinking feeling in my stomach.

"The director of *Manolos* called last night," Seth explains. "They said they're going in a new direction with the title character. They want a serious star. I told them you were one and you were just going through a rough patch, but they wouldn't listen. I think they felt you were too immature to play the character."

I want to cry. My fear of growing up has cost me the chance to play the title character from one of my favorite books. I'm so ashamed of myself.

Seth grimaces. "And that pilot you liked about Alaska actually went with another actress because they couldn't wait any longer to meet with you."

My stomach hurts. "Who'd they go with?" I have to know.

Seth clears his throat. "They went with Sky Mackenzie," he says quietly.

"WHAT?" I shriek.

"Burke, stay calm," Austin tells me. "You don't want to have another attack."

"Sky changed her mind about *I Hate You*," Seth says. "Or the director changed his mind. I'm not sure. But Sky met with the Alaska show people last week, charmed the pants off of them and now she's doing the pilot. I have to say, it's a real role reversal for her. It should do wonders for her career if it gets picked up."

I feel woozy. My hands begin to tingle and I wipe my brow. I've been so anti-new job that Sky got an offer for the pilot that I actually liked! The news hits me like a ton of bricks. I am not going to be on a TV show anymore. I won't be on a set every day. I blew all my TV prospects.

"So Kaitlin has nothing lined up?" Mom's voice is shrill.

I have no job. NO job. What am I going to do everyday? Be tutored at home? Look at what a mess I've made. My show is ending and instead of fielding offers, I'm avoiding the press and getting jobs taken away from me. I've got to take control of my life before I lose any more projects that could be good for me. "I guess the people from *Meeting of the Minds* moved on to someone else too, right?" I ask quietly.

"Actually, no," Seth says and I feel my heart soar for a moment. "They had to look at a few other people this weekend, but they promised me they'd have an answer for you this week." He smiles. "I think you have a good shot at that one."

Mom, who has hated the idea of a play from day one, actually sounds excited. "New York would be fun for a few months," she says encouragingly.

"Okay, this has all been very touching," Laney says, "but we're getting off track. First, we've got to come up with a game plan to fix Kaitlin's reputation." She paces the room. "I have to release a statement." She looks at Seth. "We'll say, 'Kaitlin became overheated at the *Sure* photo shoot and fainted.' We can say that the room was really hot and Kaitlin was dehydrated and that's why she passed out. We'll add that she is thankful to her fans for their support."

"Why do publicists always use the word thankful in their releases?" Matty asks.

HOLLYWOOD SECRET NUMBER THIRTEEN: There's probably not a day that goes by that a publicist doesn't have to issue a statement on behalf of one of their clients. Whether a star is getting married, divorced, separated, having a baby, or apologizing for a feud, there's only so many ways you can word it. If a phrase works — "we're saddened," "we're thrilled," "we're ecstatic," "we're overjoyed" — then why not keep using it?

That's what Laney has realized. She stockpiles several statements and just adjusts the wording to fit each new situation.

"We'll get *Sure* to give you an exclusive about fainting on the set and how important it is to drink water," Laney says, with a glimmer in her eye. "That's the least they can do."

"Maybe we can get Kaitlin an interview with Oprah about it too!" Mom suggests.

"Um, are you sure dehydrated doesn't sound bogus?" I am skeptical about this. The lie seems as thin as Laney's smile.

"As long as you stick to the story, no one will question it — at least not to your face," says Laney. "First we have to get through the *Pretty Young Assassins* press junket. Everyone is going to have questions about the hospital stay."

My heart sinks. I forgot about the junket. It's going to be so embarrassing to have to talk about passing out and winding up at Cedars-Sinai. How am I going to face my costars on *PYA*? Or the foreign press? They're going to eat me alive! What a nightmare. But this is a nightmare I created, I remind myself. It's about time I stopped living in denial and faced the truth.

"We'll also have to spend some time working out how Kaitlin will answer questions about her next project," Seth adds.

"Before we tackle this, does anyone want a coffee?" Dad interrupts. Everyone does. Laney, Rodney, Matty, Mom, and Seth are still talking about next week's junket as they file out.

Austin sits back down next to me. "I'm so glad you're

okay," he says. "And I'm glad you finally told them what you were feeling."

"Thanks for staying with me," I tell him. He leans over and kisses me.

"So are you hungry?" Austin asks. "I can go down to the cafeteria and get you something."

"Anything," I beg. "I didn't each much at lunch before I passed out."

After Austin leaves, it's just me and Nadine. Her silver bridesmaid dress makes a swishing noise when she walks over to my bed.

"I can't believe you left your cousin's wedding to see me after the way I treated you the other night," I say guiltily.

"I just left a little early," she tells me with a small smile. "You should have seen the looks I got on the plane." She laughs, then her face turns serious. "I came as soon as I heard. I was so worried about you."

"Nadine, I'm so sorry about the way I've acted," I tell her.

"Stop. It's me who should be apologizing," she says. "I pushed you too hard about the SATs and your meetings. Your plate has been so full. You needed an ally and I only made things more hectic."

"I know you were only trying to help me, but it felt like you switched to Team Laney/Mom just when I needed you the most," I admit.

Nadine looks away. "I feel like I've let you down." Her voice quivers. "I have a confession to make. When I went home to Chicago for Christmas and saw my parents, they gave me this big speech about my life and how I was wasting it."

"You're kidding!" I'm flabbergasted. The way Nadine has always talked about her folks, they sounded like the coolest people in the world.

"They said I had done this silly assistant thing long enough and probably saved up enough money to go to graduate school twice and that I needed to stop fooling around and concentrate on my future." She looks at me and her eyes are watery. "They said I had to stop slacking off."

Now I feel really awful. I said almost the exact same thing to Nadine, but I was just being mean. "You never slack off," I point out. "You work harder than anyone I know."

"They don't see it that way." Nadine shakes her head. "I tried explaining how important I am to you. How I'm trying to make sure you have a future that includes more than just acting. I guess when I came back to L.A., I wanted to make sure I really did that and I didn't realize how much pressure I was adding to your life. I'm so sorry, Kates."

"I'm sorry I said those awful things to you," I begin to blubber.

The two of us cry it out for a while. After we're done, I feel like a huge weight has been lifted off my shoulders. I'm finally making amends for my actions, and Nadine is only the start.

Saturday, February 21
NOTE TO SELF:

Send flowers 2 *Sure* editors.
Call Liz. (Send her flowers 2)

**Ask Seth 4 a new batch of scripts 2 read. READ
EVERYTHING!
Check on *Meeting of the Minds*.
PRESS JUNKET 4 *PYA* – next Saturday
Monday call time: 6:30 AM

FOURTEEN: *Meet the Press. Again.*

"Kates?" Nadine says softly. "Kaitlin," she sings.

I don't respond. I'm buried beneath my very comfortable 600-thread count comforter and I don't plan on coming out anytime soon.

"KAITLIN." Nadine's tone is sharper now. "I know you can hear me. It's 8:15. We have to leave at 9:30. Don't you think you should start getting ready?"

"Do I really have to go?" I want to know.

"Paul and Shelly are downstairs waiting. And Tina left a few smart outfits in your closet for you to try on." Nadine ignores me. "I think it would be best if you got up."

Argh. I know Nadine's right. I really do. But I'm not convinced I can face the press at today's junket. I'm embarrassed about telling all these journalists that I wound up in the hospital for dehydration. There's already been some press speculation that my fainting spell was code for "mental exhaustion" (aka party addiction).

"Kaitlin?" Nadine has her hand on my comforter and is rocking me back and forth. "What do you say?"

KAITLIN BURKE: FALLEN FROM GRACE. The recent *Celebrity Nation* special pops in my head. Oh God. This is almost Britney territory we're dealing with. Okay, maybe not Britney, but definitely Lindsay.

Well, maybe it's not that bad either. Mischa Barton? UGH. That's still bad.

I can't breathe. I throw my covers back and start freaking out. "Nadine, I can't do this! I can't defend myself to fifty-plus newspaper and magazine journalists! I feel silly saying I forgot to eat or drink anything that day! If I have to talk about Ava and Lauren and my recent shopping addiction, then I'll wind up spilling the beans about how scared I've been about losing *FA* and then it's all downhill from there. I'll look like a total flake!" I start coughing and wheezing and Nadine quickly hands me a glass of water.

I take a huge gulp. Ah. That's better so I take another.

"Feeling better?" Nadine asks sweetly.

"A little," I manage.

"Good." Nadine smiles. "Now get up." Her face is sterner. "You are not going to be late for this press junket."

I shake my head and stare at Nadine. She has on a gray wrap-sweater, boot-cut dark denim Gap jeans and ankle boots. "I can't face all those people. And Sky and Drew. And Hutch! Can you imagine what Hutch is going to say to me?" Sky I can deal with. I've seen her all week and she's been nice enough to not make a single rude comment about my hospital trek. But Drew, who is my boyfriend in *Pretty Young Assassins* on top of being my real-life ex, and Hutch Adams, my director who is certifiably insane, are going to send me over the edge. "Let's face it. I'm doomed. I can't do this." I shrink back under my covers and close my heavy eyes. Sleep. I just need to sleep.

"You faced your costars at *FA*, didn't you?" Nadine reminds me. "They were proud of you for trying to fix things. Tom is even letting you wait till this week to film the retrospective. You can do this too."

I shake my head. "It's not the same thing," I tell my pillow. "I can't face all those reporters. My quotes are going to be all over the papers and Web by nightfall. I feel like a big, fat liar using the dehydration excuse."

"I thought you'd react this way after a restless night's sleep," Nadine reconsiders. "That's why I sent for help. Come in." I hear Nadine say.

My door creaks open. Who could it be? Austin? Tina? Paul and Shelly? Laney?

"I'll leave you two alone," Nadine tells us and then I hear her walk out.

Curiosity gets the best of me and I peek out of my covers to see who my guest is.

"Liz?" I'm shocked and my voice reflects that. What's she doing here?

I tried calling her several times this week. I left a bunch of messages saying what an awful friend I was and how sorry I was for everything. But she didn't call me back. Austin said to give her time and now she's here.

"I am not letting you be late for this junket. We're saving your butt today," Liz says sternly, but I can see she's smiling. She looks great. It's been almost a month — a whole month — since I've seen her and I could swear her dark, kinky curly hair, which never grows, looks longer. She's got her signature look working for her — a Pucci head scarf — and has a black knit top over a cream tank with black leggings and Chanel flats. Liz goes straight for my closet. "Now let's see. Tina told me she picked out three outfits. Ah. Here they are!"

"Liz," I squeak, trying not to cry. "I've been such a jerk. I should have told you what was going on with me. I should have made more of an effort to see you."

"I think you should wear the green Rebecca Taylor top with Minx jeans," Liz ignores me. "Green really brings out your eyes and the cotton will feel soft on your skin so you'll be comfortable."

"Liz?" I try again. Liz doesn't say anything. "Stop picking out clothes for me. I don't deserve it." I pull off my comforter and pad over to the large walk-in closet in my polka-dotted Gap yoga pants and blue tank top.

Liz gasps. "When did you get this great Nicole Miller?" She holds up a black studded dress with a pocket on the chest.

I knock it out of her hand and the hanger clangs to the floor. "Forget about the Nicole Miller! I'm trying to apologize," I insist. "I'm sorry for everything — for not being there for you when you needed me, for the way I behaved with Mikayla, and how I treated you when you called me."

"I'm the one who should apologize for being a lousy best friend," Liz says. "When I saw the news about you being in the hospital I got so upset. I was in Chicago with Dad this week on business; otherwise I would have come right away. I was going to call you, but I didn't know what to say." She sounds choked up. "I had to see you in person. We got back last night." She starts to cry. "I'm so sorry I wasn't there for you. How could I have missed how stressful *Family Affair* ending has been on you? I was so wrapped up in my own drama with this NYU application and college visits that I couldn't see you were in the same boat I was." She starts to hiccup. "I didn't mean what I said about us growing apart and not being able to relate. I was just mad that that you weren't around. I know I said some awful things. I got so wrapped up in Mikayla's stories about New York and NYU that getting into that college was all I could think about," Liz continues.

"Mikayla made me feel like I was so far behind everyone else," Liz adds. "She made me feel like all the Hollywood stuff I did was frivolous." Liz grabs a tissue from my counter and blows her nose loudly. "My whole life has been this town!" She sounds angry now. "My dad's in the business! If he wasn't, and I hadn't met you, I wouldn't even know that I *wanted* to be a producer. This town works for me. Anyway, I got tired of her lecturing me all the time. I haven't spoken to her since she went back to NYU."

You mean I have Lizzie back to myself again? That's so wrong. I started rereading Nadine's and my favorite self-help book — *Embrace the True You* — and chapter twelve is called *There's No I in Friendship*. The title doesn't really make sense, but the point is, you're supposed to raise your friends up, not be happy when they fail.

"I did the same thing with Lauren and Ava," I tell Liz. "I didn't see who they really were till it was too late. They didn't act the way real friends would. You're my best friend and I should have been there for you when you needed me. I shouldn't have let one stupid fight get in the way of that. I should have apologized to you weeks ago, but I was being stubborn."

"I was wrong to say that stuff about college, Kates," Liz stresses. "Our friendship doesn't ride on whether we're both going to college. We'll be friends no matter where we wind up. What we have is so much deeper than a four-year school."

"I know," I wail. We both start bawling and hug again and that's when I hear Nadine come back in the room. She sees us and smiles.

"That's what I was hoping for," Nadine tells me. "So now that your real life is fixed, can we fix your Hollywood one?"

"I don't know." I wipe my eyes. "Liz knows and loves me like no one does. The press isn't going to be as easy."

Liz puts her hand on my shoulder. "What are you planning on saying?"

I look at Nadine. "I can't help thinking Laney's lie is not the answer, but I'm not sure how to get around it."

"Whatever you decide, we'll be right there rooting you on." Nadine looks at Liz.

That will help a lot. I take a deep breath. "Okay then. Let's do this."

*　　*　　*

A press junket is a huge day in the life of a movie. Fifty to a hundred journalists from all over the country, and sometimes the world, show up for a chance to spend twenty minutes interviewing a star who normally wouldn't be caught dead answering questions from a paper in Smalltown USA. Even if the movie in question is less than extraordinary, a good round of interviews with your cast and director can erase even the worst review.

With junkets being so important, it's no wonder a studio spares no expense to put on a good one. After the reporters have seen the movie, the studio reserves space at a swanky high-end hotel (today we're doing the junket at the Four Seasons Hotel Los Angeles at Beverly Hills). They ply the reporters with good food and give them a great gift (anything from a T-shirt with the film's logo for a low-budget flick to a weekend tote for a big movie) and schmooze them like mad. But the most important part of the day, of course, is the cast interviews. Journalists are split into small groups and the film's stars move from room to room every twenty minutes or so to answer everyone's questions. No one gets a one-on-one unless they're *Access Hollywood* or *Celebrity Nation* and there's TV coverage involved.

After four-plus hours of this, you can imagine how tedious it can get answering a question like, "What did you like about playing Carly?" (That's why you read similar quotes in different magazines a hundred times. There's only so many ways you can describe your film character, no matter how cool she is.) Even so, some stars hate the monotony of it all, which is why there is . . .

HOLLYWOOD SECRET NUMBER FOURTEEN: If you're a huge A-lister who can barely handle more than an hour talking about the film you were paid fifteen million to make, a regular press junket is not going to cut it. Why spend half a day answering the same questions when you can do it once for a huge audience? That's why the Toms of the world don't do junkets — they do press conferences. A hundred journalists are packed in a room and they get *one* chance to ask their questions. They'll all also wind up with the exact same quotes since Tom only has to answer the same question once.

No one is doing a press conference for *Pretty Young Assassins*, that's for sure. Our movie may be starting to pop up on early "must see" movie lists, but no one on our cast commands that status yet. Even if a few already have the egos to match it.

CLAP. CLAP. CLAP. CLAP. "Ladies and gentleman, the girl of the moment has arrived — Kaitlin Burke!"

My *PYA* costar Drew applauds me as I enter the suite we're using as a waiting room. Drew looks good, of course — great upper body, gorgeous tan jacket and jeans, perfectly styled dark hair hanging in his eyes, tan skin — but that obnoxious grin ruins the whole picture. "And wow, you look, dare I say, normal? No under-eye bags, no dehydration. Wait a minute," Drew eyes me closely. "Are you Kaitlin's stand-in?"

How could I have ever dated this guy? "Hi, Drew," I mumble and take a seat on a couch at the opposite end of the living room. I'll just ignore him.

I look around the opulent room. Gorgeous striped fabrics on the wingback chairs, gold mirrors, huge flower arrangements, exposed beam ceiling, perfect lighting. The only thing that isn't beautiful is the fact I'm stuck in a room with Drew. Laney, Mom, Nadine, and Liz are waiting for me across the hall. Apparently Hutch wants to give us a cast pep talk before we start so our people have to wait outside.

Drew plops down next to me.

"I don't want to hear it, Drew," I say. I straighten my shoulders and I push up the sleeves on my Donna Karan flowy black shirt. I'm glad I wore the wide-leg dark denim dressy jeans and my favorite Gucci boots with this outfit. "Didn't your mother ever teach you not to talk about things you know nothing about?"

"Oh, I know a lot," Drew says. "So does the rest of the world. This story is everywhere! Seriously, Katie Bear, I couldn't have written your fainting spell better if I faked it for the press myself." He hovers over me, smelling like coffee. "Give me a break. You fainted because you partied too much. Admit it." Drew asks. "Ava and Lauren would knock anyone out."

I will not let Drew get to me. I have to save all my strength for these interviews. I will not start a fight. But ... "You should know," I snarl. "You dated them both."

"Snap!" Drew laughs. "Nice one, Katie Bear, but it doesn't change anything, does it? The press thinks you're a total screwup. Your fainting excuse is thin and that stupid song you did pissed people off. You're so damaged, you make me look good."

Drew's laughter is driving me crazy. My blood is beginning to reach its boiling point, but I try to remain calm. I do not need another headline-making fight on my hands. Especially when every reporter in the civilized world is right outside this door. Still I have to say something. "Maybe I did handle the situation poorly," I tell him, "but we all know the only reason anyone is paying attention to what happened to me is because I'm a celebrity. If I was an ordinary girl who partied too hard, the world wouldn't know about it."

"But you're *not* a regular girl, you're a star," Drew says. "Or at least you were one till now. Without *Family Affair*, you have nothing."

It takes all my energy to not punch him.

"Leave her alone, Drew."

Drew and I turn around. I don't know if Sky was here the whole time or if she just slipped in unnoticed. She struts toward us wearing a white silk tank, matching white pants, and white heels that give her the appearance of an angel. I know better.

Drew snorts. "Don't worry, Sky," he says. "I've left you enough time to make some jabs at her as well."

"The only one I'm going to be making jabs at is you," Sky says icily.

What? Sky is sticking up for me? Maybe I never got up this morning and I'm still dreaming.

"K may act stupid sometimes, but there is nothing stupid about fainting," Sky tells him angrily. "I happen to do it all the time because I, um, forget to eat." She looks at me. "I've just never passed out in public because of it, but being discreet has never been your strong suit."

"Thanks," I say dryly.

"I'm proud of K for not wimping out about this press junket," Sky says. "A lesser star — like you, Drew — would have been so mortified they would have canceled the whole thing. But that's not K. She is tough when she needs to be."

I'm so surprised by Sky's compliment; I don't know what to say.

Drew rolls his eyes. "Is there a hidden camera in here that I don't know about, Sky? Since when do you stick up for *her*?"

"K has been my costar for more than a decade, while you're a C-list star who is better known for your conquests than your work," Sky snaps. "Of course I'm going to stick up for her."

"I'm bored," Drew says. He walks over to the food table and pops a grape in his mouth. He actually looks too nervous to come back over.

I turn to Sky. "Thank you," I say gratefully.

Sky shrugs. "I'm protecting myself too, you know," she says with a twinkle in her eye. "You're worth more to me as an ally than Drew will ever be." We both laugh.

"I may have to tell Trevor that you really do have a heart in there somewhere," I say lightly.

Sky smiles. "I guess that's okay with me." She's quiet for a moment. "So how are you? I haven't wanted to ask while we're at work. Did you really faint because you were dehydrated or is something else going on?"

I bite my lower lip. "I don't know. It's everything lately. Aren't you scared at all about life after *FA*?" I ask her seriously. "We've spent our whole lives on that show. What if we never have another hit like this one? What if we never overcome our teen star status? Those thoughts keep me up at night."

Sky looks away. "Okay, maybe I am a *little* scared. Even if I do have a hot pilot on my hands."

"Congratulations on the show," I say and try not to sound jealous. Both Sky and Matty have great pilots that could be picked up for the fall. I could have had a TV pilot too, but I messed up. I guess I can't worry about it now. There's always next pilot season or even mid-season shows. New projects are being announced every day. And if I'm lucky, I'll get to do my first play this summer. That would be really cool.

"I'm excited," Sky tells me.

If Sky knows I wanted that part, she doesn't let on. "You should be," I say honestly. "You've got a great director."

"Who knows?" Sky says with a sly smile. "If you're unemployed next fall, maybe I'll get you a *one-time-only* guest spot. I don't need another Alexis Holden on my hands."

I laugh. "I'm sure I'll be too busy with my *own* hot project to try to take over yours, but thanks anyway."

Sky's face clouds over. "Wait? You have something lined up? What is it?"

There's a knock on the door and Hutch races in, looking as harried and frantic as ever. He's still thin, and he hasn't dressed up for the occasion. He's wearing one of his concert tees and jeans and has his yoga mat rolled up under his right arm. His publicist is two steps behind him and doesn't look pleased. Hutch sees me and breaks into a grin.

"Kaitlin!" he says. He shakes my hand vigorously and doesn't let go. "Thank you, thank you, thank you!"

"For what?" I ask, confused.

"For your well-timed hospital stay!" Hutch looks at me like I should know what he means. "It couldn't have been timed better. We had to turn people away for this junket. Everyone wanted in to have a chance to interview you. We're guaranteed to get a lot of press and it's all going to be about you."

Drew's jaw drops. "You're kidding me."

"Nope," Hutch says happily. "They're here to see *her*." Hutch shakes me strongly. "Say what's on your mind, Kaitlin. Don't hold back. I'll see you guys out there."

I'm speechless. Hutch is happy that I've timed my hospital visit to our junket? Should I tell him it's a coincidence? I bite my lip to keep from laughing till Hutch is gone. Laney, Nadine, Mom, Liz, Sky's team, and Drew's people file in.

"What's so funny?" Laney asks me.

"Nothing," I say.

"Are you ready for your interviews?" Laney asks. "You've got your fainting spell story down pat?"

"Um . . ." I start to say.

"Laney, girls, do you think I could have a moment with Kaitlin alone?" Mom interrupts. Everyone looks at each other and I glance nervously at Nadine. Mom motions for me to join her out in the hallway, where I follow her across to a suite that she must have been waiting in with the stars' families and entourages. The room is empty now. She shuts the door behind us and locks it.

Uh-oh.

"Kaitlin, I was hoping we could talk a minute before you go out there," Mom says, looking more awkward than I've ever seen her. "I feel like I owe you an apology."

I sit down on one of the couches and Mom sits next to me, leaving a huge gap between us. "Mom, it's okay, you don't have to say anything."

Mom grabs my hand. "No, I do!" she insists. She shakes her head miserably. "*Fashionistas* is right. I've been a horrible mother." She starts to sniffle.

"You're not a bad mom," I say. "If you didn't look out for me, who would?"

"But I take it too far," she blubbers. "I just want what's best for you, but sometimes I blur the lines too much. You should be my daughter first and my client second. Not the other way around."

"Mom —"

"No, let me say this," Mom tells me sternly. "I want you to be the best version of yourself, Kate-Kate, and sometimes I think that means the biggest actress there is, but in actuality, I realize, it doesn't have anything to do with acting at all. It has to do with you being you, and growing into the woman *you* want to become. That means allowing you to make some of your own decisions, even if I don't agree with them."

"Mom, I told you at the hospital, I know you're only trying to do what's best for me," I say quietly, but I have to admit, it feels good to hear Mom say these things. "And I trust your decisions — sometimes — but sometimes, I want you to listen to what I have to say. I've been in this field a long time and I know what kind of roles I want to take at this point."

Mom shakes her head. "I just don't want you taken advantage of. This town can be so tough and I don't want them to destroy you. I've seen it happen to too many other girls your age."

I squeeze Mom's hand. "They won't. I've got you, I've got Seth, I've got Laney. You're all helping me make good decisions. You just have to listen to what I'm telling you once in a while."

Mom leans over and hugs me tightly, practically suffocating me. "Okay," she sobs. "I promise I'll try! And if I'm not listening, you just tell me, okay? Sometimes I need a small nudge."

Small is an understatement, but why split hairs at a moment like this? "I will."

We walk arm in arm back across the hall and into the other suite, which is pretty loud with everyone crammed inside it. Laney, Nadine, and Liz are waiting anxiously in a corner.

"Everything okay?" Laney asks, looking concerned.

Mom and I smile at each other. "Everything's great," I say.

"Good." Laney smiles. "Now about your statement for today. Remember what we went over: You fainted. You didn't eat that morning. You hadn't drank anything. It was a fainting spell and nothing more. Got it?"

I look at their expectant faces. Nadine is fidgety, Liz is

looking at the floor. Even Mom suddenly looks pensive. "Laney, listen, I was thinking," I start to say.

"Oh no! Don't do this to me now," Laney begs.

"Just hear me out," I say calmly. "This fainting cover-up is thin. You know it, I know it, even the press knows it."

"So what?" Laney says. "They can't prove anything. They'll be a few more days of press about this and then it will all blow over."

"But I'll remember it," I stress. "And this will come up again in some other interview. Maybe not tomorrow. Maybe not six months from now, but I'll know I was being fake. Laney, listen. I was scared before, and I thought this fainting story made sense, but what am I being scared of? Isn't the truth better than what the press believes right now? They know I wasn't dehydrated. The truth is, what happened to me in the grand scheme of the world is not that bad. So I freaked out. Teens do it all the time. Yes I partied a little hard, hung out with girls I shouldn't have and spent a little too much money, but I didn't kill anyone. I didn't do drugs," I remind her. "I'm just a girl who has a lot of responsibilities for someone my age and I needed to take a break from it all. It's pretty common, you know." I look at Mom. "I don't want to read some scripted quotes that lie about what really happened. I want the girls that look up to me to read my quotes and be able to relate. I shouldn't be ashamed of myself."

"I think Kaitlin's right," Mom speaks up, and Nadine's jaw

almost drops to the floor. "I think we should let her tell the truth." Mom and Laney look at each other.

Laney sighs. "If you feel that strongly about this, then okay, do it your way," she says. "I guess you're right. You shouldn't have to lie about just being a teenager."

I smile at Laney proudly.

"The first roundtable will start in five," an assistant announces.

"Are you really going to tell them everything?" Liz whispers to me as I walk away to get a bottle of water.

"Yep." I feel so confident all of a sudden.

"This is going to be good," Liz says.

My phone rings and I answer it. "Hello?"

"Have you run from the hotel screaming yet?" I hear Austin's voice and instantly feel calmer.

I tell Austin what happened. How Mom apologized and actually agreed with me for once. I tell him how Laney eventually saw my side of things. I also tell him what happened with Liz. And how Sky defended me. The combination of all these things happening in the course of one morning made me realize if I can handle all of them, I can handle anything. A room full of reporters doesn't scare me.

"Thatta girl," Austin sounds truly proud. "Knock 'em dead."

"I will," I promise. And for the first time in a long time, I feel prepared to do just that.

"Kaitlin?" The studio publicist appears at my side. "I'd like to take you to your first room."

I leave Mom, Laney, Liz, and Nadine and follow the woman down the hotel hallway. People are staring, but I don't care. The publicist opens the door and I see a group of about eight journalists sitting around a table with tape recorders in hand.

"Hi, everyone. Your first interview will be with Kaitlin Burke," the assistant tells them.

I eye the table full of food. Stars really don't eat at these things. The most we usually take is water. Otherwise you wind up with an article describing everything you ate that day. I grab a water and take a seat. I smile pleasantly as the publicist leaves the room.

"So," I begin. "We'll get to *PYA* in a moment, but first, should we start with what you really want to know?"

Saturday, February 28
NOTE TO SELF:

Last week on *FA*
Monday calltime: 6 AM

TV Tome

Kaitlin Burke Comes Clean
"I let fear get the best of me."

Week of February 29

Why Kaitlin Burke had a near total meltdown—and how she fought her way back

By Joyce Waters

Kaitlin Burke has made many headlines over the past few weeks. When her sudden inner party animal was released, thanks to new pals Ava Hayden and Lauren Cobb, Kaitlin's photo was everywhere—she was seen dancing at Shelter, shopping at Belladonna, and lunching at the Ivy. For a celebrity whose usual photo ops are charity events and *Family Affair* fan meet-and-greets, the new Kaitlin was much discussed in the media. A leaked demo, touting the star's revved-up image, called "Pa-parazzi Princess," hit airwaves and caused even more drama. (Kaitlin's publicist, Laney Peters, says the demo was nothing more than that, and was not meant for the public. "Kaitlin WILL NOT be making an album and she did not agree with the philosophy of that song," says Peters. "We regret that someone invaded Kaitlin's privacy by releasing it.") Even Kaitlin's mother, Meg Burke, wound up in the press thanks to an infamous interview she gave to *Fashionistas*, which branded her a momager.

But nothing compared to what went down two weeks ago when Kaitlin was at a *Sure* cover shoot. When the afternoon supposedly went haywire (courtesy of an unannounced visit by Ava and Lauren), Kaitlin collapsed and was rushed to Cedars-Sinai Medical Center. Later came this statement from Peters: "Kaitlin became overheated at the *Sure* photo shoot and fainted. The room was really hot and Kaitlin was dehydrated. That is why she passed out. She is so thankful to her fans for their support."

Tongues were immediately wagging with speculation that the star had a drinking problem, or that excess partying was the real cause of Kaitlin's trip to the hospital. What the world wanted to know was what happened to the confident star *TV Tome* named the hottest young star on TV? At the *Pretty Young Assassins* junket over the weekend, Kaitlin finally came clean about that fateful trip to Cedars-Sinai. "You're right—I wasn't dehydrated. I did faint, but it was for a very different reason. I guess you could say I didn't handle the news that *Family Affair* was going off the air very well," she admits. "I should have talked to my friends and family about what I was feeling, but, instead, I bottled it up and tried to just go about my business. I kept pretending that it wasn't happening. I put off meetings about future projects. The truth is, the end of this series is a huge deal and I let fear get the best of me. I didn't know how to spend time away from a set I had been on since I was a pre-schooler.

"I tried to escape my problems rather than deal with them," she adds. Escape came in the form of shopping. (She racked up a four thousand dollar credit card bill in one month, something she claims to never have done before. She is currently paying her parents back with her monthly allowance.) Kaitlin also started hanging out with girls that really weren't her speed. "Lauren and Ava are great," Kaitlin says cautiously, "but I think we have different ideas of what is fun, and mine is being in control, not out of it." (For their part, when asked about Kaitlin at the Hugs Not Drugs charity event on Sunday, Ava, who was hanging out with former *FA*er Alexis Holden, reportedly said, "We're over Kaitlin. This is our new BFF, Alexis.")

Even though Kaitlin tried to escape, her problems found her in different ways. "Every time I would get upset, I would get these frightening heart palpitations, have sweaty palms, and start freaking out," Kaitlin explains. "I tried to ignore what was happening. That's what really happened at the *Sure* shoot. I wasn't dehydrated. I did faint, but the real reason—which I was afraid to admit up until now—is that I had a panic attack." Her doctor explained that Kaitlin was suffering from panic attacks and that she had to find a way to keep her fear in check.

Kaitlin is sorry that she gave her family and friends a scare, and says she is ready to move forward, whatever the future brings. She's considering several new projects at the moment, but says she won't rush into anything unless she's sure it is right for her. She says her brief flirtation with the dark side of Hollywood taught her a good lesson about herself—even if she does wish she hadn't learned it while the whole country was watching. "I may have partied too much, but what I did wasn't illegal," Kaitlin points out. "If the worst thing I do in life is shop too much or dance on a table at a club one time, I think I'll be okay. Sure, I'm embarrassed by my actions, but I'm learning from them. I'm a teenager, and we mess up sometimes. I mess up a lot. But I still think we should be worrying about a lot more important things, like starving children in Africa or global warming. Not whether or not Kaitlin Burke shows up at Shelter."

18. INT. BUCHANAN MANOR—LIVING ROOM —FINAL SCENE
The living room is bare, except for a pile of packed boxes.
The rooms in view are also empty. Moving men continue to
carry furniture past PAIGE, DENNIS, SAMANTHA, and SARA, as
they stand together, watching the men work.

> PAIGE
> I guess that's everything, isn't it?

> DENNIS
> I think so. I told Penelope we'd leave our keys on the
> kitchen counter.

> SARA
> What time is our flight to Miami?

> PAIGE
> I told the pilot we'd be at the private runway at 4
> PM. (She looks at her watch.) We still have a little
> time before we have to go.

> SAMANTHA
> Good. I feel like I need a few more minutes here, you
> know?

> SARA
> Were you okay saying goodbye to Ryan this morning?

SAMANTHA

I think so. Ryan and I are going to try to make the long-distance thing work. (Sara snorts.) He's forgiven me for the way I've been acting and it just makes me realize all the more how special my relationship with him is. (Looks at Paige and Dennis) I'm just glad you guys lifted my grounding long enough for me to say goodbye to him. There is something else I want to say too: I know this doesn't change the way I've acted lately, but I think I'm finally okay with moving to Miami.

PAIGE

I'm glad to hear that, sweetie. I know this is a little scary because it's happening so fast, but I think it's a great move for us. You can't be afraid of change, girls. Change happens whether you want it to or not. And sometimes, like now, it's for the best. This is the time to shake things up. Try new experiences on for size and see how they fit. You never know what you'll find out about yourself when you stretch outside of your comfort zone. There could be a new, better version of you just waiting for the opportunity to come out.

SAMANTHA

I hope you're right.

PAIGE

(Grabs Sam and hugs her. Paige reaches for Sara, who leans in too.) This isn't the end of your story, girls. I promise you, this is just the beginning.

SAMANTHA

You're right. I know things will work out the way they're supposed to. No more fighting fate, right?

PAIGE

(Holds Sam close.) Think of it this way: you realized that a lot quicker than I did. I don't think I picked up on that till I was thirty.

DENNIS

Maybe thirty-five. (Paige punches him in the arm.)

MOVING MAN 1

The truck is all loaded. Is there anything else? (The family looks around the room.)

SAMANTHA

Mom, the painting. (She points to the fireplace and to the family portrait of the four of them, taken several years back.)

PAIGE

Oh my God, you're right. How could we have forgotten to pack that? I guess it's been up there for so long, I think of it as a permanent fixture. (to the moving man)

Could you get me some bubble wrap? We need to wrap
this up. (The man nods and exits the room.)

                        SARA
I don't think Aunt Penelope will want our family
portrait hanging in her new living room, do you?
(giggles)

                        PAIGE
Probably not. But I don't care what hangs there. I'm
just glad your granddaddy is giving her this place so
that it stays in the family. Who knows? Maybe one day
you two will want to move back and live here.

                        SARA
I call first dibs!

Everyone laughs. Paige walks over to the fireplace and Dennis
helps her lift the picture off the wall. They rest it on the
fireplace and stand back to admire it.

                        DENNIS
I've always loved this picture of the four of us. We
looked so happy, didn't we?

                        PAIGE
We are happy, but do you remember what was going
on that day? I think Sara had broken Granddaddy's
favorite vase and we had given her a major time-out

so she was still mad at us. Samantha was coming down with the flu. I was fighting with Krystal over the company finances, and Dennis, you had that hostile takeover you were worried about. We were all so stressed, but we couldn't reschedule so we tried to grin and bear it.

DENNIS

Sara, you had such a pout. We couldn't get you to smile for anything! (laughs) I think I had to bribe you with money to get you to cheer up.

SARA

I remember that! And Sam was sneezing all over me and her nose was running and I kept complaining that she was dripping all over my Burberry dress.

SAMANTHA

I think I was doing it on purpose because I was mad at you for ruining my American Girl doll's hair that morning.

PAIGE

You girls were so cranky that day! (laughs) The whole family had issues, but we all managed to pull together and take a beautiful portrait. I love this picture so. It goes to show that the Buchanans really pull together when we need to. (The four of

them gather together, arm-in-arm.) Nothing can stop
this family, can it? It reminds me of that time we
all had to pitch in at the Buchanan charity ball a
month after you two were born. Do you remember that,
Dennis?

                    DENNIS
How could I forget?

                    SAMANTHA
What happened?

                    DENNIS
(looks at his watch) We can make the pilot wait, can't
we? We do own the jet.

                    PAIGE
I guess it couldn't hurt to stay a few minutes more.
I'm really going to miss this place.

                    SAMANTHA
Me too.

                    SARA
Me three.

                    DENNIS
So let's stay just a few minutes more.

SARA

So that means we have time for that story. Please?

PAIGE

Okay. Well, your father and I were...

PAIGE continues to tell the story, ad-libbed, and the camera
pulls away from the family. The CAMERA SPINS DOWN to focus
on the portrait of the four of them.
MUSIC UP: Coldplay's "Viva la Vida" FADE OUT.

THE END

FIFTEEN: *Read It and Weep*

This is it.

This is my last day on the set of *Family Affair*.

It feels like only yesterday that I walked through these studio doors for the first time. Okay, I don't really remember that day (I was only in pre-school!), but I know it happened. And now *Family Affair* is coming to the end and I feel . . .

Okay.

Seriously. The world doesn't have to worry about me anymore. My family and friends were right. I have to believe in myself. Sure, I don't have a job lined up, but I'll get one. And if it's not as great as I would like after the mess I've made for myself, well, that's okay. Even Drew Barrymore had to climb back up the Hollywood food chain at one point. (Does anyone even remember that she made *Poison Ivy*? I think not.)

"How are you doing?" Nadine wants to know. She's still clinging to my left arm as we walk through the long hallway to my dressing room and then to hair and makeup for the last time. "You're shaking. Do you want some water?" Nadine is rambling. She's wearing her *The Affair Isn't Ending, It's Just Beginning* rhinestone-studded black tee that everyone in the cast and crew got as a gift from Melli last Friday. I've got mine on too. "Do you need to stop for a minute? Because it's okay if you're upset, you know. This is a big day and you can cry if you want. Do you need a paper bag? Do you feel like you're going to throw up?"

"Maybe you should eat something," Rodney suggests. He looks concerned too. "I wasn't sure what you'd be in the mood for this early so I got you chicken fingers and a bagel."

"Nadine! Rod!" I laugh. "I'm okay. I swear." I say this even though my legs are shaking. I can do this. I have to do this. I know that now. "I can handle the walk to hair and makeup. And I'm not hungry yet."

"Okay." Nadine and Rodney don't look convinced. This is what you get for going off the deep end. Serves me right, I guess. Hopefully they'll snap out of this over-protective routine as soon as the magazines stop running those "Kaitlin Burke at the Brink and Back" stories. Laney says they're rating really well. In a recent *Hollywood Nation* poll, 87% of the people polled said they felt sorry for me and knew I'd be okay.

The *Family Affair* hallways are quiet. It's only four AM so I guess they should be. The lights aren't even all on yet. The main switchboard at reception is silent. No one is going to be on set till at least seven. But I have something very important I have to do before we film our final scene.

As we pass the place where the cast portraits hang, I can barely make out my own in the low lighting. I wonder what they're going to do with them when we finish filming and a new show takes over our soundstage. I round the corner and I can see lights on in the hair and makeup room. Paul and Shelly are waiting for me.

"There's our girl," Paul sobs. He yanks my arm away from Nadine and pulls me in tight. He's a mess.

"I told him to get his crying out before I do your makeup," Shelly declares, even though her eyes look a little puffy as well. "He's a mess. I told him he's being ridiculous. It's not like we won't see you. We're doing your hair and makeup for the Avon event next weekend and your *PYA* press is just around the corner."

"If you want you can do my makeup for my SATs. Maybe some bronzer would help me concentrate," I joke. The test is this Saturday and you know what? I actually feel prepared. I haven't gone out at night in two weeks so I've had loads of time to study.

"Don't tease," he wails. His brown curls are tickling my nose as Paul buries his face in my shoulder. "I can't bear the thought of taming someone else's coarse strands every day. I finally have Kaitlin's hair right where I want it. I only want to do hers."

"Paul, could you try being less emotional?" Nadine asks. "Kaitlin really has to be on her game this morning and I don't want her getting extra upset."

"That's right." Paul lets go of me and wipes his eyes. "I didn't mean to freak you out."

I giggle. "You didn't. I'm okay," I tell them all. "Really. Giving that speech at the junket did wonders for my emotional well-being."

"Your quotes were perfect," Shelly says. She steers me to the makeup chair where Paul begins to comb out my frizzy hair and put it in rollers. Shelly gets on the other side of him and begins to work on my foundation. "I've never heard a celebrity be so honest before. And what you said was so true — you're a teenager, and if the worst you do is shop and dance too much, that's not all that bad."

"I couldn't agree more," someone else chimes in. Paul and Shelly stop what they're doing and I turn my chair around.

"Melli!" I'm shocked. "What are you doing here?" She hasn't had hair and makeup yet so her pale face is bare and she's dressed casually in cropped Juicy terrycloth pants and a matching zip-up sweatshirt. Her *Affair* T-shirt peeks out from beneath.

"You didn't really think I'd let you do your *FA* special interview on your own, did you?" She asks with a huge smile.

"Melli, it's four AM! You shouldn't have gotten out of bed for this," I tell her, even though I'm incredibly touched. "I'm the one who has been putting this off for weeks and deserves to be exhausted, not you."

"Please, I'll be sleeping in for months after today," she says with a laugh. "I *want* to be here for you. I don't have to sit in on your interview. I know that would be weird, but I wanted to be ready, outside the door, in case you need anything. I should have been here for you a long time ago."

"Everyone needs to stop feeling sorry for me," I beg. "No one did this to me. I'm just lucky my flirtation with the dark side didn't affect the show. I'd hate if people were so focused on my mini breakdown that they forget about the real story — our awesome show going off the air."

"Well for what it's worth, I think your quotes from the junket were great," Melli offers. "You sounded incredibly adult. I wish I'd had had your poise at that age."

"That's what I told her," Shelly agrees.

"I've never been more proud of you, Kates," Nadine seconds. "You really overcame a lot of pressure these past few weeks. Any director would be lucky to work with you."

"This one sure is," Tom answers as he walks in behind the rest of us. He and Melli embrace. They're so tight. I don't know how they're going to handle not being together every day. "Are you ready to do this?" Tom asks me.

I take a deep breath and nod. Time to face the music. I hop out of my makeup chair. I know Paul and Shelly will have to touch me up after this anyway to get ready for the final scene. We're shooting it in the family living room, which has been dressed down to almost nothing except a few moving boxes. It's so weird to look at.

"Did you use waterproof mascara?" I semi-joke to Shelly.

"Are you kidding? I've been using it on all of you this week!" Shelly tells me.

"Do you want me to go with you?" Nadine asks.

I shake my head. "I think I have to do this by myself," I tell her and Melli. "Besides, you'll get to see this when they air it at the wrap party this weekend."

"Good luck," Nadine says.

Melli and I make our way to my dressing room, where I've decided to tape my film retrospective. In the background of the shot is the Buchanan family portrait, which the crew will have to take back to film our last scene later on today. The picture was what I wanted as my set memento. I also took my locker from school and a tile from Summerville Breads, but the family portrait is what I really wanted. I'm not sure where I'm going to put it ("That is not going up in our living room," Mom declared when I told her what I picked), but I knew I had to have it.

"Knock 'em dead, kiddo," Melli says. "I know you're ready."

"I am, Mel," I tell her. And this time I mean it.

*   *   *

When I finish, it's almost six AM. By now the set is in full-swing. I see Trevor walk by on his way to makeup, and Matty yawns at me as he heads to my dressing room. The hall outside my dressing room door is filled with crew members all in the same black *Affair* T-shirt. Even though it's a sad day, everyone is in a good mood. I'm so glad Tom and Melli didn't agree to let *Celebrity Insider* be on set for our last day. They felt, like I do, that today should be just about our TV family. That's probably for the best. I'd hate for Austin to see me cry any more than he has the last few weeks. And I've already shed a bunch of tears for the camera this morning. Those tears were real, and I'm sure the ones I let fall a few hours from now will be as well.

HOLLYWOOD SECRET NUMBER FIFTEEN: How to cry for the camera. When we shoot scenes with several people, like the final one we're shooting today, they can take a long time to film. You need to get every person's angle, everyone's close-up, and rearrange the cameras and furniture a hundred times to get it done. A scene that takes two minutes on film can take six or seven hours to shoot. You wind up saying the same ten lines over and over for hours and each take has to be just as fresh and perfect as the take before. That's hard when you have to cry like a baby each and every time and make it look real. So how's it done? Some actors keep a raw onion nearby. Others stare at the sun without blinking, or stare straight ahead till their eyes begin to water. But for the rest of us, you really do have to think of something super sad. You know, like your dog dying or the worst moment of your life. For our group, crying should be a piece of cake. We really are saying goodbye to the "house" we've lived in ever since I can remember. I turn my Sidekick on and it buzzes to life. I stare at the screen. I have two new messages. At this hour? I scroll down. It's Austin.

> WOOKIESRULE: Knock 'em dead today. I'll B thinking of U. I can't wait 2 C U tonight.

I smile. And the second one is from Lizzie.

> POWERGIRL82: Hey U. Remember what my Sensei always says: At the end, you find the beginning. Not sure what that means, but sounds appropriate! LOL. Good luck today. I know ULL B great, Kates. Call me when U can. xoxo

It feels so good to see a text from Liz. I'm smiling as I walk onto the set after a hair and makeup touchup. Sky and Melli are standing together and . . . wait. It can't be.

"Are you all right?" I ask Sky.

"No," Sky bawls. "The show is ending, K! Over. Finished. Last day. No more dressing room. No more Pete from crafty! O.V.E.R." She wails.

I look at Melli. "She just realized this?"

Melli gives me a look as Sky sobs even harder. I put my arm around Sky. "It's going to be okay, Sky."

"Yeah, right," Sky whines. "It won't be the same thing. You won't be on my new show. Who am I going to make fun of?" Melli hands her a tissue. Sky blows her nose loudly.

"I'm sure you'll find someone new to loathe," I say hopefully.

"It won't be the same thing." Sky shakes her head. "It's hard finding someone as naïve as you to beat on."

For the final scene, we're all wearing jeans. (We're supposed to look like we've been packing. Yeah, right. What billionaire family actually packs?) Sky has on Citizen of Humanity jeans cuffed at her mid-calf and an olive tank top that makes her look thinner than she already is. I'm wearing Stitch jeans and a cute black Banana Republic top that hugs my chest and then flows to my mid-thigh. I've also got on a long string of beads that keep smacking my belly button when I walk.

Melli clears her throat. "In any case, I want to tell you both that I have loved working with you." Her eyes begin to well up. "You two are like daughters to me and I'm so proud of the fine women you've become."

Now I'm going to cry! "We've got you to partially thank for that," I remind her. The three of us are teary when Tom approaches. I'm not sure if he's going to laugh or cry himself.

"Hey, hey, now, let's save it for the cameras," he jokes, but I can tell he's a bit mushy himself. While only Spencer, Melli, Sky, and I are in the final scene, which is truly the final scene in the show (normally we almost never shoot in order), the rest of the cast has turned up to watch us film. Trevor, Hallie, Ava, Luke, Matty, and the others are all here. Nadine and Rodney and the rest of the crew are on the sidelines too. Even Matty is choked up. "Why don't you three take a breather while we light the scene and we'll call you when we're ready?" he tells us.

I walk over to Matty. "How are you holding up?" he asks.

"Okay," I tell him. "You?"

"I'm a little freaked out," he admits. "I know I have Scooby, but what if it bombs?"

"And you wondered why I was having panic attacks," I joke. "That's been my fear every day for months! Walking away from a hit is never going to be easy."

"You're going to have plenty of other hits," Matty says encouragingly.

"I hope so," I reply softly as I watch our stand-ins. Matty reaches over and squeezes my hand.

"If not, maybe I can get you a walk-on role on my show." He smirks. "After a few seasons, of course."

"Thanks a lot!" I tell him as I watch the scene wind up. One crew member is taping our marks on the floor so we know where to stand; another is filling the water bottles on the living room floor where the Buchanan clan is eating their last meal, picnic-style. Those bottles will be filled and refilled all day for continuity so that they always look filled the same no matter what angle we shoot the scene from. After what feels like an eternity, Tom calls for us.

The first few times we shoot the scene, it feels like any other. I mess up my lines and ask to go back and start over. Sky trips walking to the fireplace. Tom changes the lighting a few times. Spencer and Melli begin ad-libbing their lines more and more till Tom steers them back to the script. Four hours and a lunch break later (Crafty cooked us an extra-special feast of fried chicken and scalloped potatoes, a Buchanan favorite, for our last day, and the whole crew ate together. No one hid out in their dressing rooms for once.), we're finally ready for our last angle.

"This is it, people," Tom tells us. "Our last shot."

"Last looks!" someone yells. That means the crew has one last chance to correct anything before we shoot. Spencer, Melli, Sky, and I get into position.

"I can't believe it," Sky says under her breath. "This is it. This is really it."

"I know." It hits me again and I'm shaking. Sky and I instinctively reach for each other's hand and squeeze tight.

"Quiet, please," Tom tells everyone. The set is rowdy today, but on Tom's command, everyone hushes and a chorus of "shush!" is the only thing heard. When it stops, Tom says, "And we're rolling."

The scene runs smoothly. It should. We've only said these lines twenty zillion times today. But when the actor playing the moving man removes the last box from the room, I feel my eyes overflow with tears. I look around. I'm not alone.

"I remember that!" Sky says in character. "And Sam was sneezing all over me and her nose was running and I kept complaining that she was dripping all over my Burberry dress." She laughs through her tears.

My turn. "I think I was doing it on purpose because I was

mad at you for ruining my American Girl doll's hair that morning."

"You girls were so cranky that day," Melli says and laughs. She admires the family portrait hanging over the fireplace. "The whole family had issues, but we all managed to pull together and take a beautiful portrait." Spencer puts his arm around her. "I love this picture so. It goes to show that the Buchanans really pull together when we need to."

And even though it's not called for in the script — we're supposed to link arms — the four of us wind up in a tight embrace, all sniffling. Tom doesn't call cut though. He lets us keep going. You can hear us crying.

"Nothing can stop this family, can it?" Melli finally says. She wipes away her tears. "It reminds me of that time we all had to pitch in at the Buchanan charity ball a month after you two were born. Do you remember that, Dennis?"

Spencer laughs. "How could I forget?"

"What happened?" I ask.

Spencer looks at his watch. "We can make the pilot wait, can't we? We do own the jet."

"I guess it couldn't hurt to stay a few minutes more," Melli says. "I'm not ready to let go yet," she says, ad-libbing.

"Me either," I say softly, ad-libbing too.

"Same here," Sky sniffs.

"So let's stay," Spencer hesitates, "just a few minutes more."

"Okay," Sky says and smiles. "So that means we have time for that story. Please?"

Melli smiles. "Well, your father and I were on our way to this big charity thing that your granddaddy insisted we go to and . . ." Melli continues to ad-lib with Spencer breaking in for a few minutes until Tom finally says the magic words.

"CUT! That's a final print for *Family Affair!*"

And suddenly everyone on set is clapping and cheering and it's so loud you can barely hear anyone sobbing. We're all hugging each other and crying. Someone starts blasting Rihanna and Pete from crafty is passing around cookies that look like every cast and crewmember there. Matty hugs me and then Trevor gives me a huge kiss on the cheek, before making his way over to Sky, who he practically suffocates with a passionate smack on the lips. (I told him how supportive Sky was of me at the *PYA* junket and I think he was really touched.) No one else notices them making out. We're all too busy celebrating, and grieving, and enjoying the moment. One that I kind of hope lasts for a long time. I grab Rodney and Matty and start dancing. We throw Nadine in the middle of our circle and she lets loose. We dance to four or five songs. I don't even care about my Sidekick buzzing and buzzing in my back pocket.

This is my final *FA* moment and I'm going to make it last.

The rest of my life can wait.

Seth@CC: KAITLIN, WE'VE GOT TO TALK. I'VE GOT NEWS AND I NEED AN ANSWER ASAP.

LaneyPeters: Kaitlin???? Kaitlin Burke??? HELLOOOOO! Seth is trying to reach U! Why aren't U or Nadine picking up your phones? Is everything okay? PLEASE promise you'll have no bad press today.

BurkeMgt: KAITLIN??? Now is not the time to go shopping again! WHERE IS NADINE??? CALL US AS SOON AS YOU GET THIS!!!!!!!!!!!! Love, Mom

ROADRULZ84: Hi Kaitlin. It's Dad. Mom got me a BlackBerry, but I still can't figure out all the buttons. I think I'm emailing you. Mom said to keep it short. She's trying to reach you. She got a call from Seth and Laney about *Meeting of the Minds*. They want to meet with you again, but it has to be tonight so Mom wants to know what time you'll be done with shooting. Can you find out from Tom? I know it's your last day, but do you think you'll be done before 8 PM? That would be great because I END MESSAGE

ROADRULZ84: Oops. Guess I hit send before I was END MESSAGE

SIXTEEN: *An* Affair *to Remember*

"To Kaitlin and Matty for a job well done on a fabulous TV show," Dad holds his champagne flute high in the air.

"Kaitlin and Matty!" Our table cheers.

It's been a week since we wrapped *Family Affair*'s final taping and tonight is our wrap party at Parc, this cool restaurant/club on Hollywood Boulevard. Our entire cast and crew plus friends and family were invited, so we're a pretty large group. Good thing we've closed this place down for our private bash. Austin, Liz, Matty, Nadine, Rodney, Laney, Mom, and Dad are sitting in a deep booth with me. None of us can stop smiling.

Parc is a really pretty spot for a party. The modern space is decorated in all grays and creams, with walnut wood paneling and archways. There are great booths, beautiful ebony table tops, and a high lacquered bar, but the piece de résistance is the fourteen-foot tree in the center of the dining room that is surrounded by twenty-four Swarovski crystal smoked globe pendants. Our table is covered with food. Most of the dishes are meant for sharing, so we've ordered everything from clay pot–baked black pepper caramel cod to grilled black angus tenderloin with truffled soy bearnaise.

"You look happy." Austin leans over and nuzzles my neck. I blush, wondering who is watching.

"I am happy," I admit. "I mean, I'm a little sad. It was weird getting up all week and having nowhere to go. I just hung around waiting for Monique to tutor me. But I think I could get used to not running every day of my life."

"For now." Austin makes an interesting face. "I don't think you're the type to sit still for long."

"Well . . ." I laugh. "I'm not going to be sitting around long anyway, I guess."

"I'd like to thank Tom," Matty keeps the toasts going and holds his vanilla Coke. He looks around the room for *FA*'s creator and director, but he's nowhere in sight. "He knows talent when he sees it. Scooby is going to rock!"

"I love how modest your brother is," Liz whispers in my other ear. We both giggle.

It's been a good week. Liz and I are back to being our inseparable selves, Austin got his license and gets to borrow his mom's Ford Explorer now to take us around town. (Mom lifted my grounding. She still makes Rodney tail us.) Matty finished his Scooby pilot. I took my SATs and felt pretty confident that I would get a decent score. And . . .

"To New York and Kaitlin's Broadway debut!" Mom holds up her glass and grins.

Yep. I'm moving to New York for a few months this spring to make my stage — and Broadway — debut. On the last day of *FA* shooting, Seth got the offer for me to play Andie in *Meeting of the Minds*. I'm really nervous and excited, but I haven't had any panic attacks. I know I can tackle live theater. And maybe doing something other than TV or movies for a short while will be a good change for me.

"So I was thinking we should start planning some activities for Kaitlin while she's in New York," I hear my Mom confide in Laney. "Some appearances at some great parties and Broadway premieres, and let's see if we can get a list of Hamptons events."

"You do realize Kaitlin is working six days a week and is usually only off on Mondays, right?" Laney tells her. "She's not going to have a lot of time for parties."

My mom ignores her. "She'll make time. I just want to have everything in order since you won't be with us." Mom actually looks worried.

"I'll be there plenty," Laney insists. "Russell has to do *GMA* and *Regis* and God knows I can't let him go on alone, and Reese is accepting an award from *Glamour* in July, and then there's my summer share in the Hamptons with Cameron."

"Basically, what you're saying is we're going to be seeing you a lot," Nadine fills in the blanks and winks at me.

Thank God she's coming with me too. The whole family

decided to pack up and join me in New York. (If Matty's show gets picked up for the fall, he'll need to be back in July, which is when my three-month run ends anyway.) I'm not sure if it's to keep me out of trouble or just to run my life, but I'm glad I won't be alone. I just wish Austin and Liz were coming with me too. But we all have different lives to live, I know.

"We should discuss the apartment situation," Dad says. "I've been looking at a bunch of real estate and I'm torn between something expansive in the Village or a high-rise near midtown so that it's easier for Kate-Kate to get to work. It's going to be rough not having wheels to take us everywhere."

Dad is having a tough time getting used to the fact that he won't be driving a lot for a few months. Me, I'm glad, since I'm no closer to getting my license today than I was three months ago. Taking driving lessons is at the top of my to-do list — as soon as we get back from New York.

"Now Kaitlin, you realize your room in New York is going to be much smaller than the one at home," my dad tells me. "As a matter of fact, you're going to have to bunk up, like the rest of us."

"I have to share a room with Matty?" I freak.

"I am not sharing a room with her, Dad," Matty pipes up. "Everything she owns is pink! And her clothes will take over the whole closet. I can't get my Prada squished!"

"You two aren't rooming together. Your sister has another roommate," Dad says.

Matty and I look at Nadine. She shakes her head firmly. "I already told your parents that if I'm coming, and we all have to live together, I get my own room. I need *some* privacy."

Now I'm really confused. "Who am I rooming with?" I want to know.

"Me," Liz yells.

"What?" I shriek.

"I got in the program," Liz says. "At NYU. The summer one. My dad talked to your dad and instead of living on campus, I'm going to be your roomie this summer!"

We both scream and Laney holds her ears.

"I don't believe it!" I freak. "Why didn't you tell me?"

"I only found out on Wednesday," Liz explains. "And I wanted to surprise you. Can you believe it, Kates? You and me in New York together. Like we've always wanted."

"I know!" I exclaim. "This is going to be amazing."

"Hopefully it will keep her out of trouble," Mom says to Dad.

"I can hear you, you know," I remind her.

"Hey, Burkes," Tom walks over to our table in an Armani suit and tie. He's never this dressed up on set so it's funny to see. "Have you put in your bids for the auction yet?"

We're auctioning off the wall-size portraits of the cast that hung in the *Family Affair* studio. They actually cut the sheet rock right out of the wall so that we could take each wall down and sell them to the highest bidder. The money raised from each person's portrait will go to a different charity. (Mine is going to DonorsChoose.org, a group that funds books and classroom materials for schools that can't afford it.)

"Tom, if we win, do we have to take the portrait?" Mom asks sweetly. Dad nudges her. "I just mean, I'm not sure Kaitlin's wall-size portrait really goes with what we have in our house and I just had a decorator redo the living room, so . . ."

"You can donate them, Meg," Tom says, his face twitching slightly. "Maybe Kaitlin would sign it and we can give it away. What do you think, Kates?" I nod yes.

"I would have been happy to do that myself, but I never got a portrait," Matty sniffs. The regular cast members all have cast portraits, but the recurring stars, like Matty, didn't get them.

"Maybe you'll have one for your new show," I say encouragingly and Tom winks at me.

"That's a good idea! We should talk about that, Tom," Matty looks excited now.

"Why don't we wait for a full-season pickup," Tom laughs. "Who knows? If we take off, we can hire your sister to guest-star."

"That's what I said," Matty admits.

"That's what everyone keeps offering me!" I laugh. "Well, I will be unemployed after July."

"I'm sure it won't be for long," Tom tells me. "I bet someone will woo you back to TV before you know it."

"I don't know," I smirk. "I have to say I enjoy not getting up at five AM anymore."

The more I think about things — and I've had a lot of time to think this week while I've been lying by our pool — I secretly think I would like to be on another TV show. I know some actors complain about playing the same character for months or years, but if you have a great character, and awesome scripts, there's so much ground to cover. I loved playing Sam, but I would kill to take on an action series, kind of like the stuff I did for *PYA*. I can so see me scaling buildings in leather pants. I could be a modern day Princess Leia! But if I do get the chance to go back to TV, I won't charge a fortune like some people I know.

HOLLYWOOD SECRET NUMBER SIXTEEN: How much stars get paid to stay on hit shows. Networks will do anything to have a hit show and they still seem to think a bankable name is a way to make money. I know some small film stars that command $80,000 an episode to head to the small screen. But some insiders are starting to worry that the fan connection can be ruined when they hear a star makes over $150,000 an episode. You don't want to be seen as a gold-digger. One of these days, salaries are going to take a huge nosedive. I just know it.

"I think I'm going to bid on one of the portraits," I tell everyone. Mom raises her right eyebrow. "Do you think I could get an advance on my allowance?"

"At this rate, you're not going to have an allowance again till you're twenty," Mom tells me. I give her a pleading look.

"But I guess this is for a good cause so go ahead. But don't bid too much!"

Austin follows me. He grabs my hand. His is warm and I hold it tightly.

"What am I going to do without you all summer?" He asks. He's smiling, but he looks serious. Almost sad. I realize we haven't talked about this separation yet. Austin got into his lacrosse camp so he and his buddy Rob Murray are going to be in San Antonio, Texas, all summer working on their lacrosse moves.

"I don't know," I admit softly. "What am I going to do without you? New York is one of the most romantic cities in the world and I'm not going to have my boyfriend to share it with."

Austin moves us into a dark corner near the wine storage area by the bar. We stare at each other. This is the first time we'll really be apart since we started dating. Three whole months is a long time. But this is who I am and this is who Austin is so I guess it was coming eventually. If it didn't happen now, it would probably happen next year when he went to college. But now that the time is staring us straight in the face the whole thing feels very real and I'm afraid to hear what Austin thinks.

"What do we do?" I ask nervously. Does Austin think we should take a break? What if he falls for some hot sporty lacrosse player? His camp is co-ed.

Austin gives me an odd look. "What do you mean? Did you want to take a break?"

"NO!" I say it a little forcefully. "I mean, not unless you wanted to." Please say no. Please, please say no.

Austin smiles. "I like you, Burke. No, in fact, I love you. You're the one I want to be with — whether you're thousands of miles away or standing right in front of me."

Awww . . . he still loves me! That's a relief. He hasn't said it in a long time so I was getting kind of worried.

"Good." I look down shyly. "Because I love you too. And who knows? Maybe you can come visit me."

"I plan on sitting in that theater and seeing you at least once," Austin promises. I look up and see his face, staring at mine so intently. His blue eyes so serious, his windswept bangs hanging in his eyes, his neck smelling like Beckham, his navy Polo button-down, which makes him look better than any guy here in a Prada suit . . . I am so into this boy. And when he stares at me like this, I still go weak in the knees.

"Who knows? Maybe I can come see you in Texas." I start to ramble as he traces a finger along my bare shoulder. Tonight I'm wearing a strapless white dress with black lace and tiny black DKNY heels. "I don't have a weekend off or anything, but I bet I could fly out Sunday night after my performance and come back Tuesday AM. Nadine could probably book me a flight or if she can't I could get a jet or something. I'm sure I could convince Mom to let me do it if I —" Austin kisses me and I finally stop talking.

"We'll work it out," he says. And I know when he says that, he means it.

"Okay," I agree and push my hair off my neck. It's down and super curly tonight and suddenly I'm feeling very warm.

"You two need to get a room," Sky says as she tries to slide past us. She's wearing what looks like a John Galliano. It's a tan halter-style empire waist dress with little black flowers. Her hair has been ironed pin straight. On her arm is the best accessory she could hope for — Trevor. I think they're finally seeing each other again.

"You're one to talk," I tell Sky. "You two haven't come up for air all night!"

Trevor and Sky look at each other and blush. "Congrats on your play," Sky tells me. "I saw that show when I was in London and it was fabulous."

"Thanks," I tell her. "I'm looking forward to it."

"Maybe when you get back we could go on a double date," Trevor says hopefully.

Sky and I look at each other. Double with Sky? We're both at a loss for words at that one.

Thankfully, Melli interrupts before we have to answer that question. "There you all are!" she says. Melli looks dazzling in a shimmery blue dress, her hair pulled back in a small tight ponytail. She puts an arm around me. "I was just talking to your moms, girls. I was telling them how much I missed seeing you two this week. I feel like one of my kids went to college."

"We talked every day," I remind her. "But yeah, it was weird not to bust into your dressing room and complain about Sky or boy problems." I glance at Austin. "Not that I have any."

"You are the queen of smart PR moves," Melli tells me. "I'm so excited that you're going to do Broadway. I did it once in my twenties and it was exhilarating. Grueling, but a ton of fun working with a live audience. You're going to wow them. I'm trying to convince my husband to take a trip to New York so we can see you. Tom says he wants to come too."

"Really?" I'm so touched I don't know what to say. "I would love that."

"Good." Melli's eyes look watery. "Because you're not rid of me just because I'm not down the hall."

Now I feel the sniffles coming on. "Thank God for that," I tell her. I give her a kiss on the cheek. "Thanks, Melli."

"And as for my other daughter," Melli says, putting an arm around Sky, "I love your new pilot. I read the script and it sounds like it's a shoo-in for the fall schedule."

Sky's show does sound incredible. The *True You* book says to be happy for her, but it's kind of hard. A tiny part of me is still jealous that I screwed that one up.

"Thanks," Sky gushes. "The role is to die for and my director said I killed on the pilot. If we get picked up, the show is going to be Emmy-nominated for sure."

I smile sweetly because I'm afraid I'll accidentally say something I regret.

"This could be the last time you two see each other for a

while," Melli tells us, sounding a lot like Paige, "and I want to make sure you two part on good terms." I feel my shoulders tense. "You don't want to burn too many bridges in this town, girls," Melli continues when neither of us speaks up. "Hollywood may seem like a big place, but everyone knows everyone here and chances are you'll find yourselves doing a project together down the road or bump into each other at the same functions."

Sky and I look at each other.

"I don't think you have to worry about us anymore," I tell Melli, even though I'm still looking at Sky. "We understand each other now and I think if our work paths cross again we're going to be okay."

"More than okay," Sky says and then actually smiles.

"Could I have everyone's attention?" Tom interrupts. He has a microphone and is addressing the large crowd. "We're going to get to the auction in a little bit, but I know several people wanted to make speeches and I want to be the one to start."

Austin, Melli, Sky, Trevor, and I make our way to where Tom is standing. I can see Mom, Dad, Matty, Rodney, and Nadine, and Austin and I walk over to them. In the crowd, I see Pete from crafty, Paul and Shelly, and Renee from wardrobe. We listen as Tom talks about his first season on the show, his favorite episode, and how proud he is of everything we've achieved over the years. Melli is the next to take the mic and she tells a hilarious story about shooting her first kissing scene with Spencer. One by one, cast members volunteer to speak. Finally, it's my turn.

I make my way through the crowd and take the microphone from Sky. Then I turn and face the room. I see all the faces I know so well and I smile.

"If there is anyone in this room who might be in denial about *Family Affair* ending, we all know it's me," I say and everyone laughs. "I've taken this really hard, but I know I'm not alone anymore." The crowd grows quiet. "You guys are like a second family to me." I feel myself begin to get choked up, but I try to fight it. "The thing that helps me get through all this is that I know we're going through it together. This show and the people who make it are a big part of all our lives and just because we stop taping the show doesn't mean that won't continue. I'm going to take with me everything you've taught me and hopefully the next project I work on will be that much better because of everything I learned from you. I love you guys so much," I say and now the tears are coming. "Thank you for a great run."

Everyone applauds. Trevor whistles. Even Sky looks weepy. I hand the microphone to Trevor and make my way back over to my family and friends. Mom is crying. Dad pats me hard on the back a few times and I know he's trying to hold it together. Liz squeezes my hand tightly. Then I turn and kiss Austin.

"You sounded great up there," he tells me softly. "And you're right, this is not the end for any of you," Austin says.

"You've got the play to look forward to, and me to come home to, and so much more."

I grin. "You're right." I hold him tight. "It's kind of exciting, isn't it?" I have goosebumps.

Who knows what I'll be doing next week, or three or six months from now? But you know what? It doesn't matter. I'll make it work. Whatever happens next, I'm sure it's going to be a great adventure.

Kaitlin Burke Tackles Broadway!

by **Marleyna Martin**

Family Affair's **Samantha is all grown up and taking on her toughest role yet—live theater—in the Broadway smash** *Meeting of the Minds*. **Does she have what it takes?**

Kaitlin Burke is a pro when it comes to television drama. After years playing Samantha Buchanan, this 17-year-old has perfected the art of a good catfight, how to brawl with her mom and cry over boyfriend problems. But is she ready to do it all live? Come this May, she'll have to. Kaitlin begins a ten-week run in *Meeting of the Minds* playing wise-cracking Andie Amber. She takes over for original, beloved castmember Meg Valentine. The surprise casting choice has many wondering: Does Kaitlin have the chops for such a part? "Kaitlin was genius as Sam, and had some great film roles to date, but it will be a real test to her strength as an actress for her to take on Andie," admits one casting agent. "Hollywood will be watching very closely." We checked in with Kaitlin to hear how she's readying for a move to New York.

HN: Kaitlin Burke on Broadway! How does it feel to know your name will soon be up in lights?
KB: Exciting, nerve-wracking, thrilling ... I still can't believe it's happening. I'm so thankful that the cast has given me the opportunity to work with them.

HN: Have you ever done live theater before?
KB: Um, no. (laughs) I've done acting workshops that teach you how to ready yourself for the stage, but this will be my first time in front of a live audience.

HN: Emma Price, who plays Jenny, is a bit of a firecracker, as well as a trained theater actress. Are you

ready to go toe-to-toe with her?

KB: I hope I will be when the time comes! (laughs) I've only met Emma briefly, but she was really nice. I head to New York in April, after I finish press for *Family Affair*'s final episode.

HN: Dylan Carter, your love interest in the play, is easy on the eyes, isn't he?

KB: He's definitely cute, but I'm taken!

HN: What are you most looking forward to doing in New York?

KB: Everything. Seeing the museums, shopping, checking out all the landmarks. My mom is looking into a trip out to the Hamptons too. I keep telling her I don't get much time off. I don't think she's listening. •

Kaitlin's run in Meeting of the Minds *starts May 1.*

DON'T STOP READING YET . . .

You didn't think that just because my show ended, my story had too, did you?

No way!

My career is far from over. First stop: New York, New York. The stage is going to be a whole new experience for me and what better place to have it than Manhattan? Mom says I'm already getting invitations to fetes from the Upper East Side to the Hamptons. But don't worry, I'm going to keep things low-key this time around. I've had my fill of being a gossip girl. This summer, I'm all about work. I just hope the critics don't pan me. Nadine says the tabloids already started quizzing every casting agent out there about my chances of getting a standing ovation. Sigh.

At least I have my family and friends for support. Everyone is coming to New York, and with Liz as my roomie, I know we're going to have a blast. I just wish Austin was coming too. What's an extended vacation in New York without your boyfriend to treat you to a carriage ride through Central Park? I'm sure it will work out, though. Hollywood is all about happy endings.

But wait. We're not talking about Hollywood anymore, are we? I'm going to be in New York and that's a whole different ballgame. What do they always say about the Big Apple? If you can make it there, you can make it anywhere. I hope I'm ready.

BROADWAY LIGHTS
SECRETS OF MY HOLLYWOOD LIFE

Coming in May 2010

Acknowledgments

I have nothing but love for my amazing editors, Cindy Eagan and Kate Sullivan. Not only are they well-versed in all things Kaitlin, they also come up with cool *Secrets* titles, like this one — *Paparazzi Princess*! (Special thanks go to Kate for helping me fine-tune Kaitlin's "Paparazzi Princess" song. Even with her help, it is safe to say I will probably never add songwriter to my resume.)

My agent Laura Dail deserves huge praise, not only for always having my back, but for putting up with endless phone calls from me worrying about plot points, deadlines, and the like, all of which — as she patiently points out — come together nicely in the end. And to Tamar Ellman, for helping me brave foreign waters and their confusing contracts.

To the amazing team at Little, Brown Books for Young Readers — Ames O'Neil, Melanie Chang, Andrew Smith, Lisa Ickowicz, Melanie Sanders, and Tracy Shaw (for yet another brilliant cover design) — I can't thank you enough for showering *Secrets* with so much love.

To Mara Reinstein, who I bombarded with e-mails and calls about paparazzi practices, catfights, and celebrity melt-downs — I'm eternally grateful (as always).

Special thanks go to my tireless mom, Lynn Calonita, who has logged more hours with Tyler than a grand-mother/babysitter should have to, just to make sure I al-ways make my deadlines. I really couldn't do any of this without you. Love also to my dad, Nick Calonita, Nicole and John Neary, my grandfather Nick Calonita, Gail Smith, and Brian Smith for their endless support.

Finally, to my wonderful family — my husband Mike, my son Tyler, and our way-too-pampered Chihuahua, Jack — thank you for making home the sweetest place to be.

If you love
SECRETS OF MY HOLLYWOOD LIFE,
you'll adore Jen Calonita's
Sleepaway Girls

a novel by SECRETS OF MY HOLLYWOOD LIFE author
Jen Calonita

When Sam's best friend gets her first boyfriend, she's not ready to spend the summer being a third wheel. So she applies to be a camp counselor-in-training at Whispering Pines. But it's not going to be all kumbayya and s'mores. If Ashley, the camp's queen bee, doesn't ruin Sam's summer, then her raging crush on the cute and flirtatious Hunter just might. At least she has the gang of girls who become fast friends with her—the Sleepaway Girls.

Keep your eye out for *Sleepaway Girls*.
Jen Calonita's newest novel is a fresh look into
the world of sleepaway summer camp— where the
queen bee can make life hell for a new CIT.

Coming in May 2009.

SLEEPAWAY GIRLS

Two hours later, Mom and I were practically running to the mess hall, which according to the map was right down this super green, grassy hill. My heart was in my throat as I raced up the wood building's well-worn wood steps and pulled open the double doors. The large, open room had high ceilings with wood beams that held up rows and rows of camp banners. THE GREEN MACHINE — 2003 COLOR WAR VICTORS! announced one. WELCOME (BACK) TO THE PINES! declared a large red one. And across the back wall was a glass cabinet full of trophies. The only thing missing were the people. Mom and I were standing in front of rows of empty picnic tables covered with folders and papers and discarded jackets. "They're not here." I freaked out. I was actually yelling. One of my biggest pet peeves was being late.

"Samantha Montgomery?" I heard someone bellow, and I turned around.

"Yes?" I said uncertainly.

A tall man wearing camouflage fatigues and holding a mega-phone was walking toward us. He had white hair, was tan like it was the middle of August instead of late June, and his teeth were an eerie shade of white. The man bounded up the steps and shook my hand vigorously. "Alan Hitchens, but you can call me Hitch."

"Hi, Hitch," I shook his hand lightly and smiled nervously. "I'm really sorry we're late. There was an accident on the ex-pressway and . . ." I stopped talking.

Hitch had dropped my hand and was looking at my mother. "Pamela, it's so nice to finally meet you," he said with a large smile.

My mom made that weird gurgling sound again. "It's nice to meet you too, Alan," Mom gushed, smoothing her fitted, white button-down shirt self-consciously. "I'm sorry Sam is late." Now that we were out of the car and I could get a good look at Mom, I realized she had dressed up for this meeting. Gone were her usual working or weekend attire (suits or sweats and oversized tees, respectively) and in their place she had on tailored khaki capris and Coach ballet flats that didn't mask her height (5' 9½"), but did look nice. She was wearing makeup on her pale face and her brown hair, so similar to my own in all but texture, was its usual straight self.

"A few counselors are late and I suspect they're all in the same position," Hitch said and turned to me. "Sam, why don't you say good-bye to your mom, and I'll help her unload your bags so you can head down to the field and join the game. Ask for Alexis. She's my eldest daughter."

"Game?" I had only been here five minutes and I was already confused.

Hitch looked from me to my mother. "I find the best way to figure out which CITs belong with which counselors is to get them involved in teamwork. There's time to go over rules and paperwork during grub or campfires. Today they're playing dodgeball."

"Dodgeball?" I asked. I hadn't played dodgeball since the sixth grade and I wasn't good at it back then. I had a hard time playing any game that involved flying balls, which ruled out most gym activities and really aggravated my gym teacher, Mrs. Pepper.

"That's a wonderful idea," my mom gushed. Now that I'd met Hitch, I wasn't so sure he was my mother's type. Where he was all outdoorsy and tanned like a camp director should be, Mom's skin was milky white from too many hours at the office. The last time she did something outside, it was directing the guys from Crate and Barrel on how to unload her new dresser from the truck. Mom gave me a hug. "Well, this is it," she said, sounding choked up. "Have a great time and I'll talk to you in a few days, before I leave on my business trip."

"Thanks, Mom," I said, feeling awkward in front of Hitch. As I walked away, I could still hear Mom laughing at something Hitch said, but suddenly I felt very alone.

What was I thinking, going to camp? I had no idea what camp involved, and I certainly had never flown solo before. I didn't know anyone on that dodgeball field. I didn't have a best friend to stand next to or even a semi-good friend I could chat with about stupid stuff. I was the newbie, and being the newbie was awkward.

Baby steps, I thought to myself. Just take baby steps. I breathed in the pine scent of the evergreens that lined the dusty dirt path that was spraying dirt all over my feet. One step. Two.

I could do this.

When I got to the bottom of the hill, I could see the game had already started on a slightly muddy field that was boxed in by white spray-painted lines. Just a few yards away were the tennis courts and another field that had bags of athletic equipment waiting on it. There was an overwhelming scent of manure and I realized that the horse stables were on my left. I stood there, taking the scene in, and tried not to pass out from nerves.

That's when I saw him.

He was running across the field — shirtless, I might add — and he leapt in front of me and caught the dodgeball seemingly in slow motion. This guy was like an Abercrombie ad come to life. He was tall, but not so tall that I'd have to stand on my tip-toes to reach his lips. He had longish, dirty blond hair that would make Zac Efron's look lame, killer tanned abs that looked like they'd been airbrushed in, and eyes as green as my jade bedroom comforter.

"Hunter!" A pretty girl screamed as the guy threw the ball and it whisked by her face. "You almost hit me," she whined.

His name was Hunter. Hunter and Sam "LastNameUnknown." It had a nice ring to it.

"Sorry, Ash," he said, out of breath. "It's a game. You've got to move or be moved."

At that moment Mr. Ab-solutely perfect, aka Hunter "LastNameUnknown," looked up and saw me. "Water break!" he announced, not taking his eyes off mine, which were blinking rapidly. "Hey," he said and smiled.

I looked around. Yep, I was the only one in this direction. My future husband was talking to me. ME! If I wasn't nervous enough before, I was ready to freak out now. My experience with guys was limited, but when they were that cute, I could barely function.

"You're the new CIT, right?" he asked.

"The new," I repeated dumbly. "You mean I'm the only new one you have?" The thought was terrifying. That meant everyone already knew everyone. I was the only new girl my age. The only one? How could that be? My lack of camp experience was going to stick out like a sore thumb.

He laughed. Not in a mean way, just loud and deep. "As far as I can tell," Hunter said. "What's your name?" he asked me as tried my hardest not to drool over his sweaty torso. "You look familiar," he added.

Uh-oh. I knew that look. I really hoped to avoid this, but I guess that was asking the impossible. The Dial and Dash commercial was so popular it had aired on the Super Bowl twice and been dissected on everything from CNN to the pages of US Weekly. People at the Pines were bound to have seen it.

"My name is Sam." I couldn't take my gaze off his eyes. Up close I could see they were green with flecks of gold in them.

"Hunter," he said revealing a mouth full of perfectly straight, white teeth. Any sense of recognition he had a moment ago seemed to vanish, thank goodness. "Join us for dodgeball," he suggested. "We're short on my side so I guess you're with me. You can stand over there." He pointed to a line of girls who were staring at me curiously.

In a daze, I walked over to my designated spot, trying hard not to slip in the mud that came from the week's worth of rain we had just had in the tri-state area. I smiled awkwardly at the girl next to me. She had red hair and glasses and was wearing a Hello Kitty T-shirt. I looked at her feet. She was smart enough to wear sneakers.

"He's hot, right?" she whispered and took a puff of what looked like an inhaler.

It didn't take a genius to know who she was talking about. "Yes." I sighed. "I'm Sam," I said shyly.

She smiled, revealing her braces. "Emily Kate. But you can call me Em. You're the new CIT, right?"

I guess it was true then. I really was the only new girl. "That's me," I said, trying to sound at ease.

Em nodded. "At the opening breakfast this morning they said there was one new CIT. Everyone else in the program graduated from campers. I'm a CIT too." Em stopped talking and stared at me curiously. "I'm sorry. It's just . . . have we met before?"

Stupid Dial and Dash moment. I couldn't escape it! "Do you live on Long Island?" I asked. I put a hand over my forehead to pretend to block the sun when I was really trying to cover up my face.

I heard a loud laugh and turned around. The pretty, whiny blond girl from earlier was flirting with *my* Hunter. Okay, maybe he wasn't mine yet, but a girl could hope! I watched as she touched his chest and pretended to push him. "That's Ashley," Emily told me. "She's a CIT too."

"Are they dating?" I had to ask.

"No." Em shook her head. "Hunter is a counselor. CITs can't date counselors. It's against the rules. Not that Ashley hasn't broken them before." Em grinned. "Ashley usually gets whatever guy she wants. They worship her."

It was easy to see why. Ashley looked like she belonged on *America's Next Top Model*. She had perfectly straight, non-frizzy blond hair, bronzed skin, and gray eyes. She was also super-skinny. She'd have to be to pull off that baby blue ribbed tank top she was wearing. I repressed the urge to hate her on sight. There was something very familiar about her. I felt like I'd seen her running across a field, or swimming laps in a lake. But how? "I feel like I know her or something," I said as several people started to take the field again. Water break must have been almost over.

"You probably saw her on the camp video," Em offered. "Ashley is the camp model. She's on the cover of the camp brochure, in the commercials, the camp video, all over the merchandise catalog. She's pretty much the Pines spokesgirl." I followed Em onto the field and waited anxiously for the game to start up again. I just hoped I didn't embarrass myself.

So that explained it! She's the one who told me and Mom — on video of course — that the Pines had world-class camping facilities and a list of activities to choose from that any camper would dream of. Before I could ask Em anything else, Ashley and a few other girls took places next to us and started talking.

"How was your year, Ash?" someone asked.

"Busy," Ashley said, with a flip of her blond hair. "I had to shoot a whole new line of stuff for camp, on top of the cheer-leading calendar I agreed to do at school. My coach saw the Pines stuff and thought my face would so sell a charity calendar."

"Wow," a few girls said breathlessly.

"I met with some modeling agencies in New York too," Ashley added as she examined her bright pink nails.

"Did you sign with one?" another girl asked.

"Not yet," Ashley said quickly. "I'm still trying to decide who I like best. They all seem to want me, you know?" Ashley thumbed the girl next to her's blue shirt. "Cute tee, Candace!"

"Thanks," the girl said shyly. "You really like it?"

"Absolutely," Ashley said sounding chipper. "Old Navy, right? I have the exact same one. Well, the designer version. Mine is Juicy."

"Hey," a blond girl said to me as she jogged over and stood next to Em. She looked buff and super tan, but I got the feeling it came from being the outdoorsy type rather than a tanning bed queen. Her whole look screamed sporty. "I'm Grace," she said. "Are you the new CIT?"

"Yes, I'm Sam," I said.

Grace was staring at me intently. "Do I know you from somewhere?" she said. "Do you play field hockey?"

"That's exactly what I said!" Em nudged Grace in the ribs. "I feel like we've met before."

Oh no. They'd seen it. Any second now they were going to figure it out. I searched the group for Hunter. He was standing a few feet away throwing and catching the dodgeball into the air as he talked to a few other guys. Start the game, I begged him silently. Before they realize that I'm —

Grace gasped. "You're that girl from the Dial and Dash commercial!"

Shoot. I glanced around. Grace was so loud, people looked over to see what the fuss was about. Including Hunter, and Ashley and her group, who had turned around and were suddenly listening.

"That's right!" Em seconded. "I love that commercial."

"It's so genius," agreed Grace. "Your cell phone dies and you can't call your boyfriend to say good-bye before his trip," Grace narrated as a small crowd started to gather.

"And so you swim through that river, jump over a building, and steal a motorcycle all so you can get to a store that sells a Dial and Dash phone so you can call him immediately," Em finished excitedly. The two of them looked at me expectantly. "That was you, right? Did you do your own stunts?"

There was no denying it now. "That was me," I said and people began to murmur. "But I didn't actually leap over a building or ride a motorcycle."

Stupid Dial and Dash moment. There were hundreds of commercials on TV every day, but for some reason the *one* I made, stuck. I liked making video diaries that were just for me, or video messages for my friends. I never wanted to be the next Jessica Alba.

"That was the best commercial," Grace gushed. "So are you a model?"

"No," I said quickly and sighed. "It's a long story, but the short version is that I did this low-budget test video for my mom's company. It was part of an advertising pitch they were making to Dial and Dash Phone. The actress they hired dropped out last minute so my mom enlisted me. No one was supposed to see it but the Dial and Dash people. But when they did, they loved it so much they wanted to shoot the commercial for real. The catch was, I had to be in it. I can't even get up in front of class to make a speech or read a report so it was kind of terrifying. But it was the only way my mom's company could get the deal so I caved."

"Lucky you," Ashley interrupted. Her arms were folded across her chest and I could tell she was taking me in from head to toe. "I'm Ashley," she said with a bright smile. "I'm actually a *real* model and actress. I've done some commercial work myself."

"Sam," I said for what felt like the tenth time today. Ashley was staring at me so intently I felt uneasy.

"Ash, isn't that commercial the best?" One of her friends nudged her. "I loved the part when you jumped the building," she said to me.

"She didn't actually jump," Ashley interrupted. "Didn't you hear her?"

"Stunt double," I told the girl.

"Have you ever done anything else other than that *one* commercial?" Ashley asked. "Because the business is tough, you know. I've been working for years and —"

"You made a commercial, Ash?" her friend interrupted.

"For the Pines, yeah," Ashley snapped.

"But a national commercial?" the girl asked again.

"You guys ready to play?" Hunter interrupted the increasingly awkward conversation at the perfect moment. I had almost forgotten he was standing nearby the whole time. Now he knew my dirty little secret. Hunter had the dodgeball under his arm and he was grinning at me.

"Yes!" I said a little too loudly.

"Great," Hunter said. "I like a newbie who's ready for action." I tried not to blush.

Ashley and the girls dispersed after that, and I walked onto the field and continued to stare at Hunter and his cute, tight butt, covered in navy nylon shorts, as he walked in front of me. "Hunter, wait! Time!" A girl on the other team said and waved him over to talk. I stared at Hunter's bare, sweaty back as he ran. That's when I heard a low groan.

"Oh no. I know that look," a guy next to me said.

I looked left, then right, and then realized the guy was talking to me. "What look?" I asked him before I actually turned to face him, which was probably good considering he was beyond cute. He had slightly curly short brown hair that fell in his blue eyes and he reminded me of a Jonas Brother — tall, thin, and dark-haired. He was wearing red nylon shorts and a white T-shirt that was already muddy. I could make out the outline of his toned abs and muscles through the slightly sheer shirt and I quickly looked away and then couldn't help looking back again.

He gave me a sly grin, revealing a dimple in his right cheek. "The look that all the girls here get when they're falling for Hunter Thomas," he pointed out.

I inhaled sharply. "I'm not falling for Hunter." I folded my arms. "I was actually looking at the other team. I'm just trying to scope out our competition."

He laughed. "Whatever you say," he said. "I'm Cole, by the way, not that you'd notice when you're drooling over Hunter."

"I wasn't drooling," I said, feeling a swell of indignation. I had no idea my Hunter infatuation was so obvious. What if Hunter overheard Cole? I'd seriously pass out right there and they'd have to play over me. "I do not like him, okay?" I seethed.

Cole looked at me curiously. "Good," he said softly.

Wait. What? "Why? I mean, what do you care?" I asked.

Cole shrugged. "The truth is, a girl like you could do a lot better than Hunter."

"What makes you say that?" I had to know.

"Maybe I'm wrong, but you look normal. And nice." Cole said. He had an arrogant grin on his face that I wanted to wipe off. "Nice girls with potential acting careers have a lot more going for them than to spend their summer fawning over Hunter."

"I'm not an actress," I pointed out. I guess Cole had overheard our conversation too. "I'm anything but."

"You could be," Cole said. "People flipped for that commercial. I bet Hollywood came banging on your door."

"They did," I admitted without thinking. I usually didn't tell people that. "But I wasn't interested. I'm not. I really don't . . ." How could I explain it? "I'm not one for being the center of attention," I said. "I like to help people, and I like to get involved, but I don't really want to be the star." Wow. I had never really told a stranger that before.

Cole shook his head. "I get it," he said, "but I have a feeling that you're going to be one around here. Hunter is going to be all over that."

We both looked over at Hunter, who had finished talking to the girl from earlier and was now leaning on two short CITs, laughing. Why wasn't he starting the game already? I wanted all these awkward conversations over with. "Don't get me wrong,"

Cole added. "I like the guy. He's a decent friend to other dudes, usually, but to girls, well . . ."

I was starting to feel defensive of my crush. "He's friendly," I said.

Cole sighed. "He is friendly. Too friendly, and I feel it's my duty to warn you that he's also a major flirt and a serial dater. He loves hitting on CITs because he knows it will never go any further than that."

I looked at Hunter again. I didn't see anything particularly flirty about him, even if he was talking to two CITs. Cole moved closer to me then and I took a step back. Wow, his eyes really were unreal. They were as blue as the cloudless sky, and he had long eyelashes that I would have killed for.

"Don't fall for Hunter Thomas, okay?" Cole told me, sounding serious, instead of just teasing, like before.

Em already told me we couldn't date counselors and besides, I hadn't come to camp to find a boyfriend. "Don't worry, I won't," I assured him.

"Good." Cole looked satisfied. But why?

"Game on!" Hunter yelled, interrupting my thoughts.

I hadn't taken more than two steps to get into position when the unthinkable happened.

BOOM!

The dodgeball smacked me in the face, dizzying me. The next thing I knew, my flip-flops were slipping on mud. I tried to regain my balance, but like a movie in slow-motion I felt myself slide backward. I was falling into the muddy grass below me and I couldn't stop myself. I felt a sharp thud, then blinding pain in the back of my head. I closed my eyes before the dizziness could take over and groaned.

What a way to make a first impression.

Read the rest of

SLEEPAWAY GIRLS

Coming May 2009